WILD SCOTTISH LOVE

THE ENCHANTED HIGHLANDS
BOOK TWO

TRICIA O'MALLEY

LOVEWRITE PUBLISHING

WILD SCOTTISH LOVE
THE ENCHANTED HIGHLANDS SERIES
Book Two

Editors: Marion Archer; David Burness; Trish Long

"The right ingredients can create a legend."

– Coco Chanel

GLOSSARY OF SCOTTISH WORDS/SLANG

- "Away and shite" – go away
- Bit o' banter – Scots love to tease each other; banter is highly cherished
- Bladdered – drunk
- Bloody – a word used to add emphasis; expletive
- Bonnie – pretty
- Brekkie – breakfast
- Burn – river, small stream
- Clarty – dirty
- Crabbit – cranky, moody
- Dodgy – shady, questionable
- Drookit – extremely wet; drenched
- Eejit – idiot
- Get the messages – running errands, going to the shops/market
- Give it laldy/laldie – do something with vigor or enthusiasm
- Goes down a treat – tastes good; successful

- Hen – woman, female
- "It's a dreich day" – cold; damp; miserable
- Mad wi' it – drunk
- Och – used to express many emotions, typically surprise, regret, or disbelief
- On you go then – be on your way; get on with it
- Scunner – nuisance, pain in the neck
- Shoogly – unsteady; wobbly
- Spitting chips – angry, furious
- Tatties – potatoes
- Tetchy – crabby, cranky, moody
- Tea – in Scotland, having tea is often used to refer to the dinnertime meal
- Wee – small, little
- Wheesht (haud your wheesht) – be quiet, hush, shut up

CHAPTER ONE

Lia

"Grasshoppers?"

An alarm sounded in my head as Damien, the new owner of Suzette's, a fine-dining restaurant tucked away in Boston's cozy North End, dropped a box on my spotless prep table. As head chef, *I* should have been the one ordering the ingredients for the menu, not Damien.

At least that was the way things had been when Suzette had been alive. Now I was shouldered with dealing with her sleaze of a son who couldn't leave well enough alone. Suzette's was one of the hottest restaurants in Boston, thanks to my inventive, themed surprise menus, and Damien had taken his new role as an opportunity to strut his authority around the restaurant. Every night, like cock of the walk, he'd stroll through the dining room and publicly find fault with something, often reducing one of the servers to tears. We'd all been on edge for months now, and I knew that several of the staff were actively looking for other jobs.

It was hard enough to grieve the loss of Suzette, a kind woman who had shared my dream of building a restaurant that was both cozy and innovative, without having to also navigate a new boss who never bothered to learn anything about the service industry. Even worse? I woke up each night, drenched in sweat, panic gripping me that the one goal I'd devoted my entire life to was slipping from my grasp.

"Yeah, it's all the rage," Damien said, picking up my custom chef's knife. The knife had been a gift from Suzette when Boston Magazine had run a feature article labeling me as the hot up-and-coming chef in Boston's elite culinary scene, and it had been designed to perfectly balance in my palm. I cared for that knife like it was my baby, and seeing Damien's greasy fingers on it made my lip curl in disgust. The bright side? He likely had no clue how sharp it was, so there was hope he'd maim himself shortly and I'd be left to get on with my menu for the night.

"Damien...be careful..." I trailed off as he slit the tape at the top of the box, narrowly missing the tip of his finger, and I took a deep breath in an effort to control my temper. He needed to get out of my kitchen, *now*, and take his insects with him.

"I ordered these specially from Brazil. Overnighted them. They're incredibly expensive, so you'll need to make them a Chef's Special. I hear they're salty, like potato chips," Damien said, pausing to wipe the back of the hand holding the knife against his perpetually sweaty forehead. My heart skipped a beat as the tip of my knife just missed his eyes, because while I did enjoy a good maiming, even I would turn squeamish if he popped his eyeball out.

What happened next was like when a sports team wins a big championship, and the celebratory cannons explode confetti across the arena—except replace confetti with grasshoppers.

Live grasshoppers.

While typically I have good reflexes—an important trait in any kitchen—my brain quite simply could not process the catastrophe I was witnessing. Hundreds, no, *thousands*, of grasshoppers pinged around the kitchen, bounced off walls, and landed on any available surface.

"They were supposed to be *dried*, not alive," Damien shrieked, waving his hands in the air, and I narrowly dodged the knife he threw when a grasshopper landed in his open mouth. My breath caught as the knife clattered to the floor while Damien gagged on the grasshopper.

"You *idiot*! You almost killed me." I was also shrieking at this point, but not from fear. Oh no, the last few weeks of buried rage surfaced, as though someone had dropped a match on spilled gasoline, and now I let the inferno engulf me. Crouching, I snatched my knife off the floor and returned it to its case, before slamming the lid closed on the grasshopper box. Not like there were all that many insects still in the box. It was hard to put a bomb back together after it detonated, wasn't it?

"Idiot? You can't talk to me like that. Don't forget who

signs your paychecks, doll," Damien had the gall to say to me with a grasshopper perched on his head.

"Look at what you've done," I seethed, holding my hands out to protect my face from grasshoppers that bounced around the room like someone had tossed a bucket of superballs into the kitchen. "Everything has gone to shit since Suzette died. You keep coming in here and screwing things up. You're ruining a good thing, Damien, and I for one, am not interested in sticking around to watch you destroy Suzette's legacy. You should be ashamed of yourself. Your poor mother would be devastated at what you're turning her dream into."

"My mother didn't know what was cool. This place is old and boring. At least I'm here to make it fresh." Damien smashed his hand onto the prep table, squashing a few grasshoppers, as I gaped at him in surprise.

"This? *This* is your idea of fresh?" I swept my arms out and ducked as several grasshoppers flew past. Technically speaking, he wasn't wrong. When the food was still moving, it was about as fresh as it could be. "It's stupid is what it is. And I'm not sticking around to clean up your mess."

I made to move past him, taking my knife with me, and he shouldered his way into the hallway to block me.

"If you leave, you're fired, Lia."

"That's kind of the point, isn't it?" I needed to get out of this insectarium immediately. There weren't enough showers I could take to rid me of the creepy-crawly feeling of grasshoppers in my hair. My pulse kicked up when Damien leaned close, his breath heavy with stale cigar.

"You think you can make a name for yourself without

me? I'll blackball you in this town faster than you turn men off with your ginger hair and bad attitude."

"Excuse me?" I couldn't think straight, not between the rage that twisted my gut into knots and the sizeable number of insects that were currently doing their best to vacate the kitchen through any means possible.

"Screw it. I never liked this restaurant anyway." Damien crossed his arms over his chest and huffed out a breath. "I think I'll make it a club. Lots of young, hot women in here dancing each night. Yeah, it's gonna be slick as hell."

I gaped at him, honestly at a loss for words, as I thought about the beautiful restaurant that I'd devoted years of my life to.

"I *hate* you. You're gross, and it makes me sick what you're doing to this place," I said, not caring if I burned any bridges. I didn't want to work with someone like Damien anyway. He was as dishonorable as the day was long, and I'd rather start my own gig than take orders from a sleaze like him.

"Maybe, but I don't care what you think, doll." Damien winked at me. My lip curled in disgust. Being called "doll" was a pet peeve of mine. "Gingers aren't my type anyway. I like them rail-thin with the big titties."

He was slime. Repulsive slime, and I...I had to go. Right now. Before I did something stupid like burn the restaurant down so I didn't have to watch him ruin it. At this point, that might be the best option anyway what with the grasshoppers taking up residence.

"Eat shit, Damien. I quit." I went to move past him, and Damien put his arms out, stopping me in my tracks.

"It's Saturday night. We've got a packed house." Damien didn't budge.

"Get out of my way," I said, stepping forward. "If you think that I'll stay and clean this up, you're out of your damn mind."

"You *will* stay. And you *will* cook. Because that's your job." As soon as Damien put his hands on my shoulders and shoved me backward, I did what I'd been dying to do for years now. I brought my knee up solidly between his legs just like my brothers had taught me. With a pained grunt, Damien crumpled to the floor, a soft keening noise coming from his lips, like a balloon letting out air.

"Big tree falls hard," I mumbled.

"Lia! What's going on?" Savannah, the head bartender, came upstairs with a case of beer in her arms, which she immediately dropped upon seeing the grasshoppers. The smash of glass was beyond satisfying as I stepped neatly over Damien.

"Damien's turning the place into a club. Oh, and he wants to feed people grasshoppers." Other servers were walking in the door for their shift, and at my words, they scattered back outside. "I'm leaving."

"I'm with you. I knew this place would go to hell with him in charge," Savannah said, reaching behind the bar to grab her purse. As one, the waitstaff and I pivoted and left Damien, curled on the floor and covered in grasshoppers, screaming after us.

"Screw that guy. Want to go get drunk?" Savannah asked, looking around North End. "I think this is the first Saturday night I've had free in ages."

"Yes, yes, I do." I mean, I didn't, not really. I wanted to

go home and shower for weeks on end. But I'd just quit the single most important thing that I'd done in my life, and alcohol was needed.

Savannah hooked my arm, pulling me down the street, and before I knew it, we were ensconced in a proper Boston dive bar, yelling at the Sox on the brightly lit screens, and eating delicious fried food. By the time I staggered into my building, I was well and truly numbed from the shock of quitting my job.

There, I plopped down onto my tiny loveseat in my tiny utilitarian apartment and looked around at my bare walls. There was no cat to greet me, no houseplant to water, only a pile of unfolded laundry on the small breakfast bar. My life, quite literally, had been at the restaurant. Suzette's. My home. My baby. My everything. But it had never really been mine, had it? I'd been running my whole life, away from the little girl who wore hand-me-downs, and now fear lodged low in my stomach as the debt I'd accrued from attending culinary school loomed in my mind.

My phone pinged with a text message.

Carlo: What's up with the picture of you and Savannah at the bar tonight and her saying you guys quit?

I rolled my eyes at the text from my brother Carlo. He was the most protective of my brothers and knew how seriously I took my job.

Me: I wish she wouldn't have posted that until I was ready to share. But yes, I quit. Or Damien let me go. Either way, I'm done. He wants to feed people grasshoppers and turn the restaurant into a club.

Carlo: Grasshoppers? What the hell? I hate him. I've always hated him. Stupid move on his part. Might as well sell the restaurant. He'll make more money than trying to run it himself.

Me: He's ruined everything.

Carlo: Come home. Ma will cook Sunday dinner for you. You haven't been home in months.

Me: I need to sleep. And take a moment to process this. Will call you tomorrow.

Carlo: You'd better be at dinner or I'm telling Ma you got fired.

Me: Dick move.

Carlo: Love you. See you tomorrow.

I sent him a photo of me flipping him off and then sighed and dropped back onto the cushions. I loved my family, loud and overbearing though they were. With four brothers, an Italian mother, and a Scottish father, my childhood had been chaotic, even on a good day. And there had been more good days than bad, even though we'd been dirt poor, and my parents had barely been able to make ends meet. However, what I'd lacked for in material goods had been more than made up for in love. We were a tightly connected bunch, sometimes too tightly, judging from my brother's midnight text message.

I couldn't move back home.

Leaving my small town to live in Boston had been an opportunity to make something of myself. Suzette had taken a chance on me, a naive and tender-hearted girl fresh from high school, and she'd been pivotal in providing me with an environment in which to flourish. I never, ever, asked anyone for help, and I'd been determined to prove myself to Suzette. Through several long years of culinary school, and late nights at the restaurant, I'd worked my way up from dishwasher to head chef at Suzette's. When the article in Boston Magazine had come out, my mother had spent almost her entire paycheck on buying multiple copies to give to everyone she knew. I'd *had* every intention of framing that article myself. My blank walls now mocked me.

Blinking down at my phone, I noticed my voicemail indicator. I hadn't heard the ring in the loud bar, and now I stared at the UK number with a shiver of anticipation. *That was odd*. Punching in my code, I pulled up my voicemail.

"Hi, Lia, my name is Sophie, and I'm calling from MacAlpine Castle in Scotland. We've heard talk of your legendary prowess in the kitchen and are hoping to lure you to Scotland to work for us in our restaurant. What do you say? Fancy a chef's job in an honest-to-goodness castle? You'll have free rein with the menu, of course. Please let us know. It's quite urgent, but we'll move on to the next name on our list if you're not interested. You're our top choice, naturally." She rattled off her contact information. Surprise had me dropping my phone, and I stood up to pace my small living room. Seven steps forward. Seven steps back.

Scotland.

The thought alone made me smile. *Oh, what incredible timing.* It wasn't that unusual for other restaurants to try and pry me away from Suzette's, but I'd never had an offer from someplace as far away as Scotland. Maybe...well, just maybe. Nerves skittered through my stomach. Glancing around at my empty apartment once more, I took a deep breath and picked up my phone.

CHAPTER TWO

Lia

Carlo picked me up from the train station, a smirk on his face, and I rolled my eyes as I got into his aging pickup truck. Paint spattered his jeans, though his sweatshirt was clean, which meant he'd changed before he'd come to get me.

"I only came because I didn't want to cook today," I said, poking him in the ribs as he started the truck. "Not because I wanted to see your raggedy self."

"Raggedy? This is my best sweatshirt," Carlo protested, honking at the car in front of us who dared to wait until the light turned fully green before moving forward. "*Come on...* learn how to drive."

The driver ahead of us offered a one-fingered salute that Carlo cheerfully returned. Driving in Boston was not for the faint of heart, and most people fell into two camps—

they either enthusiastically strode into battle each day, or like me, they defaulted completely out of the game and took the train everywhere. Plus, it wasn't like I could afford to keep a car in Boston, not with the outrageous parking fees. The city was easy enough to get around in, and the train was there when the weather became too bothersome for walking. In the winter, when the nor'easters would blow through, people would often spend an entire day shoveling out their parking spots. Once a spot was cleared, the driver would put a chair in the spot to claim it as their own, and it was considered sacrilege to steal someone else's cleared parking spot. Of course, things didn't often go that way, and I'd spent many an afternoon peeking through my window as my neighbors got into arguments in the snow. I didn't get a lot of time off, and when I did, it wasn't going to be spent arguing with strangers over parking.

Except that had all changed, hadn't it?

I still was a touch nauseous over my decision to quit Suzette's, though the email and subsequent telephone call I'd had with this Sophie woman in Scotland had eased some of the queasiness regarding my abrupt decision to leave my job. Now, thoughts of castles and Scottish cuisine whirled through my head, and I had trouble focusing as my brother wound us through the streets of Medford toward our childhood home.

"You're gonna tell them, right?" Carlo asked, as he cut a car off to snag a parking spot in front of my parents' house. A triple-decker-style house, they had rented the first-floor unit for as long as I could remember, though I was told we'd moved into the apartment when I was two. With two bedrooms, one bathroom, and a generous living area, I'd grown up without the concept of personal space. When I'd become a teenager, I'd abdicated from the room I'd shared with my brothers and had claimed a storage closet as my own. Although it had taken up much-needed storage space, my mother had recognized the need for me to have some personal space away from my rough-and-tumble siblings, and together, we'd managed to fit a narrow mattress into the space. I'd hung a pretty shade I'd found at a rummage sale over the lightbulb and had used the upper shelves that lined the walls for my meager belongings and a few knick-knacks. It was cozy, albeit at times suffocating, but having my own door to close had meant everything to me.

As the second oldest of five children to two very busy parents, I'd been tasked with raising the rest of my siblings when my parents weren't around to discipline us. Now, I found it funny how my brothers tried to muscle their way into my life and offer me their opinions on everything from whom I should date to how I should spend my money. Which was rarely, mind you, as evidenced by my empty apartment and even more empty love life.

"Like I can keep anything a secret in this family," I said as I got out of the truck and took a deep breath. I hated knowing that I was about to break my mother's heart. She'd never been so happy as when I'd become head chef, following her own love of cooking, and now I had to tell her that I'd quit. Carlo came around the truck and slung his arm over my shoulders, pulling me close.

"Want me to run interference?"

"Oh sure, now you want to be the nice guy. After you threatened to tell her I was fired yesterday?" I glared up at him. I'd inherited my mother's temper—which ran hot and burned out fast—while my dad often quietly absorbed difficult news with an air of disapproval. I couldn't say what was more difficult to handle when breaking bad news, but either way, I wasn't looking forward to this dinner.

"Ma! Lia's here." Carlo pushed the door open. "And she's got big news."

"Wow, really?" I glared at my brother as my mother came bustling out of the kitchen, a dish cloth in her hands, her brown hair springing out in ringlets around her head.

"Mia cara. Mi sei mancata." My mother, Giana Maria Elenora Blackwood, hugged me with a worried look hovering in her pretty brown eyes. I'd also inherited her brown eyes and olive skin, which contrasted with the ginger hair my father had passed down to the lot of us. To this day, my mother still shook her head at her five red-haired children, as though she couldn't believe we'd come from her blood.

"I've missed you too." I hugged my mother, a shorter and rounder woman than me, and breathed in the scent of basil and garlic. Staples in our kitchen, I'd learned to cook the most basic of Italian food at my mother's hip before my head even reached the countertop. There, she'd also taught me to add her favorite ingredient—love. How many times had I heard her? *"Cecilia Giana, when you can't determine what's missing in a recipe, look for love, because love—being in love, loving another—is always the perfect ingredient."*

"Nerd alert!"

That was all the warning I had before my brother Luca tackled me from behind. We hit the ground in a tangle of limbs, and I twisted, wrapping my arm around his neck, and squeezing until he gasped for air.

"Ma! Lia's hurting me!" Luca cried.

"Cecilia Giana Blackwood, let go of your brother this instant."

I relaxed the grip on my youngest brother's neck, rolling my eyes at his smug grin. He'd always been the baby of the family and still lived with my parents today. When he stood, my mother swatted him on the side of his head, and he ducked.

"What's that for?"

"That's no way to treat a lady, Luca. It's no wonder you're still single. I could have grandbabies, couldn't I? But nothing from *you*." My mother subsided into muttering in Italian as she strode back to the kitchen to stir the sauce that simmered in her favorite pot on the stove.

"You hear that, Lia? Time to start popping them out," my second youngest brother, Gio, teased from where he played video games on the couch with Enzo. The five of us all had Italian names, as my mother still couldn't quite get over the fact that she'd fallen in love with a Scotsman. Her argument to this day was that since we carried my father's surname, it had been her right to pick the rest of our names. My father had been wise enough to not argue the point. Not that he ever argued much with my mother, instead almost always bowing quietly to her wishes. To this day, I'd never seen a man so besotted with his wife. Their love was a towering example to live up to in my own relationships. Who was I kidding? My dating life was as barren as my *Womb of Disappointment* as Enzo had lovingly nicknamed my uterus.

"The only thing I'm going to pop is my fist into your nose if you don't shut up." I lifted my fist in warning, though I kept my voice low. The fear of a rebuke from my mother was real. This was the first time we'd all been together in ages, and I knew she'd be furious if we bickered too much.

"Lia, plates." At my mother's call from the kitchen, I brandished my fist once more at my brothers and went to help set the kitchen table that dominated a large amount of the living space in the apartment. It was another point that my mother had steadfastly refused to acquiesce. We could live with a smaller couch, but the kitchen table was where family gathered. Over the years, the wooden table had grown worn with use, and the accompanying chairs had been re-covered more than once. The table itself had taken on its own place in our family, as that is where we met to share news, have difficult conversations, or even just to sit in companionable silence while my father read the paper.

"Lia, your mother tells me you have news?" my father said after he'd eaten a good portion of his fettucine al pomodoro and could relax under the watchful eye of my mother who was convinced we were always just minutes away from starvation. My father, Colin Blackwood, was a broad-shouldered man with kind eyes and an easygoing disposition. His personality was the perfect foil for my mother's heated temper and passionate nature.

My stomach twisted, and I put my fork down, nerves making me reach for my glass of wine. After a healthy sip, I looked up at the silence that had fallen around the table. In a family of seven people, silence was rare.

"I quit my job...and I mightbemovingtoScotland." I rushed out the last bit in one long breath, afraid that if I didn't say it now, then I'd never work up the courage to say it at all. Let alone actually do it, that is. Moving to Boston was one thing, but to Scotland? I waited, holding my breath, as my family exploded in varying degrees of reactions.

"Mio dio." My mother crossed herself.

"You quit?" Luca looked excited. "Badass." He ducked when my mother reached out to swat his head for cursing.

"Damien's a douchebag. You did the right thing," Carlo said, knowing he was far enough away from my mother's reach.

"You knew about this?" Enzo turned to Carlo.

"Just last night. Her friend Savannah posted about it."

"Is Savannah the one..." Gio cocked his head at Carlo and made kissy noises with his mouth.

"You've got a thing for Savannah?" I zeroed in on Carlo, distracted for a moment. This was news to me.

"Why do you think he follows her on Instagram?" Enzo laughed, dodging as Carlo tried to punch him in the shoulder.

"Boys! Enough." Dad turned to me. "Pumpkin. Tell us what happened."

And so I did. By the time I'd finished, we were all gasping for breath, we were laughing so hard, and I realized just how much I would miss my family if I went to Scotland. No matter the situation, they always had my back. Where I'd woken up today, nervous and uncertain of my future, their support was helping me to understand that I'd made the right decision.

Plus, who really wanted to eat grasshoppers?

"Grasshoppers." My mother made a disapproving noise

with her mouth and then looked up at me, worry filling her warm brown eyes. "But Scotland...it's so far."

"It's not too bad. Six hours on a flight. About the same as to California," I pointed out. We'd only gone once to Scotland, as a family, years ago when my dad had received a promotion at work, and they'd watched flight deals for a year. It was the only international travel that I'd ever done, which reminded me, I'd have to see if my passport was out of date. Was I seriously considering this job offer?

It *was* a sweet deal.

Sophie, an American, had recently inherited MacAlpine Castle in Loren Brae, and she was working on a new campaign to encourage tourism. Part of that campaign was to build out the restaurant at the castle, and they hoped to do themed weekends for visiting tourists. She said they'd read about my surprise-themed menus and had thought I'd be a perfect fit for what they had in mind. The offer included housing, a generous salary, and even a moving stipend. My own restaurant. In a *freaking* castle.

It almost seemed too good to be true.

"But..." My mother trailed off at a look from my father. When she went quiet, the rest of the table did as well. It wasn't often that my father took the lead on things, but when he did, we all listened.

"I think this could be a wonderful opportunity. Why don't you tell us about it?" My father gestured with his fork, and I let out a breath before rambling off all of the details that I knew. By the time I was finished, Luca was nodding along with me.

"This is so cool, Lia. You have to do it. I mean...it's Scotland. I can come visit and be an influencer," Luca said.

"Influence who? Girls into not dating you?" Enzo asked and my brothers started razzing each other.

"Lia? Porch." My dad stood and angled his head to the front door, and I topped off my wine glass before following him outside. The air was brisk, but summer had been kind to us so far, and it wasn't cold enough to have to grab a coat. I settled into an Adirondack chair next to my dad, and we sat in companionable silence for a moment like so many times before. As his only daughter, my dad had often tried to take me aside when he could, giving me small special moments together in his busy schedule. Sometimes it was just like this, sitting on the porch, watching the world go by, talking about whatever was on our minds.

"Will you go?" My dad glanced at me before taking a sip of his beer. "To Scotland?"

"I...I don't know. I'm thinking pretty seriously about it." I shifted in my seat, crossing one leg over the other, and watched a car search for a parking spot on the street. "It doesn't seem real. It still feels like I'll be going back to Suzette's tomorrow to plan the menu for the week."

"Big changes don't always happen on our preferred timeframe." Dad shrugged one shoulder. "I was asked to go back as well. But well, I had your mother to consider. And we had a home here. A family. Friends. It wasn't much, but it was ours. Och, starting from scratch after we'd worked so hard to eke out a living here, well, it didn't suit." Although my father had been away from Scotland for well over thirty years now, the whisper of the Highlands still clung to his voice.

"Who asked you to come back? Your family?" I raised an eyebrow at him. To my knowledge, he didn't have much family left in Scotland aside from his great-aunt. Both of his parents had passed on before I was born.

"No. The people of MacAlpine Castle."

My jaw dropped. "What, the same MacAlpine Castle I've just been offered a job at?"

Dad nodded. "I think...there's something more there that you should know about. Gran, well, you never got to know her, but she was part of a thing there years ago. An Order. I think...well, I don't know all that much, truth be told. There was magick involved, I guess. Myths. Legends. Och, it's been ages since I've even thought about it. There's been whispers of magick through the years at MacAlpine Castle. It's kind of a known thing in Scotland. You'll need to be careful how you approach things, Lia. It's not like Boston. Some of the people who live in small towns in Scotland are often mired in the old ways, old thoughts, myths...magick."

"Magick?" I choked on my sip of wine. "Wait, you're saying your gran was a witch?"

"Aye." He turned to me, his eyes serious.

"But...like, just someone who liked crystals and stuff or..." I widened my eyes at him.

"From my understanding, a proper witch. A Kitchen Witch if I remember correctly."

Kitchen Witch. The words sent a shiver across my skin, and excitement bloomed inside me like dough rising. I smiled at my father.

"If that's the case, maybe some of her magick passed through to me."

"I don't doubt it. I don't know why I haven't thought

much of this before, but it makes sense. You're magic in the kitchen."

"I love you, Dad." He'd always been my biggest supporter, well both my parents had, and his quiet pride in my accomplishments had propelled me to take risks. "Do you really think I should go to Scotland?" I still couldn't quite wrap my head around the fact that my family might already have a connection with this same castle in Scotland. It almost seemed like this might be meant to be.

"Only if you want to do this. But if you do, I wouldn't recommend you be walking in there questioning everyone in that town, either. Watch. Listen. Learn. You may be surprised."

"Dad...are you honestly saying that you believe in... what? Magick? Witches?" While the idea of Kitchen Witches existing appealed to me, I had a hard time believing it was real.

"Of course I do. There's more to this world than we know. Remember, our roots run deep in Scotland. Many of these stories that seem like fairy tales to you spring from kernels of truth. I want to prepare you, but not scare you, if you get what I'm saying."

"This might be one of the strangest conversations we've ever had." I shook my head at him, though my interest was piqued. "Magick. Legends. Myths. Is that really what you want me walking into?"

"I wouldn't send you if you weren't capable of handling yourself, you know that." It was the quiet vote of confidence in his voice that sealed the deal for me. I wasn't sure what to make of the mystical aspect of it all, but I had to admit, it didn't sound boring. And even I could see that I'd gotten stuck in a bit of a rut. What better way to shake things up than to travel to a magick village in Scotland and cook at a castle? Frankly, I didn't have any other offers on the table at the moment, and I wasn't sure that I could handle starting at the bottom at a different restaurant in Boston. Not when Suzette's had been an extension of my very soul. No, I needed a change.

"Mia cara." My mom opened the door, coming out onto the porch, her hand cupped around something. "I've kept this for you."

"What is it?" I put out my hand and she dropped a chain with a gold heart locket on it into my palm. Holding it up, I smiled at the thistle that was etched onto the front. Inside, she'd cut two tiny photos of the family and pasted them into both sides. I immediately understood what she was telling me.

"Family is in the heart." My mother squeezed my shoulder before returning inside to yell at the boys.

"Looks like you're going to my homeland." My father reached over and tapped his beer bottle against my wine glass. "Slàinte mhath."

CHAPTER THREE

Munroe

"No proper lad drinks gin."

I watched Graham, my oldest friend and the owner of a popular pub, the Tipsy Thistle, stroll to the tee. We'd stolen a morning away from work, meeting at a golf course halfway between our respective homes, and I held on to hope that the rain would hold off until we finished our round.

"My sales sheets read differently," I said. Lachlan, manager of MacAlpine Castle, and the third in our group this morning, laughed behind me. Common Gin, the company I'd birthed in my apartment during my university days, had expanded to several locations and was becoming a hit across the UK. I had bet on gin, pivoting away from my family's interests in whisky, mainly because gin took far less time to distill, package, and bring to market than specialty aged whisky. While it might hold less panache and prestige than an aged Macallan, gin was a festive and approachable liquor with no barriers to entry. I appreciated the lack of gatekeeping—as, unlike whisky, nobody was forced to sit through a lecture on the historical significance of a batch of gin prior to enjoying their cocktail. Maybe it made me a man of the people, or maybe I'd just done it to thumb my nose at my parents, but either way, Common Gin was now one of the most profitable distilleries in Scotland.

"That's women buying it," Graham said. We quieted as he took his shot, and he hissed out a breath when the ball hooked and flew off the course.

"Aye, that's the truth of it. Surely you aren't implying that you prefer to engage in a business that *doesn't* attract women?" I asked as I hefted my club in my hand.

"Och, he's got you there, Graham. It's not like you've opened a pub just to blether on with your mates all day. It's the lasses that keep it fresh for you," Lachlan said.

"The Tipsy Thistle is an institution in Loren Brae, one which I'm honored to keep afloat even in these dire times." Graham paused.

"And..." Lachlan prodded.

"Och, fine, I enjoy a bonnie lass here and there, don't I then?" Graham laughed, and they fell silent as I hit my ball in a clean line down the fairway.

"I've never liked you," Graham muttered when I turned, beaming.

"What's this about dire times?" I asked, concern for my friend overtaking our banter. "Is the pub not doing well?"

"Nothing's doing all that well in Loren Brae at the moment," Lachlan said as he took his turn at the tee. Once more we quieted as we waited for him to take his shot, and I cast my mind back to the last time I'd been to Loren Brae. It had to have been at least five years since I'd visited, as the demands of my business had kept me in other areas of Scotland and abroad. But now, after I'd recently finished outfitting a new warehouse, I was on the hunt for new distillery locations. It was one of the reasons I'd called Lachlan and Graham to meet today. I had a mind to propose a distillery location in lovely Loren Brae, situated on the bonnie banks of Loch Mirren with MacAlpine Castle as a tourist draw. I didn't like to just build distilleries and close them off to the people. Instead, my distilleries were destinations in their own right with tasting rooms, themed events, and cafes. The distillery in Edinburgh even housed a nightclub. I'd found that people enjoyed being part of the process when it came to buying Common Gin, and I couldn't keep my homemade gin infusion kits in stock. My father had laughed at me, pointing out that I was losing customers by teaching them to produce their own flavoured gins, but I had learned that brand loyalty went a long way in this industry.

"What's wrong? Is Loren Brae struggling?" I raised an eyebrow when my two friends exchanged a look but didn't say anything. We shouldered our bags and moved onto the fairway, and I waited for them to speak. It was Lachlan who cleared his throat and finally broke the silence when we reached his ball.

"It's the Kelpies."

Dread filled me. The Kelpies had long been a myth that had clung to the misty shores of Loch Mirren, whispered tales of ancient water beasts working fear into the hearts of young children. Periodically, the myth surfaced through the years, casting a stain across Loren Brae that kept people away.

"Och, that's not good. How'd the talk come about this time?" I asked, easing my bag from my shoulder when we reached my ball. I fished around for the club I wanted, and drew it out, pausing when I caught the odd look exchanged between Graham and Lachlan again. "What's that look about?"

"Right, so, what if the Kelpies were real?" Graham asked, rocking back on his heels as he studied me. I barked out a laugh and shook my head, knowing how Graham liked to have a joke at my expense.

"Santa Claus, too, right?" I shook my head and took my shot, amusement drifting through me. I wished I had more time to see Lachlan and Graham, as I had very few close friends who were willing to banter with me. Mainly due to my debilitating shyness, which I'd worked for years to overcome. While it still surfaced occasionally these days, if I stuck to talking about subjects I was knowledgeable in, like gin, I often could break through that barrier. With Graham and Lachlan, I could be myself, and that was just one of the reasons I was interested in building in Loren Brae. "Or has Santa himself brought the Kelpies? Rode them in on a rough winter's day and now the beasts are raging that he's gone back to the North Pole without them?"

"I wish that were the case," Graham said, an odd look on his face. "As I'd dearly love to meet the old lad. And as much as we like to take the piss out of you, Lachlan speaks the truth of it. The Kelpies are back. It's not a myth, laddie. They're real."

"Wait." I grabbed Lachlan's arm and turned my friend to meet his eyes. "You're *not* taking the piss? What do you mean the Kelpies are real? I thought...it's been..." A shiver drifted across my skin, like the kiss of winter's dawn, and my heart picked up speed.

"Trust me, mate, I had a harder time than any accepting that the beasts were real. Then they tried to kill me. Just like they killed my mum. Can't really argue with it when you're staring them in the face, now can you?" Lachlan's mouth twisted wryly at his words, and I saw the flash of pain behind his eyes. In all the years I'd known Lachlan, he'd rarely spoken of his mother's death, so for him to bring it up now meant that he was serious.

"Och, and you're just dropping this on me now? After all this time?" Hurt mixed with confusion. I had to admit, I didn't like being kept out of the loop. It made me feel left out, just like all the years when my parents had made decisions about my life without any input from me.

"Trust me when I say I *didn't* want to believe it myself, mate," Lachlan said. "I couldn't come to terms with it. The Kelpies? Being real? Nope. I absolutely refused to accept it. Because if they were real, well, I'd have to change what I knew about how my mother died and try to avenge her death against, well, magickal beasts. It's been a process to get here. I wasn't keeping you out, Munroe. I was hiding from it myself."

"He's not lying, either. It took Loren Brae basically closing its doors and the Kelpies screaming in his face for the man to believe. I've been after him for a while now to handle it, but...it's complicated, I guess." Graham shrugged.

"And with his mum? It just didn't feel like my place to talk about it."

"I think I need a moment to process." My thoughts whirled. How could this possibly be true? Yet, the little boy inside of me who'd buried himself in books and found comfort in fantasy worlds full of heroes and dragons stood up and cheered.

"You can have it. It will take more than a moment for Graham to find his ball anyway."

"Bloody hell," Graham said as he stomped over to the edge of the woods where we had seen his ball land.

I looked at Lachlan, *really* looked at him, and instantly understood just how uncomfortable this conversation was for him. I'd long known my friend to be an upstanding and honest man. He'd all but declared himself the unofficial mayor of Loren Brae, and I had never once, in all our years of being friends, been given reason to distrust the man. If Lachlan was telling me that the Kelpies were real, then I needed to suspend my disbelief and listen. And, if I was being honest? There was a very tiny, giddy, part of me that dearly hoped this news was real. *Kelpies*. My day had suddenly taken a very fascinating turn.

"So it wasn't just a straightforward drowning?" I asked, referring to Lachlan's mum. His mum had drowned when we were all on the cusp of being teenagers, though I had only ever summered in Loren Brae when my parents had sent me to stay with family. That particular summer had been tough for all of us. Now that my friends had brought it up, the rumor about the Kelpies tickled my mind, and I remembered more than a few fearful nights walking the shores of Loch Mirren, my eyes straining in the strange light of Scottish summer nights that refused to go full dark.

"It appears not."

There was a wealth of emotions behind Lachlan's words, and I didn't know what to say. Instead, I reached over and clapped my friend on the shoulder, and Lachlan nodded his understanding. Sometimes, words weren't needed.

"Bloody hell," Graham shouted. The crack of his golf ball ricocheting off a tree reached us.

"He's really off his game today," I observed as we walked over to annoy Graham.

"Have you tried not hitting it into a tree?" Lachlan called.

"Or perhaps staying on the fairway?" I offered.

Graham muttered a few choice words and dropped a new ball on the ground.

"You might as well tell us what your news is, Munroe, otherwise this entire morning will be utter shite," Graham said.

"It might help with your troubles. Might not." I shifted the golf bag at my shoulder as the first drops of rain that had been threatening all morning splattered at our feet. "I wanted to get your insights on opening a distillery in Loren Brae."

"No kidding? That's great news, man." A smile split Lachlan's face. "The town could use the boost, and I know more than one person out of a job."

"Is it the wrong time to build? What with the, um..."

"I mean, it's not ideal. But distilleries aren't built in a day. Plus we have a plan to sort the Kelpies out. It turns out there's an Order that keeps them contained. It's long been a responsibility of the castle owners to see to it. So, well, we're seeing to it," Lachlan said.

My phone buzzed in my pocket, and I pulled it out, only answering it when I saw it was my mother. She rarely called, and worry spiked in my gut.

"Mother? Is something wrong?"

"Certainly not, Munroe. I'm just calling to let you know that I've spoken with Cassidy about blocking off the last weekend in September for the Gordons to have their daughter's wedding at your distillery in Edinburgh. I can't possibly understand what they see in the place, but they've informed me her heart is set on it. Cassidy insisted that she wouldn't reserve the time until I'd spoken with you." *Impertinent girl.* The last bit was left unsaid, but I could hear it in her tone.

I thought you said my little gin business was a disgrace.

I didn't say that, of course, because I'd never been able to stand up to the icy-cold force that was my parents. Instead, I gritted my teeth.

"That's her job, Mother. You simply can't ask her to close down an entire distillery at your whim."

"A wedding for one of the most prominent families in Scotland is hardly a whim."

If they are so prominent, why do they want to host it at my little distillery then?

Again, I bit my tongue.

"Apparently, they find the building charming, and they love the Old Town location. You know how brides are... they get what they want. I can't possibly disappoint them. You'll approve the weekend, of course." It was as close as my mother got to asking, and I felt my resolve buckle. I'd promised myself that I would stop capitulating to their demands through the years, but thus far I hadn't succeeded.

"Of course, Mother. I'll tell Cassidy to schedule it in, on one condition..." I paused as silence greeted me. "You will book Cassidy a nice day at your spa. Full treatment. She needs the time off and I know it would be a real treat for her."

"Honestly, Munroe. You're too frivolous with the help." Cassidy was far from "the help." She was a highly trained executive manager that kept my business running smoothly.

"I'll wait for your confirmation of her spa day, and then I'll give her the go-ahead." My mother disconnected without saying goodbye, a sure sign that I'd annoyed her, but that wasn't anything new for me.

"The Ice Queen liveth," Graham proclaimed, bowing deeply with his clubs as though he had an audience with the royals. After meeting my parents only once in all of the summers I'd gone to Loren Brae, Graham and Lachlan had instantly coined them the Ice King and Queen, and the names had stuck.

"She'll outlive us all." I sighed. It might be a bit inconsequential of me to force my mother to do something nice for someone else in return for a favor, but it was the only way I'd found to gain some foothold with them and their demands through the years. I absentmindedly rubbed at the ache in my chest that always blossomed when I spoke to either of my parents.

Never good enough. Never smart enough. Never enough. Same story, different refrain.

"What now? Still mad you didn't go into Macallan's?" Lachlan asked.

My parents were silent partners in Macallan Whisky, one of the most respected whisky brands in the world. When I had decided to follow my own path, instead of taking a job at Macallan's as a handout from my father, my parents had been livid. Since then, they took every opportunity they could to needle me about my gin business. Even worse? The name I'd picked, Common Gin, chafed at their upper crust sensibilities. It didn't take a psychologist to unravel why I'd chosen that name, but I liked the appeal of creating a drink that everyone could enjoy. There had been so many lonely days as a child, curled up with my books, aside from those glorious summers at Loren Brae, that there had been something in me that wanted to create community. Maybe I needed to do it to spite my parents, or maybe I needed it to fill a well that was empty inside me, but either way, I was deeply proud of how Common Gin had grown.

"Nah, Mother wants to let her friends have a wedding at the Edinburgh distillery in September."

"I didn't know you did weddings." Lachlan narrowed his eyes. "You charge a lot for that?"

"Sometimes." I shrugged and ignored the question about what I charged. I hadn't charged any fees for the weddings I'd done as they'd all been by request of my mother. The rain picked up, and I dug in my bag for my coat. "Shall we call it, lads? I'm not sure I'm in the mood to play through this."

"Och, and here I was having such a fine game," Graham said, a delighted grin spreading on his face. "Let's grab a beer and talk more about this wee distillery of yours, Munroe."

"You're buying. You clearly lost even though we didn't finish," I pointed out as we hurried toward the clubhouse.

"You'd think a man as rich as yourself could afford to be buying his mates a drink," Graham grumbled.

"Och, I can afford it. I just don't want to." I laughed, shaking my mother's phone call off so I could focus on something far more interesting.

The Kelpies.

I chuckled to myself, even though I understood the gravity of the situation. But maybe, just maybe, I needed to believe in something fantastical—something outside the norm—in order to lift my spirits from a life of constant work and loneliness. Even if it meant that I'd be putting myself in danger, there was no way that I was staying away from Loren Brae. No, my friends needed me now more than ever.

It looked like Common Gin would be coming to Loren Brae.

CHAPTER FOUR

LIA

I still couldn't believe that I was here.

Scotland.

Of all the places I had thought about moving to in my future, Scotland had never once crossed my mind.

You don't have to stay.

It was the mantra I had repeated to myself as I'd subleased my apartment to Savannah and had packed my meager belongings into several boxes that were now in storage at Carlo's condo. It had almost been too easy, really, to get up and go.

Had I had one foot out the door this whole time?

Still, Scotland had never been on my list of places to move. In the cold Boston winters, I had often dreamed about moving south, perhaps to coastal South Carolina or maybe the Keys to gaze over sparkling turquoise waters while I cooked. An international move felt so...*adult.* Adventurous. Like the type of thing that all those influencers and digital nomads did, showcasing perfectly staged videos on their TikTok and Instagram feeds, while seemingly never having to worry about money. A luxury that I'd never known. I stared at my image in the tiny mirror in the tiny bathroom of the tiny room I'd rented for the week and laughed. Dark circles smudged my eyes, my face was as shiny as an oil slick, and my hair sprung out around my head in a riot of frizzed and tangled curls.

Turns out—I don't sleep well on planes.

Having only ever flown once before, the entire experience had been overwhelming, exhilarating, and nerve-wracking for me. I'd quickly learned that I kind of hated not being in the know, so I ended up asking a lot of questions of my kindly seatmate—a grandmotherly sort who had instantly seen the fear in my eyes and had taken me under her wing—and once I'd understood the basics of what to expect on our flight, I'd quieted down and watched a movie on the little screen in front of me.

I'd been delighted to find that wine was included in the price of the ticket, which MacAlpine Castle had provided a more than generous budget for, and two glasses with dinner had sent me right to sleep for the rest of the flight after we'd finished eating. I'd only awoken when the grandmother had nudged me, and it had taken me a full minute to remember where I was.

After a harrowing taxi journey along narrow roads in the murky twilight, a trip I wasn't hoping to repeat any time soon, I'd been deposited at the door of a cheerful bed and breakfast in downtown Loren Brae. I suppose I couldn't really call it a downtown, as it seemed to be more of a small village, actually, but I planned to explore more in the morning.

My decision to come to Loren Brae early fell in line with the mantra that I kept repeating for myself. *You don't have to stay.* Silly, maybe, as I understood at any point we could up and change our lives, but still, I clutched that reminder close to my chest like the little heart locket I wore. I wanted to scope Loren Brae out before meeting people at my new job so I could get an unencumbered view of the village to see if this was really the place where I wanted to start fresh. I knew myself well enough to know that as soon as I was shown the kitchen at the castle, I'd jump in head-first to designing a menu and wouldn't look up for years. Which is kind of what had happened at Suzette's. Although I was extremely proud of what I'd built there, it had also consumed my life. Damien's takeover, and his subsequent betrayal, had hurt me as badly as if I had owned the restaurant myself.

"You care too much," Dad had cautioned me through the years.

But I'd never been able to separate myself from my work. I put all of my love into the dishes I created, and that spilled over into the restaurant. If I wasn't passionate about what I did, where I worked, well, then, the food would reflect that. Customers know when a chef loves what they do. And it wasn't just passion that drove me, either. Although my family had shown me a lot of love growing up, the kids at school hadn't done the same. I'd been bullied for years for not being able to afford school sport, for wearing thrifted clothes, and for not being able to join any of the costly, special field trips. Kids were ruthless, and I'd been an easy target.

I'd left high school and had never looked back. There was no fond reminiscing on the good ol' days or where my prom date had ended up. No, I'd neatly shut that door, and aside from a few nightmares that would arise occasionally, particularly the one where the popular cheerleader had torn my only jersey in half in the locker room, I was an "eyes forward" type of girl now.

Running my hands under the tap, one of those faucets where the hot and cold handles were separate, I squirted some hair gel into my palm and mixed it lightly with the water before finger-combing my curls. After I'd tamed most of the beast, I patted a lightly tinted moisturizer across my face and smudged on some eyeliner. That was about the extent of my makeup routine, but at least I looked a bit more presentable.

Not Instagram-worthy, but passable.

It was still light out, though the clock told me it was half past nine, and I hoped the pub would still serve food. If not, maybe a corner store would be open. Loren Brae was small enough that I worried most things would be closed already, and I suspected UberEats was not a thing here. Quickly, I changed into jeans, a black, fitted long-sleeved shirt, and pulled on my favorite black leather jacket. I'd already Google-mapped the nearest pub, and it looked like it was on the same block as the B&B. I shouldn't need anything else except for my purse and room key.

I slipped quietly down the stairs, as the entire house seemed to be silent, and I didn't want to wake anybody. Easing the front door open, I made sure it was pulled tightly closed behind me before I turned and gaped at the loch.

Loch Mirren, I reminded myself.

I'd barely had time to process its beauty what with trying not to get carsick from the driver acting like the taxi was his own personal race car.

The loch stretched out, the soft evening light dancing across its calm surface, the mountains behind it reflected in the water. I took a deep breath, and then another, steadying myself against the rush of emotion that hit me. I'd been moving so fast, for years now, that I'd barely taken a vacation or looked up from my work. And when I did? It was a night out in the city. I couldn't recall the last time I'd been away from the thrum of the city, honking cars and hurled insults my background playlist, and now the stillness of the village settled on my shoulders like a comfortable blanket.

Who would I be here?

The thought rose, unbidden, as I continued to stare at the loch, unable to tear my eyes away from the beauty of the dusky light mirrored on the still water. I knew who Boston Lia was. I was firmly rooted there, entrenched in the city and the way of life, but would I know myself here? Perhaps this was a chance to reinvent myself. Lia 2.0. Maybe life was just a thousand opportunities to step into different versions of ourselves. Perhaps it was like trying on new shoes. Eventually, we'd settle on something fresh and new, while still returning to our old favorites over and over again.

Shaking my head at my thoughts, I turned away from the loch and wandered up to the pub. Already, I could hear music and laughter from inside, and tension eased from my shoulders as I stopped at the door and read the hand-carved wooden sign.

The Tipsy Thistle.

I approved of the name. Catchy. The pub was set in a good location, and I imagined it was likely the heart of the town. Most pubs were, if they were run right, and I felt at home as soon as I stepped inside. Years of working in the service industry had me taking in every last detail, as I walked through the stone passageway with a low ceiling and stepped into a proper Scottish pub. The owner hadn't missed a trick. A round wooden bar dominated the center of the room, and rough-hewn stone walls were covered in vintage bar signs and local art. A huge fireplace sat in one corner, with no fire lit tonight, but I imagined it was quite cozy on a colder evening.

The hottest man I'd ever seen in real life turned from where he stood at the bar and smiled at me.

My mouth went dry.

My heart danced.

Heat licked through my stomach as my ladyparts suddenly seemed to remember that I hadn't had a proper date in years, and *look*, here was a tall muscular Scot who could probably throw you over his shoulder and carry you across the field to his cave and have his way with you. I don't know why it was a cave he was having his way with me in, it just seemed to fit with his rugged good looks and uber-masculine vibe. Honey-gold hair, lively blue eyes, and broad shoulders completed the package. I stopped in my tracks.

"There's a bonnie lass on a slow night. What can I get for you, darling?"

I gaped at the man who spoke behind the golden god in front of me. Although he stood behind the bar, he was just as tall as the man who surveyed me from curious blue eyes. Why was he looking at me like that? Was it my hair? I thought I'd tamed the beast. Awkwardly, I patted my head while I moved closer to the bar, giving the hot Scot a wide berth. Men like him terrified me. Okay, that was being dramatic. More like men such as him, with sureness of their existence in the world, chafed at me. I'd had to fight for everything while people like him probably just glossed through life, doors opening left and right, women falling at his feet. Yeah, he was definitely one of those. Mind made up, I turned to the bartender.

Damn, but they grew them sexy here.

"I'm hoping you still have food going. I know it's late, but even a bowl of soup would be great." I smiled at the gorgeous man, praying he'd take pity on me and scrounge up some food, and his smile widened. He leaned on the bar, bringing his face closer to mine and pushed a menu towards me.

"Anything for you, hen. What can I get for you, darling?" I almost passed out at his smile, my ladyparts immediately leaving the cave with the golden god and hopping on the bartender train. Listen, I know I'd mentioned that being called "darling" was a pet peeve of mine. But when this man said it? With the Highlands dancing in his voice?

Well, *yes*, sir. I could be a bonnie lass all day long.

Also, did he just call me a hen? Was that a good thing? Or was he calling me chicken? Confusion made me flustered.

"Um," I stuttered.

"Lay off, Graham. Ignore this one. He puts on the charm as liberally as he does the jam on his toast." A slim woman with a crop of pretty curls rolled her eyes at me. "Graham was born with a silver tongue, and he makes a habit of flirting with every woman that steps through the door."

"A habit you could learn from, my acid-tongued wasp," Graham said, winking as he leaned on the bar.

"Do wasps even have tongues?" The woman turned to me, as though I'd know the answer, and I gaped at her.

"I have no idea," I said faintly. Surely they did, right?

Quickly, everyone in the pub took up the argument, and I blinked as people shouted over each other, sure in their knowledge of bee tongues.

Except for the golden god. A shiver of awareness trickled over my skin as I caught him staring at me. At least he had the grace to look away when I met his eyes.

"Well, now, you've gone and started it. Have a seat then." The woman patted the stool next to her, and I dropped into it, stunned at the voracity of arguments erupting around me.

"Wasps are different from bees," I surprised myself by saying.

"Och, fair point." The woman turned. "Our friend here says wasps aren't the same as bees. If I recall correctly, Graham referred to me as a wasp, not a bee. Would that be correct?"

"If the sting fits..." Graham murmured behind me, sliding a pink drink in front of me.

"What's this?" I eyed the drink suspiciously.

"It's rhubarb gin. From Munroe," Graham nodded to the golden god. *Munroe.* I rolled his name around on my tongue, like savoring a sweet treat, and then glared down at the drink. Did he think he could just buy me a drink without even talking to me and I'd fall at his feet?

Yes, my body screamed.

Traitorous bitch.

"I don't drink gin." It came out rudely, and I realized it was best not to get on anyone's bad side before I knew the town a bit better. "But thank you."

"You hear that, lad? Not a gin drinker." Graham beamed at Munroe, as though I'd told him he was the hottest man in the room. Which he was close...but not as hot as Munroe. "Looks like I'll have to see to her pleasure this evening."

Wait...was he saying?

"What'll it be then, darling?" Graham leaned forward again, and I blinked at him for a moment, basking in his handsomeness, before shaking my head.

"My God, you guys lay it on thick here, don't you?" I asked.

"Thick's the best way, don't you think?" Graham asked and the woman behind me mocked banging her head against the bar.

"Even for you, Graham, that's a bit much. Get the lady a glass of wine or something and some food. She asked for dinner, not a date. I swear, one of these days one of these women is going to reach across the bar and pop you across the nose."

"I'm guessing I know which one that will be." Graham blew a kiss at the woman.

"I'm tempted every day." The woman turned to me. "I'm Agnes by the way. If he gets to be too much, just let me know. He flirts as easily as he breathes, but trust me, he's harmless."

"Och, you wound me," Graham said, holding a hand to his heart. "You make me sound like a wee bairn, unable to defend a lass in a brawl."

"Who is brawling around here?" Agnes looked around as the bee versus wasp argument heightened. "Actually, never mind. We may have one on us tonight if that's the way things are going."

"A Malbec, please," I said, turning back to Graham, amusement replacing my earlier awkwardness. "And a bowl of the hearty vegetable soup with a cheese toastie on the side."

"Ah, a classic. I'll get you sorted out," Graham said, already filling my glass of wine.

"It's a proboscis, you bloody eejit!" a man shouted in the back and Agnes turned to me with a smile. Picking up her glass, she tapped it against mine.

"Welcome to Loren Brae."

CHAPTER FIVE

Munroe

My old shyness crept in and hit me across the head like a bag of bricks.

Who was this gorgeous woman who strode confidently through the door of the pub, all tough edges and rounded corners? The lift of her chin and the edgy leather jacket contrasted with the uncertain look in her large brown eyes. She worried her bottom lip, and I found myself transfixed on her perfect pink mouth, wondering what it would be like to taste her. Her riot of tawny curls said Scottish, but her accent said American. I wondered what had brought her to Loren Brae.

And how I could keep her here.

The thought was so foreign to me that I turned away, burying my face in my glass while the pub argued the anatomy of bees. Despite myself, my gaze kept getting pulled back to this lovely woman, like a bee drawn to the prettiest flower. I mentally rolled my eyes at the image. What was with the bees tonight?

I hadn't worked up the courage to speak to her yet, though I'd caught her name as she'd introduced herself to Agnes.

Lia.

It was a pretty name, like the soft tinkling of fairy chimes in the wind, and I committed it to memory so when I did speak with her, I wouldn't make the impasse of calling her the wrong name. I met so many new people in my line of work that oftentimes I would miss the first few minutes of a conversation after they introduced themselves because I was busy trying to make sure I'd remember their names.

I kept to myself, letting the conversation flow around me, nursing my Guinness as I watched Lia out of the corner of my eye. She'd already caught me staring once, so I had to try and not be a creep, though all I wanted to do was look at her. Which...sounded creepy even in my own head. Sighing, I turned so my back was to her and tried to listen to the man next to me talk about flowers that would attract pollinators.

Lia was, quite simply, the most beautiful woman I'd ever seen. I couldn't remember ever having such a visceral reaction to someone before, and I swear I could feel my heart thumping harder in my chest when I looked at her. My hands were sweaty on my glass, and I had to work to concentrate on what the man was saying to me before I made a total fool of myself and asked this woman to run away with me. If I changed her out of the leather jacket and put her in a sweeping green dress, she would be the spitting image of a Fae warrior queen in one of my favorite fairy tales. I was a nerd to my core, loving all things board games, fantasy, and sci-fi. My love of reading had carried over into adulthood, and I often found myself consumed with the latest fantasy series. Much like the argument about bee tongues, I could argue for hours over the Fermi Paradox.

"How's business then, Munroe?" Agnes pulled me back to her side, and I turned, my eyes lighting on Lia before skimming down to Agnes.

"Well enough, I suppose."

"More than well enough," Graham said, slapping a hand on my shoulder. "My mate here is looking to open a distillery in Loren Brae."

At that, the arguments about bee tongues skidded to a halt, and exclamations rose from around the bar. Instantly, I was peppered with questions, and I narrowed my eyes at Graham.

"Ever heard of privacy, lad? My publicist is going to kill you." Usually, we drew up a detailed launch plan before announcing we were building in a new location. There were many aspects to consider before investing in a new distillery, none of which I'd had a chance to brief my team on regarding Loren Brae. To say this was jumping the gun was an understatement.

"Och, lad. It's just us mates here." Graham rolled his eyes. Raising his voice, he turned to the pub. "I'd better not hear any talk of this in the papers. Munroe needs to keep his publicist in a job, or her kids will go hungry. Understood?"

"Sure, that's grand. Make me look like a jerk who'll fire his publicist if this gets out." I buried my nose in my pint.

"What kind of distillery?" Lia spoke directly to me, and

I almost choked on my Guinness. I wasn't expecting interaction so soon after she'd refused my drink, and I'd convinced myself I'd blown my shot by coming on too strong by offering to buy her a drink when I'd not even met her yet. It was out of habit, really, as liquor was my business. Typically, whenever I went into a pub, I'd offer free gin drinks to anyone in the crowd, as it was just good business.

"Gin," Agnes answered for me and slapped me on the back, furthering my embarrassment.

"Oh." Understanding dawned on Lia's face when she realized she'd unintentionally insulted me, and a pretty pink flush swept across her dusky skin. I wanted to jump in and reassure her that everything was fine with us, but I couldn't quite seem to get my mouth working properly. It was astounding to me, really, that after all these years of running my own company, a healthy number of girlfriends, and even some public speaking events under my belt, that my old shyness could still come back to cripple me on occasion.

"Nae bother, hen. It's whisky you're wanting if you want a proper Scottish drink," Graham piped up, holding a bottle of Macallan in front of Lia, deliberately needling me.

"I'm good, thanks." Lia gestured with her wine glass, and I cheered up. At least she was rejecting Graham as well as me. "Why do you keep calling me a chicken?"

The three of us turned and stared at Lia, and then I burst out laughing. She narrowed her eyes at me, and I realized she thought I was laughing at her. I hurried to correct her, but Agnes beat me to it.

"Och, we do forget that others don't use the term hen to refer to women, don't we? Honestly, Lia, it's not used that often really. We call our bachelorette parties 'Hen

Parties', so there's that, I suppose. But Graham here helps with the castle tours, and he also gets loads of tourists through the pub. He slips into a few of the stereotypical Scottish phrases more than the rest of us, just to put it on a bit for the ladies since his accent is the only thing he's got going for him. You ken?" Agnes arched a brow, and I pressed my lips together to bite back a smile. These two had been at each other's throats for years, and whenever they got into it, I felt like I was home.

"I beg to differ, darling. It's my accent *and* my dangerous good looks that the ladies fall for," Graham countered, flashing a wink at Lia.

I wanted to throat punch him.

"Honestly, he's not wrong about the accent," Lia said, flipping her hair back. "I hate when people call me 'doll' or 'darling' but I'm telling you, with a Scottish accent? It makes me want to purr."

Graham almost dropped the bottle he was holding in his haste to get back to Lia.

"Tell me more," Graham said, leaning on the bar and deepening his accent. A bell sounded from the back, indicating her food was done, and Graham straightened. "Hold that thought."

"Do not encourage that man," Agnes lectured Lia. "He's insufferable as it is. You'll do much better with a fine lad like Munroe here. Not only is he an upstanding man, but he runs a good business. He's too busy to be looking at every lass that crosses his threshold, aren't you, Munroe?"

Like I would ever want to look at another woman other than Lia again.

"It's not top priority on my agenda, no." There. Finally, words came out.

"That's a sad thing, isn't it? The good ones are always too busy to date, the difficult ones make dating their only priority," Agnes said.

"Och, come now, love should be everyone's highest priority," Graham said as he placed a bowl of soup and a sandwich in front of Lia. She danced in her seat like he'd just presented her with flowers.

"Is it actually love, Graham? Or is it lust disguised as love?" Agnes asked.

"Well, you'll find out won't you, now that you've agreed to marry me when we're older." Graham blew her a kiss and switched out her glass for a fresh cider.

"Did I? I don't remember that. It must have been in a moment of desperation," Agnes decided, tapping a finger against her lips.

"Even better. I can't wait for you to be desperate for me." Graham gave Agnes a heavy-lidded look, and Agnes sighed.

"I can't believe this works on women." Agnes rolled her eyes.

"Are they always like this?" Lia asked me, and I blinked at her, forcing my thoughts away from doing something stupid like asking her to marry me.

"Yes, for as long as I can remember. Don't be deceived. They actually *are* friends. I think it's just boredom causing them to pick at each other," I said, relieved when my brain kicked into gear.

"I've grown up with Graham," Agnes explained to Lia. "And practically this one, too."

"But I was just here during the summer," I explained. "My grandparents live up the way."

"How are they getting on?" Agnes asked, worry crossing her face. "I haven't seen them in a while."

"Och, they're grand. They're touring Greece right now, and after that, Spain. It's a shame I'll miss them this round, but I'm happy enough that they're able to still travel. They have a whole group they go with. It's all boat and bus tours. The tour makes all these stops, and they get to stay a few days in each destination so they can rest and relax as needed." I nodded my thanks to Graham when he served me another perfectly poured pint.

"I hate tours that are so tightly packed that you never get a moment to chill," Agnes said. "What's the point of going to a pretty holiday destination if you can't sit in the garden and read there?"

"Most people go on holiday to see the sights, not to bury their noses in a book," Graham pointed out.

"False. Not everyone plans their vacations around picking up women. Some of us prefer a chance to read books unbothered by others. It's a way to relax and unwind."

"Some would also argue that making love is a delightful way to relax and unwind."

"It's not love if you've just met her." Agnes slapped her hand on the bar, and Graham grinned, clearly pleased he was rankling Agnes.

"Looks like you could use a bit of...relaxing."

"She's going to kill you one of these days, Graham. I might just help her," I put in before Agnes could explode.

"Och, it's just a bit o' banter, love." Graham leaned over

and smacked a noisy kiss on her cheek, and Agnes swatted him away.

"Yeah, yeah." She turned to Lia who was devouring her food with a single-mindedness I admired. "How's the food?"

"Delicious. Exactly what I needed after a long travel day."

"Where are you coming from?" Agnes asked.

"Boston," Lia said, dipping her spoon into her soup. I caught the look that Agnes sent Graham, and he shook his head in answer. She glared back. What was *that* about?

"I've only been to Boston once," I said, wanting to keep Lia talking. "But I really liked it. It has this feel of being a big city, but also kind of cozy as well. It was nice to walk around, and the pub culture there is kind of like our own."

"Boston is great." Lia smiled at me, and I think I might have levitated off the floor. Her smile took all of the sharp edges from her face, and it felt like, *hell,* I don't know, a blessing or something. All I knew was that I would do anything to make her keep smiling at me that way. "I'm going to miss..." She trailed off and clamped her mouth shut.

Another weird look between Agnes and Graham. But all I could think about was what she had been about to say. Did missing it mean she wasn't going back? Would she be staying in Loren Brae? It was too much to hope for, as it was more likely she'd travel Scotland like most tourists did. Unless I could convince her to stay here, at least long enough for me to see why I'd suddenly developed this insatiable need to know more about her.

Yup, still sounding a bit creepy in my head. *Down, boy.*

My dating style was nothing compared to Graham's approach. First of all, Agnes was right—I rarely had time to date because I buried myself in my work. However, one could argue that I buried myself in my work because I was lonely. So I couldn't be too sure what the cause and correlation was here, exactly, but either way, I wasn't dating all that much these days. And, when I did date, I was about as polite as I could be. I hated feeling out of my element, and I never wanted a woman to feel uncomfortable with me. Typically, I even let her make the first move, though the lads always gave me a hard time for it. I didn't care. Steamrolling women was Graham's approach. Mine was to woo them with my nerdiness and good manners.

Hence me still being single.

"It's a touch quieter here than in Boston," I said, when Lia didn't continue speaking. "But I think you'll find it has its own charm. If you can call these two charming."

Lia laughed, and I felt like I'd won the lottery.

"Munroe, a word?" One of the locals in the pub, Stuart who owned a carpentry business, tapped my shoulder. As much as I hated to turn away from Lia, I didn't want to be rude.

"How's it going then, Stuart?" I asked.

"Well enough, I suppose, though work has fairly dried up these days. I'm of a mind to ask you about this distillery you're considering. I know Graham asked us not to speak of it, and I promise to not be saying a word. I was just thinking maybe we could have a wee chat about any of your building needs if the time comes that you're ready for it." The hope in his eyes was palpable, and my heart twisted. From what I remembered, Stuart ran a business with fair practices and good work, and it was my goal to use local tradesmen as much as I could for the project.

"Of course, Stuart. When the times comes, I'd be more than happy to have a chat with you about our needs."

"Do you, by chance, have an idea of when that might be?" I caught the glimmer of desperation in his eyes and realized that times must be even more difficult in Loren Brae than I had realized.

"Soon," I promised, clapping him on the shoulder. "Until I have a location, I can't start the process of going through budgets and design options with my team. That will be my first step." Technically, my first step should be analyzing the profitability of a distillery in a location, taking into consideration both local and tourist activity, high and low seasons, cost of electricity...the list went on and on. However, this was the perk of owning the business. Occasionally, I could follow a whim. And, while I thought Loren Brae would be a profitable location based on my preliminary research, I knew that I could make this into a tourist destination if I put a significant PR campaign behind it. Which meant, while I'd skipped a few important steps in coming to this decision, a location really was the next step in the process.

"I might have a few ideas. I know most of the buildings in Loren Brae and the surrounding area. If you need any help, I'm happy to offer an opinion or a look through to give you an idea of how much work a place might need."

"I appreciate that. Why don't you call me tomorrow and we can arrange to go look at a few places. I'll pay you a consulting fee, of course," I said as I reached for my wallet to pull my business card out. Relief crossed his face, but then Stuart shook his head.

"No need for a fee. I'm happy to help."

Proud. I admired that in a man, though it could cause issues at times.

"Call me tomorrow," I said and turned to greet the next man, an electrician, who had lined up behind him. By the time I'd finished speaking with several of the locals about my proposed project, I returned to the bar to see Lia was gone.

"Did she leave?" I blurted out, my gaze darting to the door.

"Och, it's like that, is it?" Graham raised an eyebrow at me. "You could've said something before I gave her a flirt."

"Yes, she's gone. Just now," Agnes offered, and I left without saying another word. I had no idea if I'd ever see this incredible woman again, and I had to at least try and see if she would give me her number. Nerves skittered through my stomach as I all but ran out onto the street, twisting my head in all directions until I saw a lone figure standing at the side of the loch.

When a shriek split the night, I ducked, unsure of what was happening and then realized it was the Kelpies that Graham had spoken of. Sprinting to Lia, I caught her as she turned, her face sheet-white with fear.

"What *was* that? What is happening? Oh my God, Munroe. I can't...they don't have this stuff in Boston. We have carjackings, and people beat each other up in the streets, but I don't know what this is...did you hear that... what is it? Are we going to die?" Lia's eyes were wide with fear as she babbled up at me. All I could think about was how well she fit into my arms.

I did the only thing I could think of to stem the panicked flow of words. I kissed her.

Everything quieted.

My thoughts settled, the world faded away, and a sense of rightness filled my soul. The kiss heated as much as it soothed, and Lia clung to me like I was her lifeline in a sea of darkness. I could have stood there forever, clinging to each other on the shores of Loch Mirren, sinking into the abyss together. When Lia broke the kiss and pulled back, I didn't let her go as her hands still clung tightly to the front of my shirt. She blinked those wide doe-eyes up at me, and I smiled down at her.

I wanted to apologize. I wanted to explain that I'd only kissed her because it stopped her panic in its tracks. But I couldn't. I *wouldn't*.

I would never apologize for kissing this miracle of a woman.

"Let me walk you safely home," I said, instead, and gently pried her fingers loose from my shirt. Hooking an arm around her shoulder, as I sensed she still needed the comfort, I turned her back toward the village. With a last glance to the calm waters of Loch Mirren, I nudged Lia forward.

"I'm just there. At the B&B." Lia pointed up the street.

"Perfect. I'll see you safely to your door." I wanted to make clear that I wasn't expecting anything else from her. It wasn't long before we stood at the front of the B&B, and I waited while Lia fished out her key with a hand that still trembled.

"Are you going to be okay? Do you need me to call anyone for you?" Okay, now I sounded like a fussy mum. I could hear Graham berating me in my head.

"What just happened there?" Lia paused and looked up at me.

"The kiss or the Kelpies?" I asked. Please, let's talk more about the kiss.

"Kelpies...what are those?" Lia asked. "Is that what screamed?"

"Aye, I believe so. They are magickal water horses. And, yes, I know, it's a lot to take in. Listen, it's late. Let me give you my number, and I can meet you for coffee to talk more about it tomorrow. I can ask Agnes to come as well, if you'd like. She owns the bookstore in town and might be helpful here."

"Sure, okay. Yeah. I'd like that." Lia took my card. "Thanks, Munroe. I'm..." Lia trailed off and looked away.

"What?" *Please ask me up to your room*. I didn't care if she wanted to talk until the wee hours of the morning on separate sides of the room. I'd take any moments I could get with her. "Do you not want to be alone? We can talk now. I can get some tea from the pub if you'd..."

"Oh, no, I'm okay. I mean, that was definitely freaky and deeply unsettling. But I promise you...I'm going to hold it together." Lia gave me a tense smile and shoved her hair back from her face. "I was going to say that I'm sorry if I insulted you about the gin. I didn't know that was your business."

"Och, no worries, lass. I'm made of tougher stuff than that." Was I? It didn't feel like it tonight with the way I was tripping over myself for this woman.

"Thanks for..." Lia waved her hand at the loch. "I'll call you tomorrow."

Leave now before you screw it up, lad.

"Great, that's grand. Really. Love to hear from you. Call any time. It won't be too early. If you need anything else, I know a lot of people in town. I could get you food for breakfast, or...och, right, you're at a bed and breakfast. Anyway. So, sleep well then." I turned on my heel and walked briskly away before I embarrassed myself further.

Just before I reached the pub, her voice reached me.

"And thanks for the kiss."

Turning, I bowed, like I was a geriatric senior, and then I ducked inside the Tipsy Thistle, torn between excitement and embarrassment. *I kissed her. I kissed Lia from Boston. Is that considered the first move?*

"What happened, lad?" Graham looked at me with his eyes wide. My expression must have reflected my inner turmoil.

"Whisky, neat," I ordered.

"Och, that's never a good thing. Have a seat, mate, and tell Papa all about it."

CHAPTER SIX

Lia

Much to my surprise, I slept straight through until my alarm startled me awake the next morning. I lay in bed, my eyes darting around the room, as I tried to gather my wits enough to determine just where, exactly, I was.

Scotland.

The B&B.

The Kelpies.

The *kiss.*

I rolled, pulling the tartan blanket up to my chin, and snuggled into my pillow as I relived the moment. Intellectually, I understood that Munroe had kissed me to shock me. It was an effective tactic that had immediately pulled me out of the quicksand of panic and thrust me into desire so fast that my body just ran along with the emotions, riding the adrenaline like its own personal wave of lust. It had taken all of my restraint not to pull Munroe up to my room and see if he could live up to the promise of his kiss.

Because, holy hell, that *kiss*.

Not only had it frozen me in my tracks and dragged me from a pit of fear, but it had warmed me straight down to my toes. I'd clung to him, not out of fright, oh no, but because I wanted to climb the big brute like he was my favorite tree. It was like when my pastry chef made chocolate croissants and one bite was never enough. Munroe had given me just a taste of something that promised so much more, and if it had been anywhere else and any other time, I would have dragged him to my room and enjoyed the whole croissant. But it wasn't the right time. I was here to learn about Loren Brae, to see what this magick stuff was all about and to decide if this truly was a place where I could build a new life for myself.

Adding a hunky highlander into the mix would only complicate matters.

That being said, Munroe had given me more enjoyment in a singular kiss than anything I'd ever felt from my last boyfriend. Now, as I skimmed my hands down my body, I squirmed against my palm as I brought Munroe's image to my mind.

A gilded god. It had been my first thought upon seeing him, the warm glow of the pub light silhouetting his broad shoulders. If I was being honest, Graham was equally as sexy, but it wasn't Graham's image that came to mind as my body warmed to my touch. Munroe. Man of few words, but one who was always watching. I'd caught his eyes on me more than once, his gaze a tender caress, and I could have kicked myself when I realized I'd insulted his gin business. Pulling a pillow over my head, I arched my hips as I relived the heat of Munroe's kiss, the press of his hard body against mine. Where he was tall and broad shouldered, I was short, round, and curvy. And yet, somehow, we'd fit.

I wanted to see how *else* we'd fit together. Gasping into the pillow that swallowed my moan, I brought myself over the sharp edge of desire and rode the wave of gentle pleasure with Munroe's name at my lips. When the last trickle of bliss faded, I pulled the pillow from my head and pushed myself up, determined to make it down to breakfast in time. The kind woman who had checked me in the night before had already taken my order for my eggs, and I didn't want to keep her waiting too long. I got the sense that I might be the only guest here, and I didn't want to hold up her day.

For someone who had been exposed to her first brush of the paranormal the night before, I couldn't seem to stop thinking about Munroe as I showered and readied myself quickly for the day. You'd think a supernatural encounter would have sent me running for the airport, but instead, I was obsessing over what color shirt to wear this morning if I did end up calling Munroe for coffee. Pink, by the way. I picked a petal-pink shirt because it warmed my skin tone and contrasted with my red hair. Not that it mattered, of course. It just happened to be the shirt at the top of my suitcase.

Who was I kidding? *Of course* I was going to call him. Not only did I want to see him again, without the influence of alcohol to muddle my thoughts, but I also needed some intel on these Kelpies. If the scream that had shattered the night and almost made me wet my pants was any indication of their power, well, my decision might already be made for me. As I'd babbled to Munroe the night before, I was a city girl through and through. I could handle rats and drunken frat boys pissing in the streets, but magickal beasts screaming in the night? This was a whole different ball game, and I wasn't sure I wanted to learn the rules.

Breakfast turned out to a be a proper Scottish one, with black pudding, thick cut slabs of bacon, beans, toast, and eggs. I waved away the offer of porridge, already far past my limit of food intake for breakfast. Typically, I woke late and drank my body's weight in coffee as a start to my day, but I needed to get an idea of the local cuisine in case it would be expected at the castle's restaurant. Thoughts of the castle reminded me that I needed to take a walk and explore later today. But first, more coffee was needed. Picking up my phone, I typed out a message to Munroe on Whatsapp.

His immediate response, along with a time and location to meet, made me smile. It was almost as if he'd been waiting by the phone. A soft trill of pleasure worked its way through me, and I tried not to read too much into it. He was just worried about me. We'd both experienced something otherworldly, and it was normal to want to debrief about it the next day. It wasn't like anyone else would believe me. I tried to imagine telling Savannah about water horses that screamed in the night.

After breakfast, I left the B&B to run to the market to pick up a few snacks to have in my room. Plus, I just wanted to get an idea if there was any local produce or what items were popular here. Food was my love language, and soon enough, I was lost in my thoughts as I wandered the aisle of the small supermarket, noting they had a very generous section for leeks. While leek soup was likely popular here, it was a versatile vegetable that I had used several times in unique recipes. One of my favorites had been grilled leeks with miso, garlic, and a touch of maple syrup.

"I'll take care of it. You've got enough to worry about."

Jolted from my thoughts, I sidled to the edge of the aisle and peered around the corner to where Munroe stood at the checkout. Next to him, a woman carried a screaming toddler at her hip, with a baby in a stroller beside her. Her cart had two bags of groceries, and her cheeks were bright pink with embarrassment.

"I can't understand why my card isn't working..." The woman trailed off and tried to dig through her purse.

"It's fine. Truly. Allow me to get this for you. You just get this wee man home." Munroe raised a hand for a high five, and the toddler eyed him suspiciously before continuing to scream. The baby, seeming to realize that the yelling portion of the day was upon them, took up crying as well.

"I can't..." The mother looked between her kids and Munroe. I noticed she wasn't wearing a wedding band, and I wondered if she was doing it all on her own.

"You can. I made a promise to myself that I'd do one random act of kindness a week. You don't want me to have to go back on my word, do you?" Munroe asked, already handing his card over to the cashier.

"No?" The woman seemed confused, and I couldn't blame her. It was like being steamrolled by a yellow lab.

"That's grand. It's all sorted then. Get this wee man his brekkie."

The woman looked once more between her cart of groceries and her screaming kids and seemed to finally accept that she needed help. Blubbering her thanks, she beamed at Munroe as he pushed the grocery cart through the door and into the parking lot.

I sighed.

Here I'd been pleasuring myself to the wicked promise of Munroe's kiss, and he looked to be about the nicest man in town. Not only had he come to my rescue the night before, but now he was saving single mothers who could barely make ends meet. I needed to school my dirty thoughts around him. Where I'd dreamt about him corrupting me, now I honestly worried it might be the other way around. Munroe might just be too good for me.

Which was fine, really, I told myself as I finished checking out and left the store. I needed a good reason to not have a vacation fling, and it was time for me to shift into business mode. I was about to embark on a huge life change, and any man would be an unwelcome distraction. *Even men that kissed like sin and, dear God...was he really helping a grandmother cross the street?* I stopped in my tracks outside the supermarket and gaped to where Munroe, his arm hooked around a grandmother who was most decidedly flirting with him, was crossing the street. When they reached the other side, she motioned to him, and when he bent his head, she kissed him on the cheek. Annoyance bloomed, and I stayed where I was, tilting my head as I considered my odd reaction. Annoyed? I should have been charmed. And I had been up until the old woman had kissed him.

Right. This was *not* good. I clearly must be jetlagged if I was getting annoyed that other women, particularly women several decades older than I was, were kissing Munroe. She wasn't my competition. Wait. Why was I even *thinking* about competition? This wasn't what I was here for. My eyes narrowed as she sent him a flirtatious kiss over her shoulder.

Back off, granny.

"Lia!" I pulled my thoughts away from knocking a grandmother over, not hard, mind you, just enough to put her in her place, and looked to where Munroe waved at me from the other side of the street. Hoisting my small reusable market bag on my shoulder, I went to cross the street when a loud horn sounded, startling me back onto the sidewalk. Instinctively, I shot the driver a one-fingered salute, and then hunched my shoulders when I saw it was the single mother from the store.

"Sorry," I called, even though she had her windows closed. "Bad habit."

"Are you okay?" Munroe trotted across the street and stopped in front of me, his hands hanging in the air like he'd been about to pull me in for another hug. Yes, please. Actually, no. No. I needed a clear head to focus on my job. Not on the way the sun splitting the clouds danced through the golden tendrils of Munroe's hair or the way his eyes crinkled at the corners when he smiled down at me.

"Yes, sorry about being rude to your friend. It's just how we communicate in Boston," I said, feeling my cheeks heat.

"You looked at the wrong side of the road," Munroe explained. Gently, he nudged my shoulder, so I turned to look out at the street. "You have to look both ways when you're a tourist, otherwise you could get seriously hurt."

Lovely. Now I felt even worse about flipping off the

single mom with the screaming kids knowing it was my fault.

"That'll be a learning curve, I imagine," I grumbled, as Munroe started across the crosswalk at my side.

"Don't worry about it. We're used to it. Although I'm sure the wee man has a fun new hand gesture he'll try out on his mum."

"Great. Corrupting small children already. That was the first thing on my list of things to do when I arrived. Check." I made a check motion in the air in front of me, and Munroe laughed. The sound was warm and rumbly, like a reluctant bear waking from a slumber, and it made my toes curl in my boots. I was really going to have to find a new crush, because this was quickly becoming a problem.

"What else was on the list?" Munroe asked, pointing to a pretty storefront with flower boxes and arched windows. As we drew closer, I could see Agnes inside arranging a stack of books in the window display.

"Oh, you know, the usual. Beat up a few grandmothers, start a rock band, leave a trail of broken hearts behind me."

"Ruthless," Munroe said. "I'll have to warn Catriona to watch out for you."

Was that the flirting granny's name? Duly noted.

"It's a braw morning today, isn't it?" Agnes greeted us. "I'm told you're a coffee drinker, so I have a pot of my favorite on."

"Is this your shop, Agnes? It's stunning," I said. Sunlight beamed through the arched windows and highlighted the warm tones of the wood floor. Worn wooden beams in the same color crossed the high ceiling, and colorful woven rugs were scattered across the floor. Bookshelves, low-slung chairs, and a fireplace in the corner created a welcoming atmosphere that invited a browser to drop into a chair and stay awhile. I instantly felt at home, even though I wasn't much of a reader.

"Aye, it is. Thanks for that. I do love a cozy space," Agnes said as she brought a tray of cups to the quaint table in front of the fireplace. I imagined in the winter it was quite a comfortable spot to curl up and dream away a few hours. I couldn't begin to remember the last time I'd had that amount of time to just laze a day away. Munroe settled next to me once I'd taken a seat on the couch, and I realized that I also couldn't remember the last time I'd relaxed with a man either.

"You're here about the Kelpies," Agnes said as casually as if she was commenting on the weather. "I understand you had a run-in with them last night?"

"Not a run-in, no," I said, the memory of their spine-tingling scream causing a shiver to race through me. "I was just admiring the water at night, since it was so calm and reflecting the village lights, and then...bam! A scream. I almost wet my pants."

"I can't be blaming you if you had," Agnes said, a sympathetic smile on her face as she returned with a pot of coffee and poured the steaming brew into our cups. "They're more than a little terrifying. And absolutely fascinating in their own right."

"You say this as if they're real..." I took a sip of my coffee, waving away her offer of cream, and glanced at Munroe who just studied me with those clear blue eyes.

"They are the stuff of legends," Munroe said, his gaze on me cool and assessing. "I grew up reading about them, pretending to battle them, searching the shores of the loch for these water beasts. It wasn't until Lachlan and Graham admitted to me what was going on here that I actually believed they could be real. I'm not that far behind you when it comes to wrapping my head around the way of things here, and that's the truth of it."

"You know, last night, when I heard the scream? Yeah, okay. I could suspend my disbelief and, rightly, be terrified. But in the light of day? I can't help but wonder if this is just like, I don't know, some joke they play on tourists to punk us." I shrugged, taking another sip of my coffee. It was a perfect cup, with a pleasant aroma and hitting a nice balance between acidity and bitterness. I'd have to ask Agnes where she got the roast. It might be a good choice for the restaurant.

"Quite the opposite, unfortunately. Tourism is our greatest economic support in Loren Brae. With talk of screams in the night and mythological beasts terrifying the town, it hasn't exactly been great for our public image. Aside from a few paranormal enthusiasts, that is." Agnes wore a mournful expression and I realized she was dead serious.

"But...but...how? Why? Like...what makes them...be? Come into existence? Why Loren Brae? Have there always been Kelpies here?" Truly, I had *so* many questions.

"Kelpies, in general, can be traced through myths that have been handed down through the centuries. They aren't contained to just one loch or one area of Scotland, unlike our darling Nessie."

"Nessie? She's real?" My eyes widened. The Loch Ness

Monster was the stuff of legends, and my father even had a small Nessie statue in his garden.

"Can't confirm that one," Agnes said with a wistful smile. "I've my own beasts to deal with here."

"Fair enough, I suppose," I said. I was beginning to wonder if everybody in Scotland was nuts or if it was the rest of the world who had turned a blind eye to the magick found here.

"On the flip side, I mean...how cool is it that they are real? It's like aliens landed here and hung out for a while. We'd finally have the proof that everyone is looking for." Munroe's face lit with excitement.

"I'm not sure everyone is looking for proof," I began, and Munroe leaned closer, ready to argue.

"How could you not at least be curious? Surely we're not the only planet that sustains life. I mean, consider the possibilities—"

"Guys. The Kelpies?" Agnes interrupted.

"Right. The mysterious water horses that want to kill me," I said, rolling my eyes.

"Well, it's not necessarily you that they're wanting to hurt. Not all of the legends speak of the Kelpies as being dangerous. If anything, they are quite often portrayed as helpers or protectors, depending on the case. In ours? It is protectors they are. Which is why they become dangerous."

"What is it they are protecting?" I looked at Munroe who only shrugged.

"Clach na Fìrinn. The Stone of Truth," Agnes said, her gaze on the loch through the window.

"What in the world is that?" It sounded like something out of the Middle Ages.

"Oh, just the holy grail of stones that holds all the knowledge of the world and could be incredibly dangerous if it falls into the wrong hands," Agnes said, casually. Too casually for my taste.

"Cool, cool," I muttered, as the weight of what this little town faced settled on my shoulders. A shiver went through me, like a cold wind careening down the mountain and skimming across the surface of the icy waters of the loch, and I felt something inside me rise to meet it. I'd never been one to back down from a challenge. Maybe it was my Scottish roots, or perhaps my Italian stubbornness, but I'd only just started on this new life path of mine, and I wasn't going to let some magickal water horses scare me away.

If the flirting granny could live here blithely, well, so could I.

CHAPTER SEVEN

Munroe

"Where are you off to then?"

We'd left the bookstore once a few customers had come in to distract Agnes, not wanting to speak of delicate matters in front of tourists, and now stood at the curb.

"It's my first day in town. I was planning to just wander about and kind of get a lay of the land," Lia said, tilting her head at the smooth waters of Loch Mirren. "Think I'll have any issues with our water friends?"

"I..." I paused and saw my opening. I couldn't ever remember talk of the Kelpies appearing during the day, however, I would take any opportunity to spend more time with Lia. Yes, my email inbox was overflowing, and even now my phone buzzed with incoming calls. That all could wait. What couldn't wait was a chance to learn more about Lia and see if she planned to spend more time in Scotland. Plus, anything I could do to put myself in the position to protect her appealed to the comic-book hero nerd buried deep inside of me. "We can't be sure when they'll next appear. Why don't I join you on your walk just in case?"

"I won't say no." Lia laughed up at me. "As I said, in the light of day? The Kelpies don't seem like a big deal. But I was scared shitless last night. I'll take the offer of company. Tell me more about Loren Brae. You grew up here?"

"Only for summers. My grandparents live up the way." I gestured to the road that led out of Loren Brae and wound around the banks of Loch Mirren. "It's a grand village, really. People are friendly, they help each other out, and everybody knows everyone else's business. I'm sure some people find it annoying or dull, but I have always loved it here. There's a sense of community...of family." Despite myself, a wistful note came into my voice. I'd been chasing that feeling my whole life. Maybe coming back to Loren Brae would be equally as good for me as it would be for the village and the business opportunities that I could offer.

"What's your family like?" Lia asked, as we turned a corner and followed the path that led away from the village and up toward MacAlpine Castle.

Cold. Controlling. Unforgiving.

I couldn't say those things though. Instead, I shrugged and picked up a couple of smooth flat rocks. Hefting one in my hand, I skimmed it across the surface of Loch Mirren and watched as it skipped, leaving small circular ripples, marring the smooth reflection of the mountains in the distance. I often felt like that rock when I returned home to my parents' pristine house, where everything had a place, and I was nothing but a disturbance.

"It's just my parents and me. They live in Edinburgh now, and travel often. What about yours?" I really needed to shift the conversation away from myself so I could learn as many details as possible about this incredible creature who stood next to me, her hands tapping the top of the low stone wall, her wild curls dancing in the wind. "Here." I offered her a stone.

"My family?" Lia laughed, joy radiating across her face. I caught my breath, transfixed at her unusual beauty, and wished she would smile at me the same way. "I have four brothers. They're loud, messy, annoying and I love them deeply. My father is Scottish, actually. Mom is Italian. Both first-generation immigrants to the good ol' US of A. We're all redheads, which seems to upset my mother once every six months or so. I think she had hoped her Italian blood would run stronger. In all fairness though, I don't burn in the sun the same way my dad does, so that's something."

"And your eyes." Now that I was closer, I could see little gold flecks glimmering in their warmth. "Witchy eyes. You could hypnotize a man at ten paces with those."

"What did you say?" Lia turned, and caught my arm, her pink lips caught halfway between a smirk and a smile.

"Witchy eyes? I'm sorry, I didn't mean that to offend."

"No, no. I get that." Lia looked up at me with expectation. *Did she want to say more?* But then shook her head before turning back to the loch. Hefting her stone, she tossed it in a neat arc where it landed with a loud plop. "Huh. Not the best."

"Here, like this." I showed her how to turn her body and fling the rock with her wrist. When her next rock careened directly into the water below us, I laughed and moved to stand behind her. Putting my hands on her shoulders, I twisted her body so that she was angled correctly. Then, lifting her arm, I pulled it back and forth a few times without releasing the rock, so she could get a feel for the motion.

And I, inadvertently, got a feel of everything else. Her curvy bum nestled against my thighs and instantly nudged me into hardness. I hastened a step back, dropping my hands, and pulled my coat lower across my waist. The last thing I needed to do was be some creep who rubbed myself against her back like a horny teenager taking any chance to touch a female.

"I did it!" Lia crowed when her rock skipped three times across the water. Turning, she beamed up at me, making everything in my world right, and I found myself leaning toward her lips. Everything about Lia was magnetic, and only when she poked me in the chest, nudging me back, did I realize that I all but loomed over her. "I don't think we should kiss again."

While her voice sounded uncertain and she unconsciously licked her lips, I immediately stepped back to give her space.

"I'd be delighted to revisit that thought any time you would like to," I said, turning to continue our walk. "But care to tell me why?"

"Because I liked it. Too much."

Instantly, my blood heated, and I had to think about how many galaxies there were in the sky to try and force my mind away from dirty thoughts.

"I liked it too. I wouldn't have kissed you if I didn't think that I would." I raised an eyebrow at Lia, encouraging her to continue.

"I know." Lia sighed. "That's the problem. I just got here. I can't fall for the first sexy Scotsman I see, no matter how much I wanted to invite you up last night and have my way with you. It's just...I need to focus right now."

Well, now, how was a man supposed to come up with a coherent sentence after I'd been trying so hard not to think of Lia, naked, writhing beneath me. And then she'd just dragged my mind right back to where I was so desperately trying to stay away from.

"You think I'm sexy?" Nice one, Munroe. Way to focus on the important bits. However, something in me needed to know.

"Oh please." Lia laughed and nudged her shoulder against mine like we were buddies. "Everyone under the age of eighty with somewhat good eyesight can see how hot you are. Even those over seventy." She said the last part as though she was annoyed at something, and I couldn't quite figure out what. Either way, I cheered up quite a bit. Even if Lia didn't want to pursue anything right now, I'd learned two new things about her. The first? She thought I was sexy. And the second? She had already thought about making love with me. My day brightened considerably.

"You're the most beautiful woman I've ever seen. When you walked through the pub door, my heart skipped a beat, and all I could see was this stunning vision walking toward me. I don't think I could even draw a breath or think clearly. It was like being visited by an angel. Except one with a wee bit of an edge and great lips." *Did I just say that out loud?* This would have been an opportune time for my shyness to kick in and shut my damn mouth.

"Oh my God, Munroe. You're *so* good for my ego. I'll take the compliments, greedy bitch that I am, but I just am not in the space for this at the moment."

Why? Had someone hurt her? I wanted to know more. From what I could see, we had a fighting chance here if we could get to know each other better. Why not give it a go? What was holding her back?

"How long are you here for?" I asked instead, steering the conversation into what I hoped was a more neutral territory. "Do you have other stops on your itinerary?"

"Ah, well, I'm not sure," Lia said, turning away. I waited, hoping she would tell me more, and when she continued to walk up the path to the castle, I followed. The sun broke through the clouds, and Lia pulled off her jacket and tied it around her waist. The pink shirt she wore hugged her curves and made me think of the blush that had tinged her cheeks the night before when she'd been embarrassed.

"You'll probably have to get back to work, I'm sure." I wondered what she did for a living. What would draw the attention of this woman who seemed so cagey with the details of her life?

"Do you really think you'll open a distillery here?" Lia asked, turning to look back at where little Loren Brae hugged the banks of Loch Mirren. "It's pretty as a picture, isn't it?"

We'd climbed our way up the hill that led to the castle and had just begun to walk along the path next to a wall of tall hedges that hid the castle from view. From here, you could look out across Loch Mirren and just see the tips of the second row of hills hidden behind those nearer to the shore. Puffy clouds dotted the sky, and a light breeze brought the scent of rain. I noticed that Lia had changed the subject quickly, something she did whenever I asked for more details about her life, and I wondered what she was hiding.

Maybe nothing, you bloody eejit. You just met the lass. She doesn't owe you anything.

A shrill bark was our only warning before a terrorist fuzzball of a Chihuahua rocketed across the grass, followed by a slightly larger puppy.

"Sir Buster!" a woman shouted, and I smiled to where Sophie, Lachlan's girlfriend and all-around good human, raced after the dogs. The second dog, one I hadn't met yet, landed in a ball at my feet, and I instantly scooped the puppy up.

"Who is this wee one?" I demanded, laughing as the puppy licked my face earnestly.

"Lady Lola. I can't decide who is more of a dictator—her or Sir Buster. But they're currently waging a serious war to see who top dog is." Sophie turned to smile politely at Lia, clearly waiting for an introduction from me. A growl sounded at my feet, and I peered over the fluff in my arms to where Sir Buster glared at me, clearly affronted that I had picked up Lady Lola and not him. Like I needed to lose a finger? That dog was ten inches of murder wrapped in fur.

"He's lying to me," I pointed out to Sophie, leaning over to drop a kiss on her cheek, while Lola snuggled more deeply into my arms. "Look at him wanting my attention, but you know he'll rage if I try to pick him up."

"Don't I know it? Cantankerous beast. God, I love him." Sophie laughed and turned to the woman. "I'm Sophie, by the way."

"Oh." A startled look crossed Lia's face. "Nice to meet you." Lia dropped to her haunches and crooned to Sir Buster who immediately danced over to her and put on his best flirt.

"Would you look at that? I've only ever seen him do that with Hilda when she has chicken for him."

"Dogs love me," Lia admitted, picking up a trembling Sir Buster and cuddling him close. "I think it's because they know I have access to food. I'm Lia, by the way, and I think you might be—"

"Lia!" Sophie exclaimed, clapping her hands together in excitement while I looked between the two women.

"Do you know each other?" I asked, as the two women sized each other up. This did not feel like a meeting between women who were friends.

"Not yet. But we will. Lia is our new chef. We stole her from a prime restaurant in Boston. Oh, Lia. Why didn't you tell me you were here already? Where is your luggage?" Sophie turned in a wide circle while my thoughts scrambled to catch up.

A chef.

A newly employed chef.

At the castle.

Here in Loren Brae.

Which meant...Lia was staying. If the Kelpies didn't scare her off. Burying my smile in Lady Lola's excited licks, I couldn't help but feel that maybe, just maybe, I'd finally met the woman I'd been waiting my whole life for.

Now I just had to convince her to take a chance on me.

CHAPTER EIGHT

Lia

There'd been no sense in me staying at the B&B after Sophie had discovered that I was in town, and she'd very gently steamrolled me into moving into MacAlpine Castle later that same day. So much for staying under cover in Loren Brae while I scoped the area out.

Lesson number one—it was impossible to hide much of anything, including myself, in a small village. Gossip was rampant, as I quickly learned when Sophie had commended Munroe for buying the groceries for the single mother earlier that day.

Munroe.

My heart sighed. His personality was like the cuddliest of teddy bears, and yet his mouth had brought the most wicked of desires to my mind. Still waters run deep, my mother had always said, and I was beginning to understand that this quiet man who looked strong enough to fell a tree with one hand, might have hidden depths.

And I didn't plan to become aware of those depths. Not only was Munroe friendly enough with Sophie to drop a kiss on her cheek, but as soon as we'd made our way to the castle, he'd disappeared with Sophie's boyfriend, Lachlan, to go do "man" stuff, which apparently meant video games and a glass of whisky in some hidden room in the castle. Either way, Munroe was buddies with my new employers, so that was just another reason not to become involved.

And oh. My. God. This *castle*. It was, like, a *real* castle. I couldn't quite wrap my head around the beauty and history of this place. I'd always been proud of the history in Boston and how we had a few cobblestone streets, but they paled in comparison to this building that I now, apparently, lived in. Sophie had shown me to one wing of the castle that held apartments, and I'd been given a key as well as the security codes for the front door. It appeared that half the castle was kept historically accurate and open for public tours, while the other half had been modernized and sectioned off for private use. My entire living quarters were almost as large as my parents' condo. After my shoebox of an apartment in Boston, my new digs felt like, well, a *castle*. I know, I know. Suffice it to say, *overwhelmed* was becoming my new best friend.

I was, however, chomping at the bit to see the kitchen. Would it also be modernized, or would that be one of my tasks? Sophie had informed me we had a ton of things to talk about, so I simply dropped my suitcases in my apartment and made quick use of the bathroom before leaving to find my way to the main lounge room, where Sophie had said she'd be waiting.

"Moooooo."

I hit the floor.

Seriously. I hit. The. Floor.

Hands over my head, face to the faded rug, I curled in a ball as I waited for…wait, had that noise been from a cow? What the hell? Peeking through my fingers, I peered up at where a shaggy highland cow tilted its head at me. It stood in the middle of the dim stone hallway that led from my apartment, and my breath caught when I realized I could see *through* the cow.

"Moo?" The cow stepped forward, and I curled into myself, my heart hammering in my chest. Was this ghost cow going to possess me?

"Mooooo." This time the sound was so soft, it was as if the cow whispered it, and I dared to look again. This time the cow was closer, its eyes alight with warmth, and its little paws were tapping the floor like it was doing some sort of mad Celtic stepdance for me. *Wait, did cows have paws?* No, hooves. He danced his *hooves* forward and backward as though he was performing for me.

"Um." I rolled and eased myself to a standing position. The ghost cow stopped dancing and stared at me expectantly. "Hey there, buddy. Nice to meet you."

"Mooo!" the ghost cow bellowed, just about giving me a heart attack, before winking out of sight. I gaped at the now empty hallway and then down at my trembling hands. I'd never been one for scary movies. I hated those stupid videos people would send around Halloween where you'd think you were watching something cute and then a zombie would pop onto the screen. I was not someone who enjoyed being startled. And yet, twice now in less than twenty-four hours, I had almost wet my pants in fright. This did not bode well for my stay in Scotland. Or maybe it would just toughen me up? Perhaps this was just the norm here. Ghost cows and Kelpies just dropped in and became part of the backdrop of day-to-day life? If so, I needed to work on strengthening my composure or I'd be laughed out of Loren Brae.

The flirting granny probably would have walked right up and petted the ghost cow.

Annoyed again, I found my way downstairs, barely taking the time to marvel at the historical décor, and followed the sound of voices to a large lounge room. There, I found two people I hadn't yet met, while Lachlan and Munroe argued over a video game on a couch in the corner and Sophie lectured the two dogs in front of an impressive fireplace.

"Hi," I said, raising a hand awkwardly.

The dogs instantly erupted in a flurry of barking and raced to me, careening in circles around my feet.

"Enough!" a tall, thin man with bushy white hair, assessing eyes, and a fishing tackle box at his feet barked from his chair. Instantly, the dogs went silent and crept to hide under a table that had been set for tea. A round woman with lively eyes and a short crop of hair, strode forward with her hand outstretched.

"Was that Clyde I heard?" the woman asked, searching my face, her hand still holding mine. "I'm Hilda, by the way."

"I'm not sure who Clyde is. But I'm Lia. It's nice to meet you."

"Clyde is our resident ghost coo, and he fancies himself quite a trickster." The man put his tackle box down and came over to shake my hand as well. "I'm Archie, and I'm lucky enough to call this lovely lady my bride. Welcome to MacAlpine Castle. Hilda and I are the caretakers, though I mainly see to the outside whereas Hilda's word reigns supreme on the interior."

"And the outside too," Hilda stage whispered, and Archie elbowed her lightly in the side. They regarded each other with warm affection, reminding me of the bond between my parents, and some of my tension eased. "If Clyde came to greet you, that's a good thing."

"Is it?" I wondered, nonplussed at the casual acceptance of a ghost cow wandering the castle. Although in the case of violent mystical water horses versus dancing ghost cows, I, too, was more likely to accept the resident ghost.

"Aye, dear. Unless he's in a tetchy mood, but that's rare for our Clyde, isn't it. Much more likely for this one." Hilda looked down to Sir Buster who trembled at her feet.

"Is he okay?" I asked.

"Sir Buster? Of course he is. He's a crabbit beast most days, but he'll put on a flirt when he's in the mood for a wee bit of chicken. Don't mind his dramatics," Archie said, as Buster's trembling increased. "It's all for show."

"We are coming up on his next meal," Hilda pointed out. She bustled over to the table and nodded to a chair. "Join us for tea, Lia. We'll have ourselves a wee chat and get acquainted. Boys!"

"Just one more game..." Lachlan trailed off when

Sophie gave him a pointed look. "Right, then. Never mind. I'll kick your sorry arse later."

"Like bloody hell you will," Munroe muttered.

In short order, we sat at the table with warm crusty bread, leek soup, and a simple green salad. It wasn't anything fancy, but the ingredients were fresh, and the taste was superb. I hoped the castle would have a space for a garden where I could plant herbs. I'd never had an outdoor space to call my own before, and now, seeing the expanse of green space behind the castle, excitement bloomed at the possibility of growing my own ingredients.

"Clyde likes to greet our new guests," Sophie said after we'd all settled into our late lunch. "I met him the first night I was here with my best friend, Matthew, and it was an experience, that's for sure."

"I can see that," I said. Nope, I was not going to mention the fact that I'd hit the floor like the castle was under attack. "It's...um, yeah. It was memorable to say the least. I guess it makes me feel better that I'm not the only one who saw him. I mean, ghosts, huh? A ghost *cow*. Like, that's just not something I've ever heard about. Regular ghosts, sure. But..."

"We pride ourselves on being different in Loren Brae," Lachlan said, puffing out his chest in a mock show of arrogance. "Nothing but the most original ghosts to be found here."

"Ah, so Clyde is like a Michelin Star of ghosts then?" I smiled into my cup of tea.

"We like to give the full Scottish experience here. It's... immersive," Sophie added, tapping a finger to her lips. I'd immediately warmed to my fellow American, though she was staunchly a West Coast girl, while I was from the East. However, once I'd learned how she'd inherited the castle and, instead of selling it and rolling around in buckets of cash, she was trying to bring the failing tourism sector back to life, I'd instantly respected her. Maybe I had a bit of a chip on my shoulder about rich people, as I was someone who refused help and worked for everything I had, but it was nice to see that Sophie was diving headfirst into saving the castle. I could admire hard work, even if she had the money to hire someone else to put the castle to rights for her. Not that it looked like it needed much help. What I'd seen of the place so far was astounding.

"I'd forgotten about Clyde," Munroe said, an amused smile hovering on lips that I desperately wanted on mine again. He looked just so...both out of place and perfectly at home. I wasn't sure how to describe the effect he was having on me. He sat at the end of the table, the sleeves of his flannel shirt rolled to reveal muscular forearms, his height and broad shoulders making him tower over his bowl of soup. The small teacup he held in his hand looked like it would snap, and much like how I'd felt when he wrapped his arms around me earlier by the loch. Tiny. Dainty. Ready to shatter at his touch. There was something about Munroe that took up space, as though he claimed his right to be there, and I found myself distinctly aware of his every movement. "We used to run the halls late at night, hoping he'd jump out and scare us. I think he had as much fun with it as we did."

"Aye, he did at that. Clyde does love a good coo joke." Lachlan laughed.

Oh, now Clyde was a jokester? Lovely. We had a

laughing ghost *coo* and murdering water horses. Surely my day couldn't get any stranger. And yet, I was enjoying the conversation and the quick-witted banter that flew across the table. If anything, staying here would not be dull, that was for certain. I already imagined the stories I would tell my father. I found myself relaxing as Lachlan and Munroe poked at each other over the time they'd tried to climb a tree to peek into a girls' sleepover party. The conversation flowed around me, requiring little of my input, while I enjoyed my soup and got a read on my new employers.

It reminded me of sitting with my staff at the end of a long shift while the servers counted their tips, and I made notes on what needed to be restocked for the next day in the kitchen. I liked being on a team, even more so for a team that took pride in their work. I didn't mind being a part of the "help" at the castle, if anything it made me feel like I fit in even more. I'd never dreamt of being a princess, after all. Those dreams were for far fancier people than me. Except in my kitchen, of course. There I could be supreme ruler.

"Lia, do you want to see the kitchen and the restaurant space after we finish eating? I can imagine you'd like to get an idea of what you're getting into before you make any final decisions," Sophie said, exchanging an odd look with Hilda. What was that about? Hilda gave a small shake of her head, and my senses went on high alert.

"Is there something that I need to be warned about?" I asked, pointing my spoon at Sophie. "What was that look for between you and Hilda? I don't like surprises, and if there's something that I need to know, it's best you tell me now, so I'm prepared."

"Aye, lass. There's a world of things you need to know.

But in due time," Archie said, his bushy eyebrows drawn low on his forehead. "You Americans are always so quick to rush into things. Running about, all day long, instead of taking things as they come."

"Och, listen to this one now? A few months ago, he was hounding me to take more action here, and now he wants to potter about in the garden instead?" Lachlan rolled his eyes.

"She's only just arrived. There's time enough for the things that need to get done." Archie glowered at Lachlan. "You've been here your whole life. You didn't have any excuses."

"I'd say I had some justifiable reasons for sticking my head in the sand," Lachlan countered, and before the two men could get into it, Hilda cleared her throat.

"Enough of that at my table." Hilda turned back to me. "Ignore these two. Yes, there's a lot to learn about Loren Brae, including some more unusual elements like Clyde, but why don't we have a wee wander about the grounds first before we delve into the rest of it?"

"Is the rest of it going to be the thing that makes me turn tail and run?" I asked. When the table grew quiet, I looked to the only person who'd been my North Star thus far.

Munroe just shrugged, his blue eyes soft and encouraging on mine. "Can't say what they're talking about, lass, but I'll be here to help with anything you need."

Not that I needed a hero, I reminded myself, but if I did, this quietly buttoned-up, hulk of a Scotsman would do just fine.

"I'm sorry. We're being annoying. It's like when

someone puts up a vague post on social media," Sophie apologized.

"I could use your good thoughts," I deadpanned.

"I don't know what's going to happen to me now," Sophie jumped in.

"If only I'd known better," Lachlan added.

"I never saw that coming." Munroe's lips quirked and I found myself smiling at him.

"What in the world are you all blethering on about?" Archie demanded.

"It's vaguebooking," Sophie explained. "It's when someone posts something on social media with no real explanation just to get attention and comments."

"Social media is for fools," Archie declared, pushing back from the table. "Why would you want to speak to more people than you have to?"

"Well, you see, some of us *like* people," Sophie explained.

"People are terrifying." Munroe gave a mock shudder, earning a grin from Archie.

"See? The lad's got the right of it."

After we finished eating, we followed the dogs as they raced outside and around the side of the castle. The clouds had drawn close, the air thick with the scent of wet earth, and rain misted lightly on the wind. Sophie shivered, and Lachlan pulled her close, whispering something in her ear that made her cheeks flush pink.

"Sophie still hasn't adjusted to our weather," Lachlan said over his shoulder as we followed a gravel path to a set of doors forming an arch.

I had barely noticed the chill in the air. I was more used

to snow than sunshine, and this moody weather suited me just fine.

"I don't know that I ever will," Sophie admitted, as she pulled out an antique-looking key and slid it into the lock. "A lifetime of living by the beach didn't exactly prepare me for Scotland's weather."

"Is this the kitchen?" I cut off any discussion of weather as light spilled into the murky recesses of a large room with stone walls, low ceilings, and an abundance of shiny new stainless-steel appliances. In an unconventional design, the large exterior doors opened directly into the kitchen, with one wall set with not one, but three massive ovens with stovetops. Two of the ovens were modern, but one...my heart danced. "Is this a woodburning stove?"

"It is. Not quite the original, but not far off either," Sophie said, coming to stand by me as I gaped at the room. It was a mix of modern and old, the best parts of the old—like copper pans and a proper spice cupboard—mixing with the new like the stand mixer on the prep table.

"I don't even know what to say. It's so...amazing? Intriguing? Why do the doors open directly outside?" It was such an unusual element that I had to ask about it.

"In case of fire," Hilda explained. "Fire was a castle's worst enemy, and it was a quick way to access the area most likely to go on fire."

"Of course," I nodded, walking around the room, absentmindedly trailing my finger over the edge of the large basin sink. I tried to imagine making food with just fire and buckets of water hauled in from outside. At least the kitchen had been outfitted with electrics and modern-day plumbing. Someone had spent considerable time here in carefully bringing the space into this century without sacrificing some of the finer historical details. "This spice cupboard." I sighed as I ran my fingers over the worn wood chest, and opening a drawer, I caught the lingering scent of cloves and nutmeg. I wondered how long this piece had housed spices. My skin tingled, warmth filling me, and my soul shivered before seeming to give a soft sigh of recognition. Taking a deep breath, I allowed myself to imagine staying here, in this place, and cooking the food of my heart. Something clicked inside me, like a key fitting a lock, and I nodded once to myself before turning to where Lachlan argued with Sophie about a device on the counter.

"It's a knife cleaner," I said, coming to stand next to them. The large wooden circle had slots for knives and a handle to turn the wheel.

"Is that right? I dearly hope you've upgraded her dishwashing system?" Lachlan looked down at Sophie who smirked at him.

"And here I was going to have you washing knives in your kilt for the tourists."

"Think again, darling," Lachlan said, tapping a finger on Sophie's nose.

A kilt. My eyes landed on Munroe, his back turned to me as he fiddled with the door to a bread warmer. Mentally, I stripped him and put him in a kilt, and I swear my insides went liquid at the thought. Heat bloomed in my cheeks, and I had to ask Sophie to repeat herself when she spoke to me.

"I had an industrial space outfitted back here," Sophie repeated, a twinkle in her eye. Had she caught me staring at Munroe? I did not need *that* gossip starting. Following her from the kitchen, I breathed a sigh of relief when she opened a door and flipped on a set of overhead lights to reveal industrial dishwashers, a walk-in freezer and refrigerator, and storage bins. I could have kissed her. With all of this new, assuming the restaurant space was in decent shape, I could have this place up and running fairly quickly. Once I hired staff, that is. These were all details I would need to go over with Sophie once I got an idea of what she was envisioning for the space, as well as what it would take to run it.

"This all looks great, Sophie. I'm loving the mix of the old and the new. I think this will be a really great space to get inspiration for the menu." My eyes strayed to the spice cabinet when we returned to the kitchen, and again, I felt that odd little hum in my blood.

"Don't get too excited yet," Sophie cautioned, beckoning me into another hallway that led from the kitchen. Hitting a light switch, she pushed a door open and stepped back, a sheepish look on her face. "I don't know what to say other than...I'm sorry? I, we, just haven't had time to get to this space yet. It's...yeah, so, I'll lend you Lachlan, of course, to help with the heavy lifting and all..." Sophie trailed off as I gaped at the massive room.

Not only was it cavernous—as the hall could feed a banquet full of visitors—but it was piled high with...everything, it looked like. Chairs were stacked haphazardly on tables, boxes were shoved in corners, rugs were rolled up and had been propped against the walls, and everything was covered in a fine layer of dust. Stunned, I wandered the room, trailing my finger lightly across tabletops and random chests of drawers and tried to wrap my head around just how much work it would take to not only empty out this room, but to go through what to keep and what to get rid of. My earlier excitement fell, like someone sticking a pin in a balloon.

"What happened here?" It came out in a whisper, largely because I'd never seen so much miscellaneous *stuff* in one place before. Growing up, if an item couldn't be used, it was donated, as storage space was at a premium in our house. Even more so after I'd claimed the main storage closet as my bedroom. I felt a bit like I'd stepped into Aladdin's cave, if Aladdin had a fetish for mismatched table settings and boxes of old kitchen supplies. I had a monumental amount of work ahead of me before I could set this place to rights.

"Well, at one time it did operate as an eating space for everyone in the castle," Archie explained. "And then, through the years, when smaller kitchens were built elsewhere in the castle, it became a bit of a de facto storage room."

"A bit? This *is* the storage room," Lachlan said, and I wandered away as Lachlan and Archie began to argue about the room's history. As their voices faded, I truly began to gain a sense for just how large the space was. The stone walls continued here, with large wooden beams crossing the arched ceiling two stories above my head. The room was cavernous, and I could only imagine what the acoustics would be if it was packed with diners. I was used to cooking for a quarter of this space, and I dearly hoped that Sophie wasn't thinking I would cater weddings here. Small-plated fine dining was a far cry from catering for a massive crowd. Both had their places in the culinary world, but I was confident in cooking for a smaller, more intimate, venue.

What did you think a castle restaurant was going to feed —twenty people?

A soft sniggering sound caught my attention, and I pushed more deeply among the clutter to the far corner of the room. It was darker here, as Sophie had only turned on the lights on the side of the hall closest to the kitchen. Once again, a whisper of a laugh drew me deeper among the stacked furniture.

My breath caught.

Eyes blinked at me out of the darkness, warm and almost human, the light glinting off the irises.

"Lia?"

Munroe's voice at my back had me glancing away from the dark corner to where he'd come up behind me. My pulse had picked up as my brain scrambled to make sense of what I thought I'd just seen. Turning, I held a hand out to the corner, pointing.

"What's the matter, lass?" Munroe asked, dropping a large hand casually on my shoulder.

But the eyes were gone.

I waited a moment, my mouth hanging open in shock, wondering if I'd hear that gentle riff of laughter again. When nothing more came, and no eyes glinted at me out of the darkness, I turned back to Munroe.

"I thought I saw something. My brain's playing tricks on me, I guess." I shrugged, though a prickle of awareness hummed over the back of my neck as though something still watched me from the dark corner.

"What? A rat?" Munroe stepped around me and toward the corner, and I caught his arm and held him back. I wasn't sure if it was out of fear for him or if I was at my capacity for absorbing unusual or otherworldly circumstances but, either way, I didn't want him to investigate.

"Probably. In a room this big...I wouldn't be surprised." I sighed, scanning the boxes surrounding me. The space itself was incredible, and if I could just clear it out, at least I could start to get a visual for how I would design the seating. "This is going to take forever to sort through. But, on the plus side, I might find some really cool items." I held up a pewter mug with a rough etching of a thistle.

"It's certainly atmospheric," Munroe agreed, nudging me away from the dark corner. I couldn't help but notice that as soon as I'd told him I thought there was something there, he'd immediately positioned himself between me and the potential threat. It was incredibly sweet, his instant need to protect, and I tried to remind my ladyparts that we weren't here to get our groove back. We were here to run a restaurant. With that in mind, I started back toward the others. I needed to get an idea of their proposed opening date.

"I'll come by to help tomorrow."

Munroe's words had me skidding to a stop and I turned, my face bumping into his chest. He grabbed my shoulders, easing me back.

He smelled like cedar and something fresher, mint maybe, and I had to fight every urge I had to lean in and take a big sniff of his shirt. *That would be weird*. Women do not go around sniffing men's chests. At least not in front of their new employers.

"What do you mean you'll come by tomorrow?" I narrowed my eyes.

"To help clear this out. Surely you aren't thinking to

crack on with this all by yerself?" Munroe's accent thickened as he looked at me with disbelief on his handsome face. He wasn't wrong, I would need help to clear the room. But...asking for help was not an area I excelled in. If I did recruit movers, it would be on my timeline and when I delegated it. Not because some hot Scotsman decided to play hooky from his job for the day because he had a need to be the hero.

"I'll figure it out. Thanks for the offer, Munroe, but I don't need your help." I needed to do this on my own. Sophie and I still had to work out some points regarding my actual investment in the restaurant. If I could buy into the place, then I'd never be in the position that I'd just been in with Damien at Suzette's. Which made me even more determined to prove myself, even if it meant not accepting help from a handsome Scotsman.

I was saved from having to argue the point when Sophie crossed to me, an apologetic look on her face.

"It's bad, isn't it? I knew it was, but...yeah. Listen, based on the spreadsheet I put together, it should take three weeks with five helpers to clear this. Two if we up the helpers to ten and make decisions quickly." Sophie's eyes lit with excitement when she spoke of her spreadsheet.

"When do you want to be open? I think that's really the main question. We can figure it out once we have a firm date."

"I don't have a firm date." A pained expression crossed Sophie's face. Was not having a specific date and solid plan physically difficult for her to stomach? "We're not in a rush, if that's what you're asking."

"I do work well on a deadline," I mused, turning once

more to survey the large room. "But if you're not needing the restaurant opened, like, yesterday...then, it's probably best to take our time here until we can create the perfect space."

And to hire an exterminator, I added silently, my eyes going to the dark corner in the back of the hall.

Munroe was probably right. It was likely just a rat.

CHAPTER NINE

Munroe

I gave Lia three days.

As much as it pained me to do so, I could tell by the way she lifted her chin and refused my offer of help, that I would need to step back and let her take on the challenge of the castle restaurant by herself.

At least for a day or two, that is.

It chafed, my inability to help this woman who had so captivated me, and under the guise of welcoming her to town, I arrived at MacAlpine Castle toting a housewarming gift. She couldn't say no to a gift, right? At the very least, it would give me an excuse to see her again and to check on the progress in the restaurant.

Each night, I'd stopped at the pub in hopes that I would see her, but Agnes had informed me that Lia was working long hours putting the restaurant to rights and designing menu ideas. Frankly, it hadn't been like I had all that much free time myself, what with every tradesperson in Loren Brae trying to secure work with me and scouting missions to find a spot for the distillery. As of yet, I'd come up dry when it came to the perfect location, but that didn't bother me too much. My patience was one of the things that made me a successful businessman, that and an uncanny ability to lean into the right decisions for where I wanted my business to grow. I trusted that the perfect location would present itself in due time.

A sharp whistle caught my attention, and I changed course from heading to the wide doors that led to the private entrance of MacAlpine Castle and turned toward where Lachlan and Archie stood by a gardening shed. Both men wore muddied boots and worn denim, leading me to believe they'd been mucking about in the gardens that morning.

"Munroe, good to see you, lad." Archie nodded to the gift bag I carried at my shoulder. "You didn't have to bring me gifts though."

"And what makes you think you deserve a gift?" I rocked back on my heels and pursed my lips at the old man.

"I take care of this place, don't I? Damn near raised you as well, at least part of the year," Archie muttered, his thick brows drawn low on his forehead as he glowered at me.

"He's tetchy today. He wants to be out on the river, but Sophie is on him to put together a space for an herb garden for Lia."

"It's an odd time to be starting a garden is all," Archie protested, squinting up at the sky. "It's half-summer now."

"Herbs hardly take all that much time to grow though,"

I pointed out, as I reached in my pocket. “It’s not like she’s asking you to plant her tatties.”

“And don’t you be putting that thought in her head.” Archie glowered at me. “We’ve a lot of rain up here. Potatoes could rot.”

“Could do,” I nodded. “And then again, could be great.”

“Bloody hell. The lad makes some drink from berries and suddenly thinks he’s a farmer,” Archie muttered. I handed him a small packet that I had pulled from my pocket. “What’s this then?”

“Open it and see.”

“Marabou feathers,” Archie said when he unwrapped his gift, a smile springing to his face.

“Sustainably sourced from a friend who has them as domestics.”

“That’s a good lad,” Archie said, clapping me on my shoulder. “They’ll be a great addition to my fly-tying box.”

“Where’s my gift?” Lachlan demanded, holding out a hand. I slapped my palm into his.

“My friendship is all the gift you need.” I fluttered my eyelashes at him.

“More like a curse,” Lachlan muttered, and nodded at the bag at my shoulder. “What’s this about then?”

“It’s for Lia.”

“Is that the way of it?” Lachlan measured me.

“Aye, that’s the way of it.” I didn’t care that I was declaring my intentions toward Lia to someone else before I told Lia herself. Graham had already figured out my interest from the first night she’d arrived, and Lachlan was well besotted with Sophie, so he wouldn’t be fussed.

"Does the lass know that's the way of it?" Archie demanded.

"Not yet, she doesn't. So don't go ruining things for me. I need to take my time here," I said.

"Versus every other time you've gone after a woman?" Lachlan rolled his eyes. "You move as fast as a glacier."

"Which means this one is likely more important. Seeing as he's already bringing gifts," Archie pointed out.

"Ohhhh, is it love then?" Lachlan said in a singsong tone.

"I'm happy to take my feathers back," I said, mock reaching for my gift that Archie still held in his hand.

"Not a chance. On you go, lad. Lia's in the kitchen fussing about with a recipe or two. We need to finish getting this garden sorted before we move on to more important business." Archie exchanged a look with Lachlan that had my friend picking up his shovel again. There'd been a lot of meaningful looks tossed around in the past few days, and I couldn't help but feel that I was missing something important. My instincts told me that I was, but, because I trusted Lachlan, I decided that I wasn't going to push the point. If it had anything to do with the Kelpies, he could tell me in his own time.

A battle cry greeted me as I approached the doors to the kitchen, and I smiled down as a tiny ball of rage raced toward me.

"Greetings, Sir Buster," I said, knowing better than to bend to pet the vibrating chihuahua who escorted me to the doors. "Lovely day, isn't it?"

Buster growled. As I wasn't fluent in Chihuahua, it could have been agreement or a complaint for all I could tell. Lady Lola sat on the grass in front of where the kitchen doors were thrown open to encourage the breeze, and she promptly rolled onto her back when she saw me.

"Giving it up so easily, eh? Shameless hussy." I clucked my tongue as I bent to scratch her tummy, and she wriggled on the grass in joy. Buster's growls reduced to a series of grunts, and only then did I reach out and give him a quick scratch behind the ear. Once I'd passed the guards, I poked my head through the door. "Knock knock."

"Oh!" Lia turned, surprise on her pretty face. Her curls were wrapped up in an intricate knot on her head, and her dusky skin was flushed pink from the heat of the stove. "I wondered what all that barking was about."

"Sorry about that. I wanted to pop in and see how you were getting on."

"Good, I think?" Lia laughed at the look on my face. The kitchen, which had been fairly organized when we'd first seen it, now looked as though the insides had been vomited out. Cutlery was stacked in piles, bowls of varying sizes were strewn about, and a variety of food items were on the prep table. Every drawer in the spice cupboard was pulled open, contributing to an interesting mix of spicy and sweet scents, and Lia's apron was dusted with flour. "I swear it looks worse than it is."

There was something about the way Lia's smile lit her face that made my heart shiver and dance in my chest. Everything in me quieted when she was around. The outside world's stress and anxiety faded away, and I could just be, existing in this moment with this beautiful woman, my only goal to keep her smiling.

"I'm certain there's a method to your madness," I said,

stepping into the chaos. I held out the gift bag. "I come bearing gifts."

"Munroe. You don't have to get me gifts." Lia put her hands behind her back, like a child who refused to pick up their mess.

"I don't have to do anything I don't want to do," I agreed, and held the bag out to her. When she just looked at me, the moment drew out until awkwardness took over. "I'm sorry. I didn't mean to make you uncomfortable. It was just a wee welcome gift."

"No, no. It's me." Lia shook her head and took the gift from my hand, pressing her lips together. "I'm not used to getting gifts. It's my own issue."

"Oh, I didn't want to..." I trailed off, my brain failing to come up with the right words. I thought I was doing something nice to make her smile, and instead, I'd unknowingly stumbled on something that made her unhappy.

"God, I'm a real bitch, aren't I?" Lia sighed and pinched her nose. "I don't really ever get gifts. I grew up in a family that could only ever afford to give practical gifts, and I've never really dated someone seriously enough to..." Lia trailed off, tapping a finger on a knife in front of her. I wasn't sure if she was going to use it on me or was showing it to me, so I kept my mouth shut and didn't make any sudden movements. "This knife was the last real gift that I received, well, aside from a necklace from my mother."

I noted the pretty gold heart hanging from a chain. It nestled at her cleavage, and I had to force my eyes away, so I wasn't a creep who stared at a woman's breasts while she talked about her insecurities.

"Tell me about the knife." *Please let it be from a friend.*

"This knife..." Lia held it up, and opened her palm flat, so that the handle of the knife rested against her skin. "See how it is perfectly balanced to my hand? It is a custom-made knife, given to me as a gift from my former boss, and I treasure it like it is my baby."

"Is that right? I had no idea they could make knives that were customized in that manner." Which made my gift even better, at least I hoped it would be taken as such, and I waited to see if she would open the bag. "You must have enjoyed working for your last boss."

"I did. I really, really did. I thought..." Lia's voice caught, and I stepped forward, wanting to hug away the pain that flashed into her eyes. "Suzette and I had built a beautiful restaurant together. I'd...well, I'd thought it was my future. The place had been my everything. In the kitchen each night? That was *my* domain. Until it wasn't anymore. Suzette died. Blood cancer. And her son, well, he didn't care. Not really. No interest in continuing her legacy. Instead, he wanted to feed people grasshoppers and try to sleep with as many women as he could."

"Wait...hold up. Grasshoppers?" I scrunched my nose up. "Surely they can't be all that tasty. Let alone filling. They aren't all that hearty, right? No meat on the bones."

"Grasshoppers don't have bones." A perplexed look crossed Lia's face. "Wait, do they? No. They can't. They're insects. Insects don't have bones, right?"

"I don't believe so, no." Was this going to be another discussion like the one about bee tongues? "What happened with the grasshoppers?"

"Oh, get this..." Once again, a smile lit Lia's face. "Damien had overnighted them from Brazil. Except, maybe because he doesn't speak a lick of Portuguese, he'd ordered them live. When he opened the box..." Lia motioned with her hands.

"No..." I laughed, imagining an explosion of grasshoppers.

"Everywhere, Munroe. It was like a bomb had gone off. I quit on the spot, and Sophie called me that night. So, here I am."

I'd never been so thankful for grasshoppers in my life.

"Who knew the power of a tiny grasshopper to change the trajectory of your path," I mused, leaning one hip on the table and flicking my finger on the gift bag. "Go on. Open it. I promise no live insects or even dead ones, at that."

"Fine, but, as I said. You didn't have to—"

"Wheesht."

"What's that?" Lia eyed me suspiciously.

"Hush." It was a nicer way of telling someone to shut up, I suppose.

"Wheesht." Lia rolled the word around on her tongue, and I desperately wanted to kiss her again. I moved around the edge of the table, just to be closer to her. She reached into the bag and pulled out a wide flat package and made meticulous work of unwrapping it. I noted how she savored the moment, smoothing the paper back and folding it neatly, before lifting the lid. "Oh, *Munroe*."

The way she said my name made me feel like a king among men. It was as though I'd given her a diamond bracelet and not a pretty walnut cutting board with her name etched in the corner.

"This is incredible," Lia breathed, pulling the board

from the box. The wood was stained in alternating colors, creating a striped pattern, and her name was underscored by a thistle design. My friend handmade these boards, and we sold them in a few of our gift shops at various distilleries. He'd had no problem putting a rush order on customizing this for Lia, and now I was happy to see that I'd hit the right mark with the gift. "What a beautiful piece. Thank you, Munroe, truly. I'll treasure this gift."

I didn't doubt it, either, not from the way she spoke of the knife she'd been given. Lia put the board on the table, running a finger over the smooth wood, and I desperately wished she'd run her finger over my...right, okay. I needed to get my thoughts out of the gutter. When she leaned up and kissed my cheek, her lips lightly brushing my skin, it took everything in my power not to reach for her. I'd never met someone who had such a profound effect on me before.

"Use it in good health," is what I said instead, and mentally kicked myself for sounding like a polite grandfather. Turning away, I wandered to the spice cabinet to put some space between us before I bent her over the table and showed her all the ways I wanted to use her. No, correction, worship her. "This spice cabinet is cool. It's quite old, eh?"

"It is. I'm kind of obsessed with it and how they just put the spices directly in the drawers. It's incredibly well made. And the little round handles on each drawer. Want to try this recipe? I'm not really a baker, but I know scones will be a must-have, and they're easy enough. I was trying out a blueberry and crushed coriander seed. Hey!" Lia shouted, and I whirled, hands up.

"What?" I gaped at the glob of batter that dripped from her hair.

"What the hell, Munroe?" Lia half-laughed, half-glared at me.

"I swear...I didn't..." I held my hands up, confusion filling me, though I couldn't help but laugh at the glob of batter running down the side of her head.

"Oh, you think this is funny?" Lia ducked her hand in a bowl, and to my complete shock, she came over and ran her palm down the side of my face, streaking my cheek with batter that smelled faintly of blueberries.

"I can't believe you just did that." I looked at her in shock.

"You started it."

"I didn't, no, but I'll end it." The thrill of battle lit inside me, and Lia must have seen it in my eyes because she squealed and ran from the room. Laughing, I chased her into the banquet hall and caught her in two steps, pinning her to the stone wall. Our eyes caught, and laughter fell away as something else heated between us.

"Munroe," Lia gasped, as I angled my mouth closer to hers.

"Lia." It was a question as much as it was a demand.

Lia closed the space between our lips, making the decision for me, and that was all the assent I needed. Her lips were hot against mine, and I teased her mouth open, tasting the sweetness of blueberries on her tongue.

This woman.

Her.

She was everything. I had no rational explanation for why I knew that she was meant for me. Maybe it was the way that the world quieted when I was with her, and how my focus narrowed to just her. It was as though she was the sun, and I was determined to spend my life in her orbit, basking in her brilliance. It was over the top, this rush of desire and need to care for her, to claim her, to make her my own...and yet I couldn't force those thoughts away.

I didn't want them to go away.

For the first time in my life, I felt, *really* felt, like I'd finally found my way home. For years now I'd been searching for something I couldn't quite grasp, until my eyes had landed on Lia, and everything had clicked into place.

We barely knew each other, and yet I already understood everything that I needed to.

My hands trailed down her sides, and I lifted her, positioning her legs around my waist, pressing my hardness to where I wanted her most. Lia arched against me, breaking the kiss, and leaned her head back against the wall. Taking the invitation, I traced my lips across the soft skin at her neck, sticky with batter, and licked my way down to the open V of her shirt. I was just following the trail of the batter, I reasoned, and I pressed a kiss to the soft swell of her breast. Lingering there, I waited for her to tell me no, or to invite more, and when she said nothing, I skimmed my teeth across where her nipple pebbled against the thin fabric of her tank bra.

Lia bucked against me, and I almost embarrassed myself by finding my release so quickly. She was warm against my body, curvy and soft, and just so...lush. I wanted to lick her from head to toe, to press myself into the soft folds of her flesh, to watch the ripple of pleasure dance across her face. She threaded her fingers into my hair, pulling my mouth back to hers, and there we feasted on each other until we both broke apart, gasping for air. My arms shook, and still I held her, never wanting to let her go.

A bowl clattered to the floor behind us, and I spun, Lia stuck to me like a barnacle on a ship. We both inhaled in shock.

A small shaggy being, with a crinkled face, curious eyes, and a wiry coat of hair peered at us from under the table. Clothed in patchwork overalls and a faded red hat, it disappeared as quickly as it had come.

"Holy shit," Lia breathed. "Did you see that? Tell me you saw that."

"Wheesht," I whispered. I backed up, carrying Lia from the dim banquet hall, and kicked the door closed behind us. Once we were in the kitchen, I put her on the prep table, and just caged her in with my arms, wanting to keep her close in case anything untoward would arise.

"What the hell was that? I thought...the other day...was that a goblin? Is it going to kill me?" Lia gasped, her head turning wildly, as she scanned the room.

"No." I knew what it was, though I'd only ever known it to exist in fairy tales. Leave it to Loren Brae, home of the Kelpies and a ghost coo to house another mythological character. Why stop at one, right? "It's a broonie."

"A broonie? What is that? Is that like...a local animal?" Lia asked hopefully.

"No, darling. You'd probably know it as a brownie. A brùnaidh." I pronounced the Gaelic term.

"No way. Like an elf? A house elf?" Lia gaped at me.

"Aye, something like that. We need to talk to Hilda and Archie. Let's go," I said, pulling Lia from the table.

"Wait, Munroe. What's this?" Lia pointed to a leather

book on top of the cutting board that I'd given Lia. The leather was old, worn in areas, and a Celtic knot was etched across the cover. A braided leather cord wrapped around the outside.

"I don't know."

"Let me see. Maybe the broonie left it," Lia said, stepping in front of me. I leaned over her, dwarfing her with my height, but needing to keep my body around her in case the broonie acted up. From my understanding, they could be quite mischievous in nature. At least now I knew who had thrown the batter. Lia carefully unwrapped the cord and opened the book, gently nudging the pages open.

"It's recipes," Lia exclaimed. "But...more like. Like cooking recipes for...spells? For ailments? Oh, a love recipe? Is this a spell book?"

"Aye," I said, leaning over to scan the page she'd landed on. "Look."

"A book of Kitchen Witchery..." Lia gasped again. "A Kitchen Witch. This was left for me. On purpose. I think..."

"You think you're a Kitchen Witch?"

Lia angled her head to look up at me over her shoulder. "I just might be."

"Fascinating," I said, a trill of joy rushing through me. "In that case, bring the book. We need to talk to the others."

Of course I would fall in love with a Kitchen Witch. Amusement and excitement bloomed inside me. It was like all my fantasy books coming to life. My inner nerd couldn't be more delighted with this turn of events.

"Oh, before we go...do you have any milk? Or cream?" I asked, stopping at the door.

"Why?" Lia demanded, her nose buried in the book.

"Best to put a bowl out by the hearth. For your new friend."

"You can't be serious." Lia's mouth dropped open. "Like for a cat?"

Something clattered in the other room.

"Wheesht," I hissed, grabbing her arm, and moving her closer to the door. "Don't be insulting it."

"Oh God, I can't believe this is my life right now," Lia hissed. "Right, okay. Um, cream is out by the mixing bowl. Just grab one of the smaller bowls and pour some in."

"On it." With that, I left a bowl by the door to the banquet hall and followed Lia out to the garden where the sun just peeked through the clouds, and everything seemed simple and normal again. It was laughable almost, to go from running into a broonie and then casually walking away as though we were out for a romantic afternoon stroll. Either way, I couldn't wait to hear what Lachlan would make of this. Of all of my friends, he had been the most resistant to believing in magick, and the fact that he accepted the Kelpies as real now showed just what huge strides he had made.

But a broonie? Oh yeah, this was going to be fun. It was almost as good as discovering aliens were real. Almost.

CHAPTER TEN

Lia

My thoughts were a tangled mess, like someone had dumped a bowl of silverware on the floor, as we crunched our way up the gravel path that led to the residential side of the castle. Sure, we could have used an interior passageway to reach the library, but I'd never lived in a building so large before and my navigation was shaky at best. Now I was fixated on the imposing stature of this pretty castle, and wondering just what a simple woman like me, Lia Blackwood, was doing here. The castle was as impressive as it was enchanting, both stately and welcoming, with a Saltire flag topping each of the four turrets. I'd never given much thought to turrets before, and now I wondered how many women had stood at the tiny windows through the years, gazing out over Loch Mirren, and perhaps also coming to terms with the fact that magick was real.

In so many more ways than I had ever expected.

Let's be honest, I'd never given much thought to magick or the mythological before. I'd never been much of a dreamer, as dreams seemed the luxury of the idle or the well-off. I'd neither had the time, nor the money, to spend lost in fantasies. Restaurant hours were unforgiving, and adding culinary school on top of that had only made it certain that I'd rarely had a moment to myself for years now. Even so, on the rare days that I had a night off, I'd often use that time to watch a thriller movie or catch a concert.

I had this weird sensation that I was drifting along, caught up in the tide of something I didn't quite understand, and that I was no longer in control of my own destiny. It was an unsettling feeling, to say the least, but what bothered me most is that I felt like I didn't have all the information. How could everyone else around me quietly accept all of this magick while I was trying not to have a meltdown about some sort of hairy little goblin who had just left me a recipe book meant for Kitchen Witches?

Right. That too.

Kitchen Witch.

Perhaps I was the same as my great-gran, though my father hadn't had much time to give me more information on that part of his family history before I'd left town. Was I a witch? I wiggled my fingers at the ground, silently commanding a piece of gravel to rise into the air, and when nothing happened, a hysterical giggle escaped.

"You alright then?" Munroe asked, and I turned to him,

making a helpless movement with the hand that wasn't holding the cookbook.

The *spells* book, I corrected.

"Um..." I said, my eyes wide. Munroe caught my shoulders, pulling me to a stop.

"Hey, Lia. Look at me. Focus on your breathing," Munroe crooned, his voice lilting with the highlands. "That's a good lass. In and out. In and out."

My vision darkened for a moment, and I realized I truly had been quite close to freaking out, but Munroe's voice kept me focused, and soon I'd tamped down on the worst of the anxiety that had threatened. Not a full panic attack, so that was something at least.

"In and out," Munroe continued, and I lost myself in his eyes, unconsciously licking my lips as my ladyparts reminded me of another activity that required in and out motions. "Not now, darling. Although I'd dearly love to sort out this powerful need I have for you, it's not the best time."

I snapped my eyes away from his and realized that I'd been subconsciously rubbing my free hand up and down his chest like a deranged woman.

"Sorry," I said, pulling my hand away from his very muscular chest. *Get a grip, Lia. You can't go around groping men.*

"Totally fine and not at all unwelcome. It's just that you're about to start something that I have every intention of finishing, at great length and with considerable attention to detail, so unless you're ready for me to haul you over my shoulder and lock us away in that turret up there, I suggest we take a step back."

My mouth rounded, but no sound came out as, I kid you not, I almost took a step forward so he *would* take me up to the turret. I mean, could you imagine? For all I knew, turrets were probably full of pigeons and whatever else haunted this castle, and yet somehow, all I could think about now was Munroe pinning me to a wall, high above the castle grounds, his strong hands wringing pleasure from my body.

A sharp bark brought my head around, and I pulled my mind away from the gutter, er, the turret that is, and waved at where Hilda stood on the steps, a grocery sack tucked under her arm, the dogs bouncing at her feet.

"Here, let me help you with that." Munroe hurried forward, but she only nodded to the parking lot.

"Another bag in the car. What...happened to you both?" Hilda's sharp look took in our appearances, and I remembered that we were both covered in scone batter.

"Um, food fight?" I suggested, my cheeks heating.

"Is that what they're calling it these days?" Hilda raised an eyebrow at me.

"I'll get the bag if you can get Archie? We need to talk," Munroe said, neatly sidestepping the question.

"Is something wrong?" Hilda asked, and I held the door for her and the two dogs that followed hopefully at her feet.

"No. Yes. I don't know." I sighed and scrubbed a hand over my face. "Do I have time for a quick shower? I can feel the batter congealing in my hair."

"Aye, by the time I get the shopping put away and we call Archie in, you'll have more than enough time to shower. On you go." Hilda made a nodding motion with her chin, and I hustled upstairs toward my apartment, more than grateful for a moment alone to just breathe.

"Mooo–"

"Nope! Not now, Clyde," I barked, snapping my fingers in the air.

Silence filled the hallway, and I skidded to a stop outside my door, guilt filling me.

"Sorry, Clyde. Didn't mean to take it out on you," I said and then shook my head at myself. Here I was talking to an empty hallway like a lunatic.

"Moo!" Clyde appeared from out of the wall by my head, bouncing joyfully forward, and I slammed against the door, my hand at my heart. Clyde looked at me, his head tilting, his big eyes full of mischief.

"Oh, right. You think you're so funny, don't you, big guy?" I wagged a finger at him. "You're cute though, I'll give you that." Turning, I opened the door to my room and ducked inside, hoping Clyde knew enough to respect my personal privacy. Granted, I wasn't sure what a cow would know about privacy, but at this point I wouldn't be surprised if he waltzed through the door and made me a pot of tea.

My apartment still startled me every time I walked into it. It was just so...decadent. The door opened directly into a large sitting area with stone walls, high arched ceilings, a small kitchenette, and two narrow hallways on either side of the room leading to separate sleeping quarters. A door on the other side of the room led to a small en suite bath, which Hilda had apologized for the size explaining that renovating for indoor plumbing and baths had to be done with a careful mind to the historical nature of the building.

It was the biggest bathroom *I'd* ever had.

Slipping off my shoes by the door, I padded across pretty woven rugs in shades of green and gold and went to the bedroom I'd chosen. Even though it was the smaller of the two rooms, it was the one that made me feel the most comfortable. Here the ceiling was lower, and the stone walls seemed to curve around the bed, cocooning it. I'd learned that if I left the curtains open, I could just prop myself up on my pillows and look out the window to Loch Mirren far below. I'd also learned that the Kelpies screamed in the early hours of the morning.

The first night, I had jolted awake, a fine tremor working through my body as I tried to figure out where I was and what sound had awoken me. Then, I'd crept to the window, wondering if I could catch a glimpse of the creatures. Instead, I'd found both Lachlan and Sophie, walking the...I wasn't sure what they called the big wall that ran the perimeter of the castle, but they looked like soldiers pacing, waiting for battle. There was something comforting to me about Sophie being out there as well, and if this plucky American could handle facing down a Kelpie, well, I guess I would have to as well. I couldn't let a West Coast girl best me.

I made a mental note to ask her if she'd liked 2Pac or Biggie better, and quickly grabbed a fresh change of clothes, before hightailing it to the bathroom. I took a quick enough shower to get the sticky batter out of my hair, but not long enough to work the tension from my shoulders, and fifteen minutes later, I was back downstairs in time to see Sophie at the door of the library. I'd towel-dried my wet hair the best that I could and had pulled on a thick Red Sox sweatshirt to ward off the chill in the air.

"2Pac or Biggie?" I asked Sophie and she paused, tilting her head at me, her lips quirking in a smile.

"2Pac, naturally. I'm a Cali girl." Sophie accentuated her words with an exaggerated toss of her auburn mane of hair, perfecting the California girl hair flip, and strutted into the library.

"I'll allow it," I said. "Mainly because I know the Sox are better than the Dodgers."

"I'd jump on that except I'm not hugely into baseball."

I gaped at her like she'd just said she slept in a coffin at night.

"You don't...but..." It was impossible to grow up in Boston and not like baseball.

"Ladies, are we here to talk about the celebrated catalogs of early nineties rap artists, or do we have something important to discuss?" Archie barked from the corner where he'd taken a seat at the end of a massive table that dominated part of the library. I'd stumbled on the library in my sheer inability to find my way back to my room the other day, and if I'd been a girl who loved books, well, this would have been my nirvana. It had high bookshelves with rolling ladders, a painted ceiling with an honest-to-god mural, and a large fireplace that likely warmed the whole room in winter.

"How in the hell do you know about rap music?" Lachlan raised an eyebrow at Archie.

"I'm hardly sheltered, lad." A faint pink color rose to Archie's cheek, and suspicion rose inside me.

"2Pac or Biggie?" I asked Archie, hands on my hips.

"In my estimation, The Notorious B.I.G was the better rapper." Archie sniffed and snapped his newspaper, folding it neatly on the table in front of him while Lachlan pretended to faint.

"Archie listens to rap music? Is...is that what's on your speakers in your toolshed?" Lachlan asked.

"I find it important to listen to a wide range of musical genres, and aye, American rap music occasionally makes its way into my repertoire. Now, why did we call a midday meeting? I thought this was for tonight?" Archie looked at Hilda who gave a quick shake of her head.

"What was for tonight?" I asked, that feeling of being kept in the dark rising once more.

"Um, now that you've had a few days to settle in, we wanted to have a talk with you. About some other aspects of your job...should you choose to accept it. Well, I mean, legally it's not part of your job, but it's..." Sophie wound a piece of hair around her finger and shot a desperate look at Lachlan. "I'm bungling this."

"Bungling what?" Munroe asked from behind me, and the low timbre of his voice sent a shiver down the back of my neck. I turned to see him with wet hair and a clean shirt, and the fresh scent of soap drifted in with him as he came to stand by my side.

"What did you want to talk about today?" Hilda asked, ignoring his question.

"There's a broonie living in the banquet hall, and it left a book of Kitchen Witch spells for Lia."

Gasps filled the room.

"I'm guessing that's not what you wanted to talk about tonight?" I asked faintly, dropping into a chair at the table.

"Tangentially, I suppose," Archie mused, tapping his finger on the paper in front of him, a faraway look in his eyes. "A broonie. Och, it's been ages since I've heard talk of one of those."

I leaned over and rested my forehead lightly on the table, my thoughts threatening to scramble once more.

"Look, you've gone and broken her, Archie," Hilda chided him.

"Och, it's not me that's broken her. It's likely the wee broonie. They can be quite difficult, you ken?" Archie grumbled.

"Oh, can they? *Can* they?" I flipped my head up and glared at Archie. "And the ghost coos are harmless, and the Kelpies will probably eat me, but the broonies, och, well, they're just difficult, are they?" I tried out a Scottish accent.

"I mean...aye...that's the way of..." Archie clamped his mouth shut when Hilda shot him a warning look.

"We've brought you here under false pretenses," Sophie began, and then her eyes caught on Munroe. "Um, Lachlan...should we maybe do this alone?"

"No." I grabbed Munroe's arm when he made to stand. "He stays."

"Munroe's solid. It's not like it's much of a secret anymore, what with the whole town involved now." Lachlan shrugged.

"Involved in what, exactly?" Munroe moved just slightly closer to me, enough that his broad arm brushed mine, and I immediately leaned into his warmth. Listen, I'm not the type to hang on a man's arm and beg for him to protect me, but I'd also never dealt with the land of magick water horses and batter-throwing kitchen goblins, so maybe, just maybe, it wouldn't hurt for me to lean on someone.

"Lia," Sophie said, drawing my attention to where she sat, her arm tucked through Lachlan's, her face wreathed in sympathy. "I had a sharp learning curve to deal with as well. It's going to sound...well, insane really. But the truth is, we brought you here, not only for your superb cooking, of course, but because you're the next person to join the magickal Order of Caledonia. Should you choose to join, of course. You can say no."

I blinked at Sophie as I took in her words. Honestly, I would have laughed out loud except for the fact that the room had gone dead silent, and the air had turned thick with tension. I waited for Clyde to jump out of a bookshelf to break the moment, to add some hilarity, but not a sound could be heard aside from Sir Buster's disgruntled grumbles as he arranged himself on a bed by the fireplace.

"You can't be serious. What is this? A cult?" I arched an eyebrow at Sophie.

"I thought the exact same thing when I first learned about it." Sophie gave me an understanding smile. "I made it well known that the only cult I was joining was one that worshipped cheese."

Archie gave a disapproving snort.

"So you brought me here to join some magickal group. It's not really about me starting a restaurant, is it?" Hurt filled me. I couldn't help it. I'd lost so much this year from Suzette to my place in her restaurant, that I had pinned my hopes on Scotland being the answer to my future. See? This is what I got for letting myself dream, even a little. I should have kept my head down and stayed working at Suzette's until I'd found a more suitable job offer. Now I was stuck in Scotland, having turned my life completely upside down, all under false pretenses.

"No, the restaurant *is* part of it, lass," Hilda said, with an apologetic look. "The truth of it is that *what* we have to tell you can't be done over the phone or with someone we don't know or trust either. We need your help, desperately, but you have a say in the matter. And believe me, it's not in our nature to ask for help. But sometimes circumstances are outside our control. This is one such circumstance. I'll apologize on behalf of all of us for withholding pertinent information from you, but trust me when I say to you, we very much still want you to open our restaurant here. This isn't about your merits as a chef."

"Of course it's not," Archie snapped. "The lass is at the top of her game. One of the best chefs in Boston, a city far more cosmopolitan than Loren Brae. We're lucky to have her here."

The unexpected compliment soothed some of my ruffled feathers, and I glanced around the table as everyone waited for my reaction. It was Munroe, though, who sealed the deal for me.

"Lia," Munroe said. He turned in his chair and wrapped an arm around my shoulders, drawing my attention to him. As soon as he touched me, my anxiety seemed to quiet, as though I could rely on this man to take care of things for me. Even though I preferred to do everything on my own, in this moment I needed someone to be my true north. "I know you haven't known us all that long, but I can vouch for these people. While Lachlan is annoying, and absolute rubbish at video games—"

"Like bloody hell I am—"

"The rest of this group are stand-up people. Archie?" Munroe nodded to the man who regarded me with an assessing look. "He's all bark, but very little bite. If he considers you one of his own, he'll stand for you. And Hilda? She'll be a mother to you whether you like it or not. And, while I was having a wee joke about Lachlan, I'll tell you the truth of it. He's one of my best mates, like a brother to me, and this is why I'll betray his confidence."

"Betray..." My eyes darted to Lachlan to see a pained expression cross his handsome face.

"The Kelpies killed his mother when he was just a wee lad," Munroe said.

I gasped, seeing the very real and visceral pain flash across Lachlan's face. Sophie leaned into him, whispering something into his ear, and he pulled her into a hug.

"Oh, no. I'm *so* sorry, Lachlan," I whispered. My fingers dug into my palms and Munroe traced a soothing circle on my back.

"I hope you'll forgive us for not being entirely forward with you, lass. And that, at the very least, you'll be open to listening to what we have to say," Archie said.

I blew out a breath and surveyed everyone at the table, before glancing to the ceiling where cherubs danced among the clouds. The scream of the Kelpies resonated in my mind, as did the curious eyes of the broonie under the table in the banquet hall. But it was the softest of moos in the background, encouraging almost, that had me fortifying my resolve. If magick was real, maybe it wasn't all bad, if Clyde was any indication of the good side of it.

"So, the Order of Caledonia? What is that? It sounds

like...a medieval thing or something like that. Is this the Knights Templar stuff? I'm great with a knife, but I don't know anything about swords or riding a horse." Munroe patted my back as the tension broke in the room, relieved looks passing across the table.

"There's a good lass," Archie said, and it felt like I'd won a prize.

Maybe I had. But I'd withhold judgment until I learned more.

CHAPTER ELEVEN

Lia

"Hi, Pumpkin!" My dad's smiling face filled the screen, and instantly my worries lessened. At times, my father was like my own personal Xanax, and I relaxed back into the couch cushion in the sitting area in my apartment. "Where are you? It looks really nice."

"I'm in the apartment that came with the job." I glanced around the room, the stone walls, woven rugs, and wooden beams in the ceiling reminding me that I was, indeed, living in a real-life castle. There was something about the luster of the woodwork that screamed luxury to me. This was no fake IKEA hack. The wooden beams were handcrafted centuries ago and, as I stared up at them, I suddenly realized that I could be as integral a part of the castle's future as these beams were. I just had to decide if I accepted my fate.

No big deal, right?

After an hour in the library, where whisky and tea had been offered to me several times as I tried to calm myself down, I'd learned a few hard truths about my invitation to work at MacAlpine Castle.

The first?

Loren Brae was in trouble. Like, big trouble.

Apparently, there really *was* the holy grail of magickal truth stones sequestered out on a tiny island in the middle of Loch Mirren, and the Kelpies were currently protecting it because the first line of defense, the Order of Caledonia, had disbanded. Or the last of the members had died. Basically, though, Hilda and Archie were trying to restore the Order to make sure this Stone of Truth didn't fall into nefarious hands and wreak havoc on the world, while the Kelpies, unable to distinguish between friend or foe, did their best to drive everyone from town in order to protect this aforementioned miracle stone.

And the second interesting tidbit of information?

It seemed that I was next in line to join the Order of Caledonia, should I choose to do so, as it appeared my great-gran *had* once been an active member of the Order.

"Wow, that's a nice perk, isn't it then? How are you doing? Are you enjoying it? I'm so proud of you, you know." My dad's eyes crinkled at their corners as he smiled at me, and I opened my mouth to speak and closed it again, unsure how to proceed. I realized now why Sophie had withheld information from me. When you put the truth into words, it sounded...well, it sounded crazy. Was I really supposed to tell my dad that I might be a Kitchen Witch, and the people of the castle needed me to join a magickal

Order to protect the holy grail? The words died on my lips as I just stared at him.

"What's wrong, honey? You've got that *deer in headlights* look when you don't know what to do. Do you need to come home? I'm sure your mom and I can scrape together some airfare if needed." Worry crossed his face, and I shook my head to stop his flow of words.

"Dad, can you tell me more about Gran? I think I'm just kind of caught up in everything here at the moment. It's so...historical. Everything has so much more backstory and history than in the States. It's making me think about my roots, I guess. And our family."

"That's my girl. Don't let your mother hear it, but you should be proud of your Scottish roots. Best people on earth." Dad said the last part in a whisper, and I laughed, knowing my mother must be in the kitchen. He'd taken the call from the Adirondack chairs on the front porch. How I missed sitting next to him. "Listen, Lia. I did some digging on your great-gran, and I've found some more information. Turns out, she also was involved at MacAlpine Castle, just like I'd thought. Look." Dad reached into his shirt pocket and took a moment unfolding a piece of printer paper. "I printed this off at work. Doesn't she look just like you?"

I waited while he fumbled with turning the phone camera around and then gasped at the black and white image on the paper. A short, rounded woman, with curly hair barely contained in a bun, stood in front of the stove in the castle's kitchen. She had the same cheekbones and deep-set eyes as I did, but it wasn't the likeness, nor the fact that she was standing in the same kitchen that I now worked in that had me reacting in such a manner.

It was the book on the table in front of her.

The same book that now sat next to me on the couch.

The broonie hadn't been trying to be difficult, though the throwing of the batter was likely unnecessary. He'd been trying to give me a gift from my very heritage. Inside me, I felt a shift, almost a visceral click, as I understood in that moment, in a way that I never otherwise could have until I came to this place, that I was home. Which meant I'd have to protect it, just like generations before me had. Broonies, ghost coos, Kelpies, and all.

"That's pretty incredible. I can totally see how we look alike. And she was a chef as well," I said, screenshotting the image so that I could look at it in more detail later before the camera was flipped back around.

"Aye, a Kitchen Witch, I'm told." My dad's forehead creased. "At first, I thought it was just a funny turn of phrase, but it really sounds like she was, well, at least at that time, considered a witch. That being said, there's a long history of witches in Scotland, and well, a lot of places, of course. Maybe they didn't mean actual magick, you know."

"Based on what I've seen here, they probably did," I admitted, and my father's eyebrows shot up in surprise.

"Is that right?"

I decided to tell him about Clyde, and by the end of it, my father was wiping tears from his eyes because he was laughing so hard.

"Who would've thought? A ghost coo who likes to banter. Aye, that's just the kind of thing I miss about my homeland. Did I ever tell you about the time I swore I heard a banshee crying across the loch when I was meant to be home for dinner? Och, it sent me scurrying home fast as can be," Dad said.

"I do remember you telling me about that now," I said, smiling at him. "I'd always thought it was just a story, but now I'm beginning to understand that Scotland has a few tricks up her sleeve."

"She's a wily one, she is. But she's a country I love with all my heart. You're lucky to be there, Pumpkin. Call me when you can. I'm hoping, if all goes well this year, that we'll be able to swing a ticket to come visit you."

"Oh, Dad." My heart clenched. I'd love to see my family here, but not until I figured out this whole Kitchen Witch thing. "I'd love to have you. Let me get my feet wet, and I'll keep you posted on how things go. Oh, anything else about Gran you can think of?"

"I'm just told she was a miracle in the kitchen. People went to her with ailments...and not just physical ones either. Matters of the heart and whatnot. Who is to say if she helped or not?" Dad glanced over his shoulder. "I gotta run, I love you."

"Love you too." I clicked off the call and then pulled the image of my grandmother up, zooming in to study her unwavering gaze. *Did her magick run in my blood?* What would that mean for me then? Cooking had always been something that I did because I loved it, but I'd also been determined to make a living from it. Was the hum I felt in my soul when I created a perfect dish actually magick? I'd always just thought it was the satisfaction from doing a good job. Or adrenaline, even. On particularly busy nights, we'd be slammed until last orders. It was those times that I would hit a rhythm, moving seamlessly from order to order, hyper-focused on performing my best. The thought that magick might have a play in my success was as fascinating as it was irksome.

Grabbing the spells book, I tucked it under my arm and left my apartment. We'd taken a break from discussions as Hilda had wanted to recruit Agnes to go through the book with me, and since I wasn't quite ready to chance the broonie in the kitchen again, I headed downstairs, thinking maybe I would go for a walk.

"So...about that turret?"

Heat flooded me, and I couldn't help the images that flashed to my mind. Me, gasping for breath, while Munroe buried his head between my legs, bringing me to the sharp precipice of pleasure. Oh *girl*. There had to be something in the water here that had me all hot and bothered. And no, I couldn't blame it on the whisky, as I'd refused the offers of it earlier that day.

I stopped and looked over my shoulder at where this gilded glorious hunk of a man strode to me down the hallway, his steps easy, his posture confident, and my mouth went dry. I really needed to nip this in the bud. Whatever had happened between us, *twice now,* my ladyparts joyfully reminded me, needed to stop. I'd thought I'd need to keep my head clear to focus on getting the restaurant up and running, but now the stakes were even higher.

"Lia! What's this I hear you found a book?" Agnes broke the spell, popping her head around the corner. She held her hands out and waggled her fingers in glee, the same way a child would for candy. Ignoring Munroe's turret comment, I broke eye contact and turned to hand Agnes the book.

As soon as it left my hands, I felt bereft, as though someone was taking an integral piece of me away. *What an odd thing to feel.* I made a note of that emotion and filed it away for further examination at another time, though at the rate I was going with new experiences and emotions, I doubted I'd have time to examine things more deeply.

Frankly, since the moment I'd arrived in Scotland, I'd done nothing but *feel*. Perhaps that was strange. Had I been operating my life on autopilot, and all of a sudden, the plane was crashing, and I needed to react? Everything felt bigger, more important, more intense here. My eyes strayed to where Munroe stood by the fire, consulting with Archie over a fly he was making for his fishing. I'd gone from a routine that I'd grown comfortable with to...whatever this was. Constant surprises, new revelations, and discovering that magick was real.

I'd always prided myself on being resilient. It was in my nature to land on my feet when life, or one of my brothers, knocked me down. I couldn't accept that, collectively, the entire town of Loren Brae was running some sort of scam to punk me, Lia Blackwood, and have a laugh at my expense. Which meant that these otherwise seemingly sensible people believed, wholeheartedly, that magick and myths were real. And I'd seen evidence with my own eyes, hadn't I? It was time for me to accept that while I might not have all the answers in the world, I needed to trust myself to handle whatever came my way.

Broonies included.

Maybe I could befriend the little guy. Absentmindedly, I wondered if he'd drunk the cream that Munroe had left out for him. Was he hungry? I should research what they ate. *Nobody* left my kitchen hungry. It was a fact that I prided myself on. On the rare occasions that I did have any time off, I'd often cook for friends or my family. It was one of my greatest pleasures about being a chef—the ability to create my own community of people I cared about while serving them food made with love. I didn't have a lot to give in this world, so feeding people was my love language.

"This book..." Agnes sighed from where she'd dropped into a chair at the table, turning each page as carefully as if it were made of glass. "Och, it's incredible. Fascinating, really. Look, Lia. Did you see this? This appears to be the previous owners. Where did you find this?"

I realized we hadn't filled Agnes in on the backstory around the book, and I glanced at Archie as I crossed the room. Hilda came through the door, a tray piled high with the makings for tea, and Munroe crossed the room quickly to divest her of her burden.

"Broonie left it for Lia in the kitchen," Archie barked and returned to tying his lure.

The man was nothing if not succinct.

"Stop it," Agnes breathed, her face lighting with interest.

Interest, I noted. *Not* fear. I was going to take my cues from these people who had lived here their whole lives. If they weren't bothered by a small furry goblin-man running around the kitchens, then I would learn to accept it as well. Maybe I could teach him to like baseball.

"I saw him with my own eyes," I admitted, sliding into

the chair next to Agnes and bending to look at where she pointed in the book. "It was...disconcerting?"

"Took about ten years off my life." Munroe came to the table, and I breathed a sigh of relief. Okay, maybe I didn't have to totally pretend that I hadn't been scared. "Never knew those wee ones were real."

"Nor did I." Agnes tapped a finger against her lips, her gaze dreamy. "But I have *so* much to research now."

"Oh," I whispered, my eyes catching on what Agnes had pointed to. It was a line of signatures, as though each person who had owned the book had added their name to the list.

Eilidh Blackwood.

Moibeal Blackwood.

Morag Blackwood.

And there, a space for me to sign my own.

"They're all Blackwoods."

"Is that your given name then?" Agnes asked, and I realized she just knew me as Lia.

"Yes," I said, a smile hovering at my lips. I traced my finger lightly across the names, feeling a rush of love for ancestors that I never knew. "Cecilia Giana Blackwood. Italian and Scottish. "Morag was my great-grandmother."

"She was one of the Order," Archie said.

"Was she?" Agnes asked in delight, turning between me and Archie. Hilda busied herself pouring tea, and Lachlan came through the door with Sophie in his arms, the dogs tumbling at his feet.

"What did we miss?" Lachlan demanded, letting Sophie to her feet, and the pink flush on her face told me just what they'd been up to.

"The book the broonie left for Lia is her great-gran's," Archie said.

"Oh, Lia. What a treasure to have," Sophie said, coming to sit next to me. Together, the three of us bent over the book and carefully turned the pages, looking at the various recipes.

"He's right," I said, caught on a recipe for a soup to soothe aching bones.

"Who's right?" Munroe asked, his voice holding a note of something that I couldn't quite identify.

"My father. He mentioned that Gran was known for being a miracle in the kitchen. People would go to her with their sicknesses and stuff, and she'd fix them up."

"Aye, that's what a Kitchen Witch does." Archie snipped a thread and looked up at me under his bushy eyebrows.

"Give the lass a wee chance to catch up," Lachlan said, clucking his tongue in disapproval as he picked up a cookie from the tray. "It's not likely that being a witch is something she's familiar with."

"I mean, I've *heard* of witches, of course. Salem isn't all that far from Boston. It's a pretty notorious spot for witch history. But it was always something that was just..." I waved my hand in the air. "Out there. Stories. Just some fun to have on Halloween and once in a while get my tarot cards read. That kind of thing."

"This isn't just for fun. It's real, and you need to accept it," Archie barked, and I blinked at him, unsure how to proceed with his directness. Listen, in Boston, I met attitude with attitude, but since I didn't fully understand the undercurrents here, I wasn't sure how to navigate. I was saved by Sophie's intervention.

"Lia hasn't said she didn't accept it, Archie. I know you're chomping at the bit to get started, but you have to remember you've lived with the knowledge of the Order of Caledonia your entire life. You need to have some grace with people getting up to speed. Lia can still decide to leave, and then we'd have to figure out our next steps. One would think, considering what an important part she plays in restoring the Order, that you might try to be more polite." Sophie's eyebrows were almost to her hairline as she lectured Archie.

"I'm not leaving," I interjected quickly before Archie could respond.

His look of approval filled me with warmth.

"That's a good lass," Archie said. "I knew you were up for it. Tough stock, the Blackwoods are."

"Did you know my family?" I asked, tilting my head at him in question.

"Just your great-gran when I was but a wee boy. She fixed me up after a nasty fall. You've the look of her."

It was just another piece fitting into place for me, and I realized that even though I might be about to embark on one of the craziest journeys of my life, I was also strangely excited about the challenge.

Echoes of the people that came before me sang in my blood.

"How do we get started?" What was the protocol for becoming part of a magickal Order? Did I need to dance naked under the moonlight or something? I sincerely hoped not, I was a horrible dancer.

"We do the ritual. You pick a weapon. You have to pass three challenges. If the Clach na Fìrinn approves, you're a part of the Order, and we're one step closer to keeping Loren Brae safe," Archie said.

"Wait...the Stone of Truth has to approve me?" I couldn't bring myself to try and pronounce the Gaelic term for it.

"It's basically the Holy Grail. It's all knowing. Consider it like...a little god or goddess. In rock form," Sophie clarified, and I slid her a look.

"You realize—"

"Yes, I'm well aware how that sounds. But once the gems started showing up in my sword, I was on board."

"Your sword?"

"Oh, right. I didn't tell you that yet. I'm the Knight." Sophie beamed at me like she'd just told me she'd won the lottery.

"You're...the Knight," I said slowly. "So what does that make me?"

"The Kitchen Witch," Archie barked.

"Archie, your tone," Hilda said.

"Well? I thought we'd established this."

"Yes, but we didn't really do a good job of explaining it, did we?" Hilda poured me a cup of tea. "My apologies, Lia. We're a bit beside ourselves with the new development of the broonie. We've long been keepers of not only MacAlpine Castle, but of the Order of Caledonia. When the Order recently disbanded, the Clach na Fìrinn felt threatened and the Kelpies act as its defense. However, a second, and lesser common circumstance can also happen."

"Which is..." I asked, heart hammering in my chest.

"The Clach na Fìrinn calls on any creatures to protect it. Creatures we may not think to be real of this world. Our myths. Legends. Stories spoken of across fires over the centuries. Until the Order is restored, we could be dealing with far more than just the Kelpies."

"Bloody hell," Lachlan said, pinching his nose.

"A host of mythological creatures coming to life?" Agnes looked torn between worry and excitement. "I know I should hate this, but my bookworm's heart is screaming in excitement."

"So, lass. Can we get started then?" Archie stood, and I looked up at him, eyes wide.

"Wait...I don't know what that means."

"You'll accept your power. We wait to see how it manifests for you, and then you'll need to pass three challenges. Since you're the Kitchen Witch, I'm going to assume that your challenges are going to have to do with healing and recipes, much like Sophie's were to do with her knightly characteristics," Agnes said.

"How will I know what the challenges are? Is this like... a game? Will a buzzer sound?" I looked around the room, waiting for someone to wave a flag or something like at the start of a race.

"You won't know," Sophie said, a sympathetic look on her face. "It's super annoying. I love things that are neat and tidy, and nothing about magick is logical or fits into a box on my spreadsheet. But what I can tell you is that each and every one of us in this room will help you."

I found myself looking to the one person in the room who brought me calm as much as he distracted me. Munroe smiled softly at me and gave me a small nod.

"I'll be here for you, Lia."

His words drifted across my skin, like a cooling breeze from the ocean, and I took a deep breath. Although I still found elements of this deeply confusing, I understood enough that I needed to make a decision.

"Okay, then. Let's get started."

CHAPTER TWELVE

Munroe

"It's a bit of a rag-tag operation you're running here," I commented to Lachlan as Archie readied whatever supplies it was he needed. I kept one eye on Lia, who seemed overwhelmed but was holding her own, and did my best to tamp down on my own reservations. "Stone of Truth? Three challenges? Myths coming to life? You're lucky Lia didn't run from the house screaming like a banshee."

"Och, don't get me started, mate. It's been a mess to figure out, let alone attempt to bring others into. And we'll have to do this again, and again, and again."

"How many times?" I asked.

"Nine to complete the Order." Lachlan grimaced.

"Seems you'll be able to streamline things by then, eh?" I couldn't help but lend my business mind to things.

"Streamline..." Lachlan laughed, crossing his arms over his chest. "Tell me how we're supposed to do anything when a bloody broonie jumps into the picture? It's bad enough we've got Clyde scaring people witless. Now, a broonie?"

A plaintive "moooo" sounded from somewhere above our heads, and I grinned.

"Now you've gone and hurt the poor lad's feelings," I said. Lachlan pinched his nose and sighed.

"Sorry, Clyde," Lachlan grumbled.

"Can I just use my own knife?" I turned as Lia stood, talking with Archie.

"I don't see why not," Archie said. "Is it meaningful to you?"

"It is. And as weapons go, it'll do the trick."

"Let's get your knife and get it sorted out then."

I hung back, not wanting to intrude on this moment for Lia, but also wanting to be there for her. I couldn't imagine what she must be feeling. I mean, it was a lot for me to wrap my head around, and I'd grown up with tales of the Kelpies and was well-steeped in the myths of Scotland. But for a newcomer? Surely it was a testament to who she was as a person that she didn't run screaming from the castle grounds. It made me admire her even more, this willingness to give it a go, and I thought back to how good she'd felt wrapped around me.

How right.

I'd wanted to sink into her, both physically and emotionally, and never let go. It was an incredible thing, this recognition that I held inside me for Lia.

It was like my heart had taken one look at her, sighed in relief, and said, *"there you are."*

I wanted to learn everything about her. To peel back the layers. To find out what her greatest fears were, to learn who'd hurt her in the past, and to make everything right for her future. I wanted to protect, uplift, nurture...all of the things. Instead, I hung shyly at the back of the group that walked across grounds sodden from an earlier rain, fighting my emotions that threatened to overwhelm me.

Watching Lia step into her power was an incredible honor. I wanted to be there for her every step of the way, cheering for her, and helping her in any way I could. That had always been my favorite part of the fantasy stories that I devoured growing up—when the hero or heroine finally claimed his or her power. It was such a pivotal moment in the character's life, and I'd eaten that shit up. I think, in some respects, I'd hoped to gain the confidence to do so in my own life, stuck in a cold and unforgiving home environment. Was it that much of a leap to understand why I'd been drawn to fantasy novels and fairy tales where the hero overcame the bad guy? I wasn't one for metaphors, really, but even that one was hard for me to miss.

I suppose, in many respects, I'd proverbially thumbed my nose at my parents with my gin business, but that decision didn't really have the same badass pomp and circumstance surrounding it as did Lia choosing her magick.

"Look at her glow," I said, and Lachlan turned, hanging back with me, as Lia stood with Archie and lit a bundle of sage. There were words to be repeated, rituals to be made, a blessing made in each corner of the estate. To me, the words didn't matter, nor did the exact nuances of the ceremony. I didn't need to hear the spells or understand the way magick worked to see, very clearly, the transformation in Lia as she partook in the ancient ritual of accepting her role as a member of the Order of Caledonia.

"She's a lovely lass, Munroe," Lachlan agreed, and I shook my head, reaching out to grip his arm. I needed my friend, in that moment, to stand with me while I felt my future shifting on its axis and recalibrating around the woman who stood before me, quietly muttering words of magick.

Was there ever anything as beautiful as a woman stepping into her power?

My breath caught as Lia finished the final ritual, and Archie closed the spell. A shimmer of light rippled across her skin, and she lifted her face to the loch, power humming around her. She'd been beautiful before, of course, but now?

Lia was heart-stopping.

I could only hope that she'd give me a chance to show her that I could be the type of man who would stand by a powerful woman's side and help her fly. Her success would be my own, and, crap, yeah...here I was going so far down the line that I could barely think straight.

"Are you going to ask her out?" Lachlan asked, as we turned back toward the castle. Storm clouds gathered low on the horizon, dark and threatening, and the wind carried the scent of rain with it.

"Ask her..." My brain was still fixated on a future with her. I was so focused on the outcome that I'd forgotten the steps required to get there. "Right, a date. Of course."

"Because the way you're looking at her? It's like a wee lost puppy desperate for love."

"I am. For her love," I admitted before I could try and hide it. "She's everything, Lachlan. I see a future with her."

"Och, mate. Slow down there. You've only just met the lass." Lachlan gripped my shoulder, and I stopped in my tracks, turning to meet his eyes with a level look.

"How long, Lachlan? How long did it take with Sophie?" I asked because I knew, *I knew*, he'd fallen fast for her.

"Bloody hell," Lachlan said. He scrubbed a hand over his face and sighed. "Right, if that's the way of it then you need to do it properly. It's a date you'll be taking her on then."

"Thanks, Dad. I'll get it sorted." My eyes caught on a stone and wooden building set a ways back from the castle. "Hey...I don't think I remember this building. What is it?"

"It used to be one of the stables. It's empty now though."

"Can I take a look?" My curiosity piqued, I left the others to walk toward the building, ignoring the first drops of rain.

"Nae bother," Lachlan said, changing course and accompanying me to the stable. There, he pulled a ring of keys from his pocket while I studied the structure. The walls were in good condition for their age, made of stone, though the roof needed repairs. I jumped as a grasshopper landed on my hand. For a moment, I blinked down at it, amused as it studied me with its big eyes.

"New friend?" Lachlan grinned at my hand.

"Och, he just landed on me. Haven't seen one in ages."

"Loads around here. Must not be out in nature much. Too busy pushing papers," Lachlan said. Turning, he trundled the door open, startling the grasshopper, and the insect bounced into the bushes at my feet.

"You're not far wrong," I admitted, shaking my head and stepping into the space.

"It's not wired with electrics, but it's a pretty space. I wouldn't go too far in, as I'm not sure of the nature of the roof, and I'm not interested in a doctor's visit today," Lachlan said, crossing his arms over his chest.

"Och, come on now. What happened to the lad who fearlessly climbed trees to peek in girls' bedrooms?" I laughed.

"He's grown up and has a woman who prefers his limbs in good working order."

"Fair enough." I, too, wasn't interested in a roof falling on my head so I only wandered a few feet farther into the structure. It was a cavernous space, light filtering through a few cracks in the roof, and accompanied by a musty smell of damp and earth. But the stone walls were beautiful, and some of the original wood beams could be saved. If Lachlan felt like it, he could make this quite the space. "Ever consider doing weddings here?"

"Here?" Lachlan cocked his head and studied the space. "I can't say I have. It's been brought up, quite often, for the castle, particularly the garden. But then they go off-site for the reception."

"Could be another avenue for income," I mused, wandering back outside. I wouldn't mind getting back to the castle before the brunt of the storm hit. "It's a great space."

"I'll add it to the list. Restaurant first." Lachlan locked the door behind me, and we picked up our pace, the rain intensifying as we neared the castle once more. "That way we could offer catering packages if Lia was amenable to it."

"She's doing well, I think. Taking this all in her stride. It's a lot to throw at a body, isn't it?" I asked. We both began to jog as the rain picked up.

"It is. But much like Sophie, Lia seems to have a good backbone. Maybe it runs in the blood, or maybe the lasses like a bit of adventure, but we've lucked out if Lia can hold her own here."

"I don't think she'll let you down," I said, reaching the steps first.

"I hope not. That being said, we've a ways to go before we restore the Order to its full glory. Only then will Loren Brae be protected again."

"Christ, Lachlan. It's a hell of a thing, isn't it? I can't believe this has been going all these years, and you've never said a word."

"I didn't want to believe it. I couldn't, not really." That old sadness crept into Lachlan's eyes, and I clapped a hand on his shoulder, immediately contrite.

"I'm sorry. I keep forgetting how closely this ties in with your mum. I'll try to be more respectful in the future."

A cheerful honk had us both turning.

"Get in, lads, we're going to the pub. I think we could all use a drink after today," Agnes called from the driver's seat of her car. Lia sat next to her, and Sophie was tucked in the back.

"Got enough room for us?" I asked. If Lia was going, I was in.

"Sophie can sit on my lap," Lachlan said, opening the back door and sliding across the seat.

"Oh please, Lachlan, I can barely fit back here as it is," Sophie grumbled, but Lachlan merely tugged her until she sprawled across his lap, and he grinned at her.

"See?"

"You dearly love manhandling me, don't you?" Sophie pretended to be cross as I squeezed in next to them.

"There's no way I can answer that in a car full of people without sounding crude," Lachlan admitted.

"Knock off the foreplay, you two, or Munroe's going to toss you out of the car," Agnes ordered, zipping away from the castle.

"Or toss the contents of my stomach," I said.

I was rewarded with a laugh from Lia, and I held on to that warm feeling all the way to the pub. Once there, we piled out and went to annoy Graham.

"I just love this place," Lia sighed as we entered the Tipsy Thistle, where Graham immediately brightened upon seeing us. At least I hoped it was us and not Lia, as I'd made my interest known to Graham a few days before. He wasn't one to poach, I reminded myself, but every time I saw him wield his easy charm from behind the bar, it reminded me how much better he was at hooking women than I was. I scowled at him in warning, and his grin widened.

"Lia, darling, I was desperate for you to visit again. Is it true what I heard? You're not just passing through on a wee holiday?" Graham grasped her hand and pulled it to his face, brushing his lips softly across her knuckles.

Right, so Graham had a death wish then.

"The rumors are true. I've recruited her to open the restaurant at the castle," Sophie said, sliding onto a barstool and patting the one next to her for Lia to join her. Agnes took her other side, leaving me at the end with Lachlan taking up the spot on the other side of Lia. I bared my teeth at him, and Graham gave me a wink.

Cheeky bastard.

"What'll it be, love? None of that nasty gin, of course, so perhaps a nice red wine?" Graham continued to hold Lia's hand even though she'd already settled into her chair.

"Actually, I think it's time I tried the gin. Which do you recommend, Munroe?" Lia divested her hand from Graham's and turned to me.

"Do you prefer sweet, botanical, or crisp?" I asked, grateful that Graham was no longer touching her, and I wouldn't have to murder a good friend tonight.

"Hmm, not so much botanical. Can you do sweet and crisp?"

"Not a problem. I'd suggest the rhubarb gin then. Tonic will make it a touch more bitter and add the crispness, but if you like it on the sweeter side, you can mix it with lemonade or even a dash of Sprite."

"Okay, I think I'll try it with the lemonade. That sounds refreshing."

"Add a sprig of mint if you have it, Graham," I said. "Put it on my tab, please."

"Naturally." Graham turned to begin building drinks. He'd already placed a cider in front of Agnes, knowing her preference.

"Oh no, please, you don't have to do that," Lia said,

turning to me. "I insist on paying my way. I can buy my own drinks."

"Just because you can, doesn't mean you should," I responded, shaking my head at her. "Lia, I own the company. I'd be honored for you to try something that I created."

"Oh, well, it's just...I don't want you to think I'm taking advantage of you because you do own the company. I can pay." A stubborn look crossed Lia's face, mixed with something else...was that insecurity? Or embarrassment? Either way, I wanted to wipe that look off her face and give her anything in the world she wanted just so she'd never have to be left wanting for anything.

"Here's the thing," I said, leaning slightly in front of Agnes to hold Lia's look. "We build this into our numbers. There are a certain number of bottles that we always plan to give away, that are used for promotions, or are comped at various events. It's part of the gig. It's built into our overhead. This is like when you get free samples at the supermarket."

"Well, if it's not a big thing, then yes, I'll accept your payment."

Agnes was turning her head between us as we spoke, a considering look in her eyes.

"Here you go, darling. I'm prepared to toss it away if you think it's absolute drivel." Graham slid Lia her drink, and I narrowed my eyes at him. Before I could speak, Agnes jumped in.

"I dearly hope you keep it up, Graham. It's been ages since I've seen you get popped one, and I, for one, would be delighted to see it again."

"You're a bloodthirsty woman, Agnes," Graham said, crossing his arms over his chest. I held my breath as Lia took a sip of the drink, and when pleasure flooded her face, I sighed in relief.

"This is really good, Munroe." Lia turned to me. "Like, really good. I don't think gin was much on my radar before, as beer was always just the cheapest option. The few times I've tried it, well it was a basic gin and tonic and I remember it being quite bitter."

"That's likely the tonic itself. The quinine in it makes it more bitter. However, tonic companies have really upped their game now. They have flavored ones, artisanal tonics, that can really play well with the different notes of a gin. It's really a whole new playing field for gin, in my opinion, and we've moved away from just serving your grandpa's gin and tonic."

"I can see that. This is almost playful, isn't it?" Lia mused as she took another sip, and warmth filled me. I didn't need her to approve of my product, but it was certainly icing on the cake. My chest puffed up a bit, and I opened my mouth to expound on the qualities of gin, when Agnes jumped in.

"Speaking of playful, I did some research on the broonie for you."

"The what now?" Graham turned around so fast that the wine in the glass he was holding almost sloshed over the rim.

"Och, didn't anyone tell you yet? Lia found a broonie in her kitchen."

"You don't say?" Graham put the wine glass in front of Sophie and stared across the room, as though he was trying to remember something.

"Lia's also the next member of the Order," Sophie added, and Graham's eyes snapped to Lia's.

"Is that right? Well, in that case, your drinks are on me."

"They are not," I put in. "I already claimed it."

"Yes, but it's my pub, and she's here to help save Loren Brae," Graham argued back.

"I called it first," I pointed out.

"Lads," Agnes said, putting her hands up like she was referee. "Enough. Lia can pay for her own drinks if she feels like it. Hell, I can buy her a drink if I feel like it. What she doesn't need is you two bickering over her when she's clearly just trying to take it all in. Give her some breathing room, will you, you bloody eejits?"

"God," Lia said, her hand rubbing at a spot under her chest. I couldn't help but notice the way her shirt shifted over her breasts when she did that, and my mouth went dry thinking about her magnificent breasts at my mouth earlier. "To *save* Loren Brae. That just...wow. Yeah, right. Okay. Putting it like that really puts it in perspective, doesn't it?"

"It's been hard on the entire town," Agnes explained. "Once the Kelpies began acting up again, it scared away tourism. I'm sure you noticed many of the boarded-up buildings. People couldn't afford to keep their places open or pay their rent. Many have left for places with more opportunities. It's heartbreaking to watch. However, we've had a kind benefactor in our lovely Knight here who has helped ease the sting of rent for the next year."

"That was you?" Graham burst out, his mouth dropping open. Leaning over the bar, he clasped Sophie's face between his hands and placed a loud smacking kiss on her lips. Lachlan was halfway out of his seat before he finished, his hands at Graham's throat. I leaned back in my chair ready to watch the show.

"Lachlan!" Sophie tugged on his arm, pulling him back. "Please don't kill the nice man who feeds me drinks."

"Aye, Lachlan. Don't kill the handsome beast who can well best you in a wrestling match," Graham said, a glint in his eyes as he waited for Lachlan to drop his hands.

"That's utter shite, and you know it," Lachlan grumbled, but he released Graham. "Don't touch my woman."

Graham, being Graham, reached across the bar and tapped a finger on Sophie's arm.

"Oops," Graham said, and Lachlan growled at him.

"I swear they do this out of sheer boredom." Agnes rolled her eyes and turned to Lia and Sophie. "Right, so here's the deal with the broonie. There's a long history of them in Scotland, but the information I pulled is all from myths. In the olden times, they were quite large—almost human-sized. But newer stories showcase them as being smaller, wizened beings. They can be quite helpful, as they like to be given chores to do. Kind of like...you know sheep dogs? They're working dogs. They like to be given tasks to do, or they just about die of boredom. It's kind of the same with broonies. They work in the night, and they'll help on the farm or in the house, but you walk a fine line with them. You can't insult them. If you give them clothes of any nature, they'll leave."

"Wait, what? Why? What does giving them clothes have to do with anything?" Lia interjected.

"I honestly have no idea," Agnes admitted. "Do any myths make sense? They're also known to be quite mischievous. They'll play pranks or kick up a fuss occasionally. You'll want to stay on his good side, so he doesn't muck things up at the restaurant."

"Wait, so I just...like, he lives there now?" Lia drained her drink. "My sous chef is a broonie?"

"Something like that. If you want him gone, you can give him a piece of clothing. Or at least that's how the story goes."

"But where would he go?" Lia asked.

"I have no idea. Truth of it is, this is my first broonie, so I'm learning along with you," Agnes said, a gentle smile on her face.

"We left some cream for him," Lia said, rubbing that spot on her chest again.

"I just remembered from somewhere that it was good to leave some food for them," I said.

"It is. He's likely quite hungry, as the kitchen has been empty for a while now. It's been decades since that restaurant was fully open, hasn't it?"

"Aye. We've been operating a coffee cart and a pop-up cafe for tourists on the weekend, but nothing like what the restaurant once offered," Lachlan said.

"I can't wait to get started," Lia admitted, smiling at Graham as he slid her another drink. "I'll need to hire people soon."

"I can help you there," Graham offered, and I looked around, needing a distraction from my thoughts of murdering Graham.

"Dartboard is open. Do you want to play?" I asked Lia, not caring if I was interrupting a conversation.

"I want to play!" Sophie piped up.

"Go on without me," Agnes implored. "I'm a danger to the pub with darts."

"She really is. She's maimed me on more than one occasion. Her aim is terrible," Graham said.

"Or perhaps it was spot on?" Agnes mused.

"Vicious woman," Graham muttered.

The four of us stood and wandered to a small room in the back with a pool table and a dart board. I was pleased to see that Lia wasn't interested in staying and chatting with Graham, and her face lit when she saw the dartboard.

"Oh, this is a proper dartboard. No bells and whistles, eh?" Lia said.

"No, we aren't that fancy here," Lachlan said, wiping clean the chalkboard used for scoring. He pointed to where the darts were. "Pick your weapon."

"Oh, my second weapon of the day. The Scots really do like their battles," Lia said.

"Boys against girls?" Lachlan asked before I could suggest that Lia and I be a team. Annoyed, I shot him a look, but he just grinned.

"Munroe? A word?" A man stood at the door to the room, and I recognized him as a local tradesman. Nodding to the others to get started, I ducked out, and by the time I'd returned, I'd spoken to five other tradespeople and had ordered them all drinks as well.

"What's going on?" Lia asked. I looked down at her, and the worry I had for the people of this town eased. *She did that*, I realized. Just looking into her pretty eyes eased my tension.

"Just some locals inquiring about work opportunities,"

I said, and took the darts she handed me. "What are we playing? Cricket?"

"Correct. Do you know how to play? You want to close out numbers," Lia began, and I looked down at her, a smile hovering on my lips. Keeping my eyes on hers, I shot my dart, and her eyes followed the movement.

"Holy shit," Lia breathed. "You just got a bullseye without looking."

"Aye, lassie," I said, leaning toward her a bit. "I don't like to lose."

"Oh, it's on." A competitive glint came into Lia's eyes, and her lower lip poked out in a delightfully stubborn pout. I wanted to lean in and taste her once more, and it was only because my thoughts were on kissing her that I missed the next two bullseyes. Instead, I closed out twenties, and got one sixteen.

The game progressed quickly, with Sophie shamelessly cheating every time Lachlan went to shoot. Without a thought to the rules, she groped him, kissed his neck, or whispered something in his ear. Even though we were beginning to lose, I couldn't help but laugh as Sophie continued to throw Lachlan off his game to the point where he toggled between frustration and amusement. I had a feeling Sophie was just using this game as foreplay.

The unintended effect of that, much to my delight, was that after two drinks, Lia decided to embrace similar tactics.

"Have I told you how handsome I think you are?" Lia breathed in my ear as I leaned forward into a throw. Of course, her breath at my neck and her words had their intended effect, and I miscalculated. The dart hit a nine, which wasn't included in the game, and Lia grinned.

"You haven't," I said, evenly. "But do tell me more." I held up my next dart, and Lia took the invitation, moving closer into me, and reached out to stroke a hand down my side while I positioned myself for my next throw. God help me, but I was just about willing to throw this game if it meant that Lia would put her hands on me.

"The first time I saw you...I thought you couldn't be real. Like a gilded god," Lia murmured, and my heart skipped a beat. I barely, just barely, closed out the fifteens and handed the darts over to Lia. My mind was whirling. Had she had a similar reaction to mine when we first saw each other? I couldn't help but be pleased.

Lia turned out to be an excellent dart player, a fact that she credited her brothers for, and I felt that two could play at this war of distraction. Leaning down, I brushed a curl away from her ear as she lifted her hand to throw. She stilled, and her eyelashes fluttered to her cheeks, her dusky skin pinkening.

"And the first time I saw you, I realized that I never wanted to look at another woman again." Whoops, maybe that was too much, but it was the truth.

Lia's dart clattered to the floor after it bounced off the dartboard.

"Damn it, Munroe," Lia seethed, turning to me. Her eyes were bright with anger, but also something more. A deeply buried need. I recognized it, because I saw it in my own every time I looked in the mirror. She may not know it, but Lia Blackwood was desperate for love. And I would be the one to give it to her if she let me.

"All's fair, darling," I said, giving her a wink.

The ladies lost the game, by a narrow margin, and Lia stomped her foot in frustration.

"You guys cheated," Lia complained as we made our way back to the bar. I noticed she was unsteady on her feet and went to offer her a hand, but she grabbed the side of the bar to catch herself. "Whoa, those drinks just hit."

"Yes, gin can sneak up on you if you're not used to hard liquor," I said. "Are you okay? Do you want some food?"

"I think I just want to go home," Lia admitted. "I'll just go. You guys stay and have fun." Lia reached for her handbag that Agnes had been watching. "Let me get the drinks."

"No, Lia. I've got the drinks." I looked up at Graham who nodded to me.

"You'll get her home?" Graham asked while Lia continued to dig in her handbag.

"Of course," I said. Turning, I looked over to the table of tradespeople that I'd bought drinks for. "And another round for them, please."

"That's a lad!" One of the men called, and Lia looked up, the light of war in her eyes.

"Pay for your own drinks, *lads*," Lia said. "You shouldn't be drinking at the pub if you can't afford it."

"Whoops, all right, that's time to go," I said. Gripping Lia's arm, I propelled her from the bar, as she shot daggers over her eyes at the table of men.

"Well? I'm not wrong, am I? What are they doing mooching off you? It seems everyone takes advantage of you," Lia muttered as the cool night air hit us. I realized then that her outburst had come because she wanted to protect me. It made me smile, even though I suspected she'd probably be embarrassed about it in the morning. I knew Graham would smooth things over with the lads, and Lia would be forgiven. There wasn't a one of us in this town who hadn't had a bad night or two in front of the rest of the pub. It was the nature of life in a small community, and the acceptance that we all were human made Loren Brae the tight-knit place that it was.

"It's not a bother, Lia. I can afford it," I said, threading my arm through hers as we walked down the quiet street and toward the path that led to the castle.

"Doesn't mean people need to use you," Lia muttered.

"I think you're just misdirecting your anger about your catastrophic loss at darts," I said, shifting the conversation.

"Catastrophic, my ass," Lia said, whirling on me and smacking me lightly on the chest. "I would've won if you hadn't gone all mooshy on me."

"*Mooshy*?" I laughed. "What, exactly, is mooshy?"

The loch was still that night, the surface smooth and reflecting the gentle lights of Loren Brae back at us. I scanned the water, nervous for the Kelpies, but silence met us. Perhaps they were happy that Lia had joined the Order today. One more person closer to keeping the stone protected.

"You know." Lia waved her hand in the air as we left the loch and started up the hill to the castle. It was darker here as we wound along the tall hedges that lined the drive and I pulled my arm from Lia's and instead put it around her shoulders, drawing her closer into me so I could shield her with my body. Just in case. "Mooshy. Sentimental. Lovey."

"Och yes, *that* mooshy." My lips quirked in a smile. "I wasn't being mooshy. I was being honest."

"Really?" Lia skidded to a stop and turned to look at me, which had the added benefit of her pressing into my body. "You really don't want to look at any other women? Only me?"

I wanted to have this conversation sober. I didn't want this to be the first time I told Lia what I saw for us in our future, or at the very least, hoped for. It wasn't the right time, no matter how romantic the soft summer night was. I could all but hear Graham and Lachlan giving me hell for moving at a glacial pace, but this mattered. She mattered.

"You're the most beautiful woman I've ever seen," I told Lia instead, and she scrunched her nose at me.

"Not possible. I mean...I'm not half bad, but there are far prettier people than me. I mean, just look at this mess of hair." Lia pointed to her curls that I desperately wanted to see curtaining my face while she rode me into blissful oblivion.

"I'm sure you know," I said, gently turning her and continuing the walk toward the castle before I pulled her to the grass and showed her just how beautiful I found her. "As a chef that is...that you might make the most perfect dish in the world, but you'll still find someone who doesn't like it, right?"

"Yes, the bastards." Lia sighed.

"It's like that, Lia. Everyone has their tastes. Beauty, like food, is a subjective thing. And for me, well, you're a five-star meal. If I was a dying man, you'd be the last meal I'd request."

Lia halted and turned to me once more. Her lips were wide, and her mouth hung open as though she wanted to say something but couldn't get it out. The moment hung suspended between us.

"Damn it, Munroe," Lia said, and then her hands were on me, pulling my head down, and I gladly indulged her.

She tasted sweet, the hints of lemonade and my gin still on her tongue. Something about that combination, knowing this woman enjoyed something that I had created, heated my blood. Without thinking, I lifted her, pulling her legs around my waist, and cupped her bum with my hands.

Lia's mouth was desperate on mine, and she made soft sounds of pleasure as she kissed me, her tongue dancing across mine. We feasted on each other, each kiss an exploration, each taste a discovery. Lust raged through me, but love quieted me. My heart had broken open, and Lia now occupied the space where loneliness had once resided. Slowly, and ever so softly, I gentled the kiss until Lia brought her forehead to mine.

"What am I going to do about you?" Lia murmured.

"Give us a chance," I whispered. I wouldn't beg, not yet, but if it came down to it, I would.

A shimmer of light caught my eye, and I turned my head, as did Lia. We froze, cheek to cheek, while I cradled her close in the cool night.

A unicorn poked its head from the hedge and trotted forward.

A soft glow surrounded the majestic animal, and it stopped a few feet from us. She was a brilliant white, with a gossamer mane, and an intricate horn protruded from her head. Huffing out a breath, the unicorn bowed once to us, her horn lighting with an effervescent shimmer, and she stomped her hoof once.

"Please tell me you see this," Lia said, her voice barely a whisper in the night.

"I do," I said, keeping her close. Although my arms shook, I would do anything to protect Lia, and while I didn't feel that this unicorn was a threat, I couldn't quite understand what it was trying to tell us.

Once more it bowed, and then, in an instant, it disappeared into the night as quickly as it had arrived. We stood there, frozen, Lia clinging to me. I could feel the pulse at her neck firing rapidly, and her breath came in rapid little pants.

"A freaking unicorn," Lia said. Turning, a smile bloomed on her face. It was a smile of wonder, of acceptance, almost childlike in its delight. "I've never seen something so beautiful in my life."

"Me neither," I said, drinking in Lia's joy.

But it wasn't the unicorn I spoke of, it was Lia.

I just had to figure out how to make her mine.

CHAPTER THIRTEEN

LIA

"I, *Cecilia Blackwood, the second in the Order of Caledonia, announce my arrival. I accept the responsibility of protecting the Clach na Fìrinn and promise to restore the Order to its fullness. In doing so, I show myself worthy of the magick bestowed upon me, the same magick given to my blood before me. It is with these words that I establish the Order of Caledonia as the first line of protection for the Clach na Fìrinn, and accept the power given to me therein. It is with a pure heart and sound mind that I accept this gift, and I give my promise to stand with the Order of Caledonia.*"

My words drifted back to me the next morning as I lay in bed, far later than I usually would, my emotions knotting in my stomach. Yesterday had been, well, it had been a day for the books, that was for sure. Between seeing the broonie, learning about the Order, all the way to meeting a unicorn on the path home, it had been incredible. *Incredible*. Overwhelming. Unbelievable. All of the things. I felt like I was in that Space Invaders video game and just cruising along, dodging all the meteors trying to blow up my ship. It was truly that wild. I couldn't actually believe all of the things that I had learned the day before.

That I had become.

I looked down at my hands and wondered what my magick would be. Archie had told me it would manifest after the ritual was completed, and while I had felt a ripple of something...awareness, maybe, go through me at the completion of the ceremony, I still felt like me.

Lia Blackwood. Fish out of water.

Which was fine, really, I reminded myself, as I took a sip of my coffee and stared out the window to the loch. The rain came down in vicious sheets today, which also contributed to my reluctance to leave my bed. That and I needed a moment or two to process.

A freaking unicorn.

I still couldn't believe it. I sincerely hoped that it wasn't my drunk imagination. But Munroe had said he'd seen it too, and I just couldn't see him being mean enough to toy with me like that. He was about the nicest teddy bear around, it just didn't seem to be in his nature to lie. I groaned, flopping back against my pillows, as I thought about our kiss. *Kisses*, my ladyparts helpfully reminded me. I was doing a horrible job of establishing my boundaries. It was like, my head told me one thing and then two seconds in the presence of Munroe, and I was climbing the man like a tree. What was it about him that was like catnip to me? I truly felt like a cat in heat, and I was certain I'd soon be wailing and strutting myself in front of him until he moved past the kissing stage and eased this ache that I had for him.

Maybe he was just an itch that needed to be scratched. Maybe, because since I'd arrived in Scotland, I'd been blind-sided left and right, which was making me feel all sorts of things. I was unsteady on my feet, and maybe I just needed the distraction of Munroe to keep me balanced. Men I could understand. Attraction I could understand. Lust I could understand. Kelpies, broonies, ghost coos, and unicorns...well, they were a bit harder to grasp.

I winced as I remembered yelling at the poor men at the table. I needed to rectify that situation immediately, or I'd get a reputation for being difficult. Although baking wasn't at the top of my skill set, I still was better than the average chef. I resolved myself to making up a nice box of treats, and I texted Agnes to see if she'd be able to deliver them for me, along with an apology note, since I had no clue who the men had been but was certain Agnes would know.

Agnes: Happy to! Only if you make some for me too. Yes, I'm greedy like that.

Me: Come by this afternoon, and I'll have them packaged up.

Agnes: I'll be by just after lunch then.

I glanced at the clock and realized I needed to get moving if I wanted to get my mission accomplished. I didn't have a car to get around, so I was happy that Agnes was willing to come by and pick up my apology gifts for me.

After a quick shower, I did my hair in two Dutch braids that ran along either side of my head. I typically braided my hair back in one manner or another when I was in the kitchen as it was an easy way to tame the beast and keep things sanitary. I often wore a hair net or chef's cap over the braids as well.

I slipped into fitted black jeans, a black long-sleeved top, and comfortable sneakers before grabbing the recipe book and heading downstairs. I wanted to get a solid day in my kitchen because I knew that I was close enough to a soft opening to start hiring staff. After a careful inventory of most of the items in the large banquet hall, I'd come to the realization that I was well stocked with enough equipment and furniture to start the restaurant. I had buckets of silverware, plenty of dishes, and more than enough tables and chairs. On top of that, there were boxes upon boxes of décor and furnishings, and coupled with the natural beauty of the restaurant space, I didn't have much to order before we could open. I wasn't one to fuss too much on overdecorating a space, particularly one like the banquet hall. The natural features of the stone castle walls and thick wood beams added to the atmosphere, and all the room really needed was some candles and ambient lighting.

That, and a killer menu, of course.

Sophie, Hilda, and I had met two days ago to discuss the vision for the restaurant. While they wanted to serve some of the Scottish staples, as tourists would be a large part of the clientele, they'd also encouraged me to have fun with some original dishes. Since I'd need to stick to a consistent menu in lieu of a surprise menu like I'd done at Suzette's, I'd suggested one themed weekend a month, and then a second daily offering of my spin on the Scottish classics. For example, I could take neeps and tatties, a traditional Scottish dish of turnips and potatoes, and add my own take. It would be almost a fusion restaurant of sorts, offering a variety of influences from other food cultures, while still offering the traditional favorites for those who weren't feeling adventurous. I'd been pleased with the outcome of the meeting, as it would allow me to stretch my legs, while also making life just a touch easier by having a consistent menu each week. We'd agreed on rotating some of the menu items each month and, of course, I could always offer any specials that I was in the mood for. All in all, I felt like it gave me a lot of creative control, while also allowing me an easier time of ordering supplies each week.

My thoughts on my menu, I almost bumped into Hilda as she poked her head out of the door to the lounge.

"Oh, Hilda! I'm sorry, I didn't see you there," I said, grasping the woman's arm.

"Nae bother," Hilda said. She was dressed today in pressed jeans and a lavender button-down shirt. "Come meet my friend if you have a moment? We were just discussing the restaurant."

"Of course." I detoured to the lounge, but only because I knew there would be cookies, and my empty stomach churned against the onslaught of the coffee I'd inhaled. I pulled up short when I saw the woman sitting in an armchair by the window, a small table set for tea.

The flirting granny.

I narrowed my eyes at my nemesis and sniffed. Was she here to flirt with Munroe? Or maybe she was after Archie. I'd have to warn Hilda to watch her man.

"This is my friend Catriona, Lia," Hilda said, smiling between us both.

"Lovely to meet you." Catriona had a voice like honey, which I'm sure many a man had appreciated.

"Nice to meet you as well," I said. She didn't offer me her hand to shake, so I followed suit.

"Do you have time for a cuppa? I just brewed a pot."

"Not really," I said, honestly. "I was just on my way to the restaurant. I have a huge list of things to get through. But I have a few minutes for a scone." I'd been eyeing the plate of scones on the table, their scent making my mouth water.

"Oh, you must try them," Hilda insisted, pulling out a chair for me. "They're really something."

"Thanks," I said. I placed one on my plate and tore off a chunk but didn't add butter. I always liked to see how the flavors worked before adding a topping to breads or scones. Taking a bite, I let the flavors settle on my tongue, and was delighted with the interesting combination. I hadn't been expecting savory, for some reason. "What is this flavor? Garlic...and is that nigella?"

"Wild garlic, cheese, and nigella," Catriona said, approval sparking on her face. "It's one of my favorite combinations."

"You made these? They're delicious," I said. "An unusual combination that works really well together."

"I'm surprised you know of nigella. Not many people do," Catriona said, taking a small sip from her teacup. Her hand shook with the effort, and I felt my heart softening toward this purported man-eater.

"I do. Black cumin, we call it too. It has some good health benefits, supposedly." I eyed up the pile of scones. Would it be rude to have another?

"Go on." Catriona smiled. "I don't get to bake much anymore. I do miss it so."

"Catriona used to make the best bread in the village, if not the country. People would come in droves for her loaves, and she'd be sold out by early morning," Hilda supplied, smiling affectionately at the woman. I was starting to feel like a real bitch for my unkind thoughts about this poor woman for flirting with Munroe.

"I can't knead anymore." Catriona held up her hands. "Arthritis. It broke my heart to close, but the pain got to be too much. Now I try to make things here and there that don't require much effort. I miss it."

"I'm sorry to hear that," I said. I understood what it was like to have something taken from me, and it was only sheer luck that had landed me in this new role. Well, that and my family's history, it seemed.

"Not much to be done about it. Just have to get on with it." Catriona shrugged.

"I'm lucky to get your scones when you're up to making them." Hilda patted Catriona's hand. "We won't keep you, Lia. But I thought I would introduce the two of you since you both have a love for cooking."

"It's really nice to meet you. Thank you for these, they are delicious." I picked up my second scone to go, knowing it was a touch rude, but my mind was spinning with an idea. "Catriona, will you be around for a bit? Would you like to stop by the restaurant, say in an hour or two? Or perhaps tomorrow? I have a few things to figure out right now, but I'd have some time to show you the place later today or tomorrow if you're interested."

"I've got all the time in the world, dear. I'll wander on

down after our chat." Catriona smiled up at me, a warm and open smile, and I berated myself for my earlier annoyance with her.

"Great, see you later." I looked down at where both dogs had planted themselves at my feet, their eyes on my scone. "Not a chance, kids. Your mom would kill me. This will give you an upset tummy."

Sir Buster growled at me, and Lady Lola rolled on her back.

"Interesting tactics. Submission and aggressiveness. And yet, neither will work."

"They're shameless, really." Hilda sighed.

I left the two women chatting, my brain busy with an idea I'd had. Honestly, I'd quite forgotten about the broonie until I'd unlocked the kitchen doors and propped them open to encourage the light breeze to work its way into the room. Only when I saw the kitchen, entirely put to rights, ingredients that I'd left out the day before when we'd left in a hurry tidied and stacked, did I remember that I was dealing with a small elf goblin man thing.

A shiver went through me as my nerves kicked up, but Agnes hadn't said he would be violent or to be considered a threat—she'd merely mentioned mischievous. I took the clean kitchen to be a good sign and that he was happy about the cream we'd left out for him.

But now...how the hell did I befriend a broonie? A part of me desperately wanted to call for help, but that went against everything that I'd ever stood for. So, instead I did what I'd always done—I handled it myself.

"Hello?" I called, stepping tentatively inside, and hitting the switch for the lights. When silence greeted me, I shrugged and walked to the table, putting the book of spells down on the box that held the cutting board Munroe had given me. "Um, well, thank you for cleaning up in here. I don't like to leave a mess in the kitchen, so it's very kind of you to help. I really appreciate it."

A whisper of something sounded in the other room, and the hair at the back of my neck rose, but nothing else followed.

"So, um, if you wanted to get to know each other, I'd be fine with that as well. Or are you hungry? I see the cream is gone. What...is there anything else you like to eat?"

At that, something clattered in the other room.

Ah-ha. The way to any man's heart—through food. Well, the poor thing couldn't subsist on cream alone, right? I'd just have to see how he felt about cookies.

"I'm going to make up a batch of cookies because I owe some people an apology. I'll save some for you. Would you like that?"

Something that sounded suspiciously like "Aye" drifted in from the other room, and I waited, my eyes on the door to the banquet hall that was cracked open. When nothing appeared, I sighed and went to the pantry to take inventory of my ingredients. I'd put an order in for some staples before I'd arrived and was pleased to see the refrigerator and pantry were well-stocked with the basics. Keeping it simple, I decided on cinnamon oatmeal chocolate chip cookies.

Testing the oven, I was pleased to see it had been outfitted with a modern burner system. It took me a moment to figure out the Celsius to Fahrenheit degrees, consulting my phone to make the conversion for me, but then it was just like old times. I picked one of my favorite soulful cooking playlists from my phone, turned it up, and bent to work, letting my mind drift back to the idea I'd had earlier.

I couldn't stop thinking about the sadness in Catriona's eyes when she spoke of baking her bread. While I could bake bread, it wasn't where my talents lay. I wondered if there was a recipe in my book that might be of help to her. It was worth a shot, right? And, at the very least, it might assuage some of my guilt for thinking about pushing her into the street when she was openly flirting with Munroe. Nevertheless, I knew a woman in pain, and maybe, with my newly discovered Kitchen Witch powers, I could fix something up for her. After I'd slid the cookies in the oven and set the timer, I rested one hip against the counter as I thumbed through the book.

"Ah-ha! I knew it," I said, delight filling me as I found a page for arthritis. "Interesting." Nigella seeds were listed as one of the potential ingredients that could be used in the recipe, and I wondered if Catriona had done some research herself. "So what I'm seeing here is a variety of options that I can put together." Talking to myself while cooking was pretty much the norm for me, and I often forgot other people were around in the kitchen until they answered me when I spoke. Now, I muttered to myself as I read through the variations. The spell indicated that I could make a tea, an ointment, a soup, or a tincture. I eyed up the recipe that involved a ginger and hot pepper tea, but I kept circling back to the one that involved stinging nettles. I'd been certain I'd seen a batch nearby recently.

Humming to myself, I dug in a drawer until I found a pair of kitchen shears and some rubber gloves for cleaning dishes. Then, I cast my mind back to where I'd last spied a patch of nettles. It had been by the tool shed when we went on our ritual walk, and Archie had warned me away from them. Grabbing a bowl, I sought them out and cut a few bunches and placed them gingerly in the bowl. Stinging nettles could be nasty if they touched the skin, and even I, a city girl, knew to take care with them. Returning to the kitchen, I pulled up short.

The rest of the spell ingredients had been assembled neatly for me on the prep table.

My alarm for the cookies went off, and I jumped about a foot in the air, barely catching myself from dropping the bowl of nettles. *Lovely.* I was going to have to adjust to having a broonie around and, until then, it seemed I'd constantly be on edge. Putting the bowl on the table, I grabbed my oven mitts and took the trays of cookies from the oven and put them on racks to cool. Then I turned to study the ingredients laid out on the table.

The healing recipe was for a garlic, nettle, and potato soup with onion and a touch of turmeric as well. All of these ingredients were simple, yet I suspected the combination of garlic, nettle, and turmeric would be the ingredients that would provide the most healing properties for Catriona. I grabbed the olive oil and poured it over the nettles, keeping my gloves on as I massaged the leaves until they were tender, and then cut the stalks from the leaves. In moments, I had the garlic and onion cooking in a pot, before I added water, bouillon, and the potatoes I'd neatly diced. While I waited for the water to start simmering, I checked the cookies and found them to have cooled just enough that I could slide a few onto a plate.

Taking a deep breath, and then another, I steeled my resolve before I tiptoed to the open doorway to the banquet hall. Peering inside, my eyes darted among the stacks of furniture for any creatures that may be hiding. When nothing moved, or jumped out at me from the dark corners, I bent and placed the plate on the floor.

"Thank you for your help in the kitchen." Turning to go, I paused and then turned back around. "Um, if we're going to, like work together, do you have a name? Should I call you something?"

A soft mutter greeted me from far across the room. My pulse picked up, and I steadied my breathing.

"Um, I didn't quite catch that. Was it David, you said?"

Something clattered to the floor, and there was an indignant sound.

"Okay, not David. Try again? It's hard to hear you." I seriously could not believe I was having a conversation with a kitchen goblin. Another muttered response, and I thought for a moment, trying to pick out the sounds.

"Rice?" I said, confused.

A snort sounded and some chattering.

"Rice? Really?"

More chattering.

"B...Brice? Brice? Is that a name?" A gleeful sound erupted from the corner, so I took that to be a yes. I decided, instead of going to try and corner the little guy, that I was going to leave him be. Listen, I'd lived in the city long enough to learn to coexist with mice and pigeons and whatnot. Certainly, I could learn to live with Brice, particularly if he was as helpful as he was showing himself to be. If he wanted to stay hidden in the corner, I had no problem with that. I'd feed the little kitchen goblin all day long if he didn't get in the way of what I was trying to build here. Plus, I was a sucker for taking care of anyone, and anything, with food. Maybe that was just the nature of being a chef, but I didn't like knowing anyone around me was hungry.

"Okay, Brice it is. Thank you, my friend, for your help. I've left some cookies for you. They're cinnamon oatmeal with chocolate chips. I hope you like them. If there's anything else I can make for you, just let me know. Or leave the ingredients out, and I'll put it together for you when I can." I waited, but there was no response. I took that as a sign that he was pleased with my offering and returned to the stove where my broth was just beginning to boil. I added the nettles, along with the rest of the ingredients, and stirred the soup before returning to the book. Now came the hard part. According to the book, I had to actually perform a spell of sorts over the food.

This was going to be my first time trying out my newly discovered magick, so to speak, and I was more than grateful that I was alone.

Well, except for Brice, of course. Granted, he was magick, so he didn't count as a judgmental audience. Or did he? Would he be critiquing my technique? I narrowed my eyes at the open door to the banquet hall. Either way, it was best to get on with it, or I wasn't sure I'd work up the nerve to try a spell if anyone was around watching me. I'd discovered that people had a habit of dropping by my kitchen quite frequently, and I needed to take this opportunity while I was still alone.

I turned the stove off, because I needed to read from the book while I stirred the soup and cast my spell. There was no way I was bringing the book near open flame, so I dearly hoped that the spell didn't require fire to work. But it seemed that the only thing I needed to do was to stir clockwise and repeat the words.

Oh, and intent. That was right. Agnes had mentioned it in an offhand comment the night before, but the meaning had stuck with me. Intention was everything when it came to spell work, apparently, but I supposed that applied to anything in life. What we paid attention to grew, didn't it? Clearing my throat, I took a few deep breaths to settle myself, and then opened my eyes. With my left hand, I stirred the pot, clockwise as instructed, and brought the book in front of me with my other hand.

A hum of recognition flowed through me. It was startling, and...exhilarating. Like, *here I am*. Here. I. Am.

This felt right. More so than anything I'd ever done in my life before. A strange sense of understanding and belonging burbled through me, riding on the edges of joy. I held onto that and poured that feeling into my words.

"As I stir with my spoon,
I call upon the power of Mother moon,
The fire that flames within must cool,
And soon the pain no longer will rule,
Set the energy free to run with the wind,
Aching joints and sore bones I do rescind."

There was a gentle flash of light, and I gaped as the ingredients in my soup melded seamlessly together.

"Well, shit. I didn't even have to run them through a food processor," I murmured. Carefully, because my hands were shaking, I turned and put the book in a clean spot on the table. I realized that I would need to create a designated safe spot for the book, because I would be devastated if it got damaged in the kitchen. Which wasn't unusual. The sign of a well-loved cookbook was the food stains that stuck to its pages.

I spooned the soup into several mason jars and added their lids before digging around in a pantry until I found a basket. I'd give these to Catriona to take home and, well, I guess I would just have to wait and see.

"Hello, dear. Is this a good time?"

I looked up to see Catriona hovering at the doorway. Her face was alight with curiosity, but also I caught a sense of longing in her eyes. I realized now, just how much I wanted to help her.

"Perfect time, I was just finishing up putting together a basket for you."

"For me? Whatever for?" Catriona came forward, her eyes bright with interest. "This is a brilliant kitchen, isn't it?"

"It really is. I'm lucky to be working here. I swear I can feel the history seeping into my bones as I work. Speaking of bones..." I tapped my finger on the basket. "I've prepared a nettle soup for you. It's meant to help with your arthritis. I'd be grateful if you could give it a try and let me know how it works for you."

"Nettles?" Catriona gave a little shiver. "Nasty plants."

"With healing properties. I promise I'm not trying to kill you."

"Even though I flirted with your man?"

My mouth dropped open. I didn't know which part to debate—whether Munroe was my man or that I'd been annoyed at her blatant flirting.

"I saw your look. I may be old, but my eyesight is still sharp. I know a lass that's got a bee in her bonnet." Catriona smirked at me. "If he's spoken for, you only have to say it."

"He's not..." I sighed and pinched my nose. Was I really going to argue with this grandmother about who got to flirt with Munroe? This was absurd. And...yet. "Listen, lady. If you're going to work here, you can't be flirting with Munroe. I don't know what he is, other than he's off limits."

A stunned look crossed Catriona's face, and her hands shook as she placed them on the handle of the basket.

"Working here?"

"See how the soup does. If you feel better, come see me. I could use an experienced baker. But only if the pain isn't too much."

"Even if it lessens, I'm not sure I can do what I once could," Catriona balked. "I don't know what the demands of your restaurant will be."

"Did you run a bakery before?"

"Aye."

"Did you hire help or manage any employees?"

"Aye."

"Then it will be much the same here. You won't have to do it all, but you will have to work. If, and *only* if, your pain goes away, *then* you can oversee the baked goods. I'm a good baker, but I'm a better chef. I'll need the help."

Catriona sniffed and nodded at the tray of cookies behind me.

"May I?"

"Of course." I put one on a spatula and passed it to her.

She bit into it, a considering look on her face, and then nodded her approval. "Tasty. A touch less baking soda and just a wee sprinkle of salt."

"Duly noted. Do we have a deal?" I asked.

"We do. I'm off to try out your soup, and I'll follow up with you on the results shortly." Catriona hefted the basket, and I resisted offering my help. It wasn't all that heavy, and she'd likely have to lift more than that if she came to work for me. Although her hands shook, once she'd hooked the handle on her arm, she moved along just fine. At the door, she stopped and turned back to me. "Oh, and Lia? I won't flirt with Munroe anymore. But I can't promise he won't flirt with me."

With a wink, and her head held high, Catriona strolled from my kitchen like the badass flirting granny that she was. See? I *knew* that I had been right to be wary of her. There was a woman that knew her own power.

Returning to my table, I skidded to a stop as my eyes landed on my knife.

A singular ring of gold now glimmered in the handle.

CHAPTER FOURTEEN

Munroe

Over the rest of the week, I'd kept up a steady text conversation with Lia, even if she didn't immediately respond. It was almost easier for me to chat with her over text, as shyness didn't prevent me from articulating my thoughts, and every time she sent me a smiley faced emoji back, I screenshotted it and saved the message in a little folder in my phone with notes on what made Lia smile.

And finally, just yesterday, I'd convinced her to go on an official date with me.

Only if I can get the furniture moved around in the restaurant, she'd quickly added, but I had come up with a plan for that. But first, I had one more property to tour. I still hadn't found a perfect spot for the distillery, and Cassidy was beginning to wonder if I was ever going to return to Edinburgh to run the company. While I assured her that she was more than capable of managing the business, I knew I'd have to take a drive to the city soon to settle a few things and sit in on some meetings.

"The view is grand." The real estate agent, a lad not from Loren Brae, swept his hand out. He wasn't wrong. The property showcased an old stone mill positioned on the edge of Loch Mirren, about a fifteen-minute drive away from the village. It was quite picturesque, in fact I'd even stopped once to take a photo of the building, and I could imagine it being a perfect tourist spot. It was just off the road, easy to spot, and the entire building with the backdrop of the rolling hills and pretty water just about made it a postcard. Something niggled at me, a disquieting feeling in my gut, but soon I pushed it aside in my excitement about discovering that this property was for sale. By the time I'd finished touring the space—it would need a total rehaul on the inside, and we'd need to reinforce the main structural components—I was ready to move forward with the location. I wasn't one to back down from a challenge, and the thrill that I always got at the start of a new project drove me forward.

"Draw up the papers. Let me know if the seller is set on the fixed price. Given the work needed here, I'd be interested to see if there is any flexibility," I said, shaking the lad's hand at the end of the tour. His face lit like I'd just given him the best Christmas present, and I felt good about my accomplishments as I returned to my rental cottage just outside of Loren Brae.

One of my biggest points of pride was that Common Gin provided a significant number of jobs for people who dearly needed them. I cared about all my employees, and I still got a thrill every time I saw the joy on someone's face, like today, when I made a decision that impacted someone else's life. I was no superhero, but once in a while, I kind of felt like one.

Lia, however, now she was the real superhero. I'd learned from Agnes that Lia had run her first spell to much success and had managed to pass the first of her three challenges. While I wished that Lia had felt comfortable sharing that information with me herself, I understood that she was incredibly busy with getting the restaurant sorted. Maybe she'd tell me over dinner tonight.

I took my time finishing putting together dinner, a simple lasagna that Hilda had assured me I couldn't mess up too much, a sliced baguette slathered in garlic butter, and a decadent bottle of red wine. Flowers bloomed in a vase at the table, candles were ready to be lit, and a nice playlist was set for music in the background. I had picked up wood for both the indoor fireplace and the outside fire pit, in case she'd want to sit around the fire and, after checking my watch, I jumped in the shower.

Nerves kicked up, and I reminded myself that I was a successful businessman who had a lot to offer a woman.

Not just any woman, my nerves reminded me.

A badass goddess of a Kitchen Witch. A powerful woman. A woman who had walked into the pub and changed the trajectory of my life. A woman who had the power to break me.

Anxiety was kind of a bitch, wasn't it?

"I am a *nice* person. I am a *good* person. I can be the partner that Lia needs," I recited to myself as I finished getting ready. Right, I sounded like an eejit. Talking to myself like I was in a motivational seminar. Sighing, I hopped in the car and turned the music all the way up to drown out my thoughts as I drove to MacAlpine Castle.

It wasn't quite dinnertime, but the surprise I had arranged was already waiting for me outside the kitchen. One look at Lia's face told me that I might have miscalculated a bit. Kicking myself for not arriving earlier, I pasted a hopeful smile on my face.

"Munroe. What are these men doing here?" Lia bit the words out, as though she was just holding back her rage.

My eyes lit on the group of men who waited for my orders. Smart men, as they all kept their mouths shut.

"I hired them to move all the heavy furniture for you. So you could come to dinner," I explained.

"Hired..." Lia put her hands on her hips, her face mutinous.

It didn't help that I thought she looked even more beautiful when she was angry. Her eyes were alight with fire, hair fell loose from her braids, and her body vibrated with energy. I wanted to massage the tension from her shoulders, but suspected she'd swipe at me if I touched her. Instead, I waited her out.

"You can't just make decisions for my restaurant." Lia jutted a finger into the air, spiking each word like an exclamation point. "I don't need your help. I don't need anyone's help, Munroe. I can do this on my own."

The stubborn lift of her chin told me there was more to the story here, and I suspected if she was as proud as I was, that she wasn't about to unpack it in front of a group of strangers.

"Can you show me the banquet hall again?" I asked, walking into the kitchen, and forcing her to follow me.

"I'm serious, Munroe. I can do this on my own," Lia insisted, and I pressed my lips together as I studied the mountains of furniture still stacked in piles in the cavernous hall. She could do some of it on her own, but even she couldn't lift all of this furniture by herself. I thought for a moment about what angle I wanted to take before turning to her. This time I did grip her shoulders and leaned closer, forcing her to look up at me.

"Here's the deal, Lia. I well know you're more than capable of handling all of this on your own. And I know you didn't ask for help. But those men out there? Those are the same men you've seen who keep coming up to me at the pub, begging for work. They have families to feed. While I can't give them much to do until I have a distillery to build, at the very least I can give them this. You'd be helping the community out if you let them come in and take care of this. Just tell them exactly what you want done, and I trust they'll handle it for you."

"Oh." Lia visibly deflated, and she bit her lower lip as her eyes darted around the room. "Well, in that case, *I'm* paying for their services."

"Too late, they're already under contract with me. When this is done, which will take several days, feed them. They'll be delighted. In the meantime, you've promised me a date."

"But only if the restaurant was done..." Lia trailed off when I gave her a chiding look, and she sighed, pinching her nose before nodding into her hand. "Right. Give me a moment, and then we can bring them in."

I moved to the door and then stopped when I heard Lia whispering into a corner.

"Brice. There are men coming in to move the furniture around the next few days. You might want to hide in the pantry. I'll put your dinner in there."

My eyebrows lifted, and I crossed my arms over my chest when Lia turned and caught me staring.

"Brice?"

"That's his name," Lia muttered, a mulish look still on her face. "And he's very nice. He's been nothing but helpful."

"I'm glad to hear it," I said. "Brice is a good name. A strong name. I'm happy you have someone looking after you while you're here."

A soft chattering from a dark corner drew my attention, and I could only hope that Brice was pleased with my words.

"I don't need looking after," Lia protested as we went back into the kitchen, and she grabbed her notepad.

"Nobody does, Lia. But it's nice he's here to help, nonetheless. I know you can handle yourself, and you are a stunning badass warrior queen. I'm just saying that I'm glad he's here. If you don't mind him and he's helpful, it's not a bad thing, aye?"

"I guess?" Lia asked, scrunching her face up as though she was uncertain if it *was* a good thing to be looked after.

A short time later, after Lia had given the men a very detailed diagram of where she wanted the furniture moved to, and Archie had arrived to oversee the removal of the overflow pieces, I cooled my heels in the main lounge of the castle. Sir Buster growled at my feet while Lady Lola flopped into my lap, content to be given all of the adoration she rightly deserved.

Sir Buster jumped up in a flurry of rage and raced into the hallway.

"Crabbit beast," Lachlan muttered as he came into the room. His face brightened when he saw me. "Munroe! How's it going then?"

"Well enough, I suppose. I convinced Lia to have dinner with me."

"Ah well, I knew this day would eventually come." Lachlan strode over and dragged a chair in front of me, concern creasing his face. Reaching over, he clasped my shoulder and looked me deep in my eyes. "The time for us to have *the talk* has arrived. Now, Munroe...when a lad likes a woman, there comes a time when they'll want to express their love in a bodily manner."

"I'd like to express something to you in a bodily manner," I said, holding up a fist, and Lachlan threw his head back and laughed. Lia came into the room just then, stopping our conversation, and warmth bloomed in my chest just looking at her. She'd changed into form-fitting jeans, a soft pink shirt that immediately made me think of her naked and had dusted some makeup across her face. I wanted to lick every inch of her skin and hear her beg me for more.

"You look beautiful," I said, standing quickly and handing Lola to Lachlan. Crossing the room, I held out my arm. "Ready for dinner?"

"I'm famished actually. As much as I love food, I'd completely forgotten to eat today."

"You two kids have fun. Don't stay up too late," Lachlan called as we started out.

"I didn't see a curfew in my employment contract," Lia called over her shoulder, and I laughed when Lachlan swore.

"You'll do well here," I said as I held the door of the car for her. "Banter is highly prized."

"So I've learned. Frankly, it's kind of like working in a kitchen. Half the day is just spent ragging on each other," Lia explained.

"It sounds fun," I said, and we chatted lightly about life as a chef. Soon, I pulled up to the brightly lit stone cottage, and Lia glanced around.

"What is this place? Is this a restaurant?"

"No, it's the cottage I'm renting."

"The cottage you're renting?" Lia arched an eyebrow. "Isn't that a bit presumptuous for a first date?"

Immediately, worry filled me. "Och, aye. I'm sorry. Of course, you're right. We can go elsewhere. I just...I get interrupted so much when we go out here that I thought it would be nice to have a quiet conversation while I cooked for you."

"You're cooking for me?" Lia's voice rose, and she tilted her head at me.

"Is that also a bad thing?" I asked, deflating. Here I'd thought I was being romantic, but maybe I had played my cards all wrong.

"No, Munroe, not at all." A smile bloomed on Lia's face, and I breathed a sigh of relief. "Nobody *ever* cooks for me. I think they're too scared to."

"Och, rightly so. I'm terrified. But I'm giving it laldie." I got out of the car and rounded the bonnet, opening her door and helping her from the car.

"What does that mean?" Lia asked.

"Just...give it my all. With great enthusiasm."

"That's one of the best ingredients, you know," Lia said as I unlocked the door to the cottage and held it open for her. "Enthusiasm. Next to love, of course."

"Love?" I asked, pausing as I shut the door behind me. My heart hammered in my chest at the word. I knew my feelings for Lia. But it was far too soon to share them. I'd barely managed to convince her to go on a date with me. It would be ages before she'd let me tell her what I felt about her. In the meantime, I could do my best to show her in every other way possible that I wanted to be the man who would stand for her.

"Yes, love." Lia smiled. "Everyone thinks that being a good chef is about following a recipe perfectly. But there's some things you just can't teach. It's instinct maybe, a gut feeling. But if you really love what you're creating, well, it shows. A good chef can make a perfectly presentable meal. A great chef adds their enthusiasm...gives it laldie...and you'll taste the difference."

"You really love what you do, don't you?" I asked. Picking up a lighter, I walked around the room and lit the candles I'd placed on the mantle over the fireplace, on the small dinner table, and along the breakfast bar. Lia automatically rounded the counter and bent to peel up a corner of the tin foil that covered the lasagna dish.

"Nope, sit," I ordered, pointing at a stool on the other side of the counter.

"Just being nosey." Lia laughed and did as she was

ordered. I poured her a glass of red from the bottle I'd had breathing on the counter, and she smiled her thanks at me. "And to answer your question, yes, I do love it. I've loved cooking ever since I was little. I learned it at my mother's knee, I suppose. She's Italian, and I think food is also her love language. She's convinced that everyone is always starving, and you never leave her house with an empty stomach. God, I don't know how she did it."

"Did what?" Crappity, crap. Lia's mother was Italian? Like proper Italian? And here I was trying to serve her lasagna? That's right. She'd *told* me that, and I had forgotten. Nerves had sweat springing to my palms, and I picked up a dish towel to wipe my hands before pouring myself a glass of wine as well. "Slàinte."

"Cheers," Lia said, tapping her glass to mine. We both drank, and I tried to tamp down on my nerves about cooking for this beautiful woman. "I don't know how she fed all of us. There were the five kids, my father, plus any of our friends we brought around. My mom fed them all. We barely had two pennies to scrape together, but she is a master at making a budget stretch. I think it's what made me so good in the kitchen as well. I learned to be creative if we ran out of ingredients or ended up having a busier night than usual. Instead of turning people away, I'd just figure it out. It's what you have to do when you're poor."

Lia said the last part almost absentmindedly, and I took that as an opportunity to learn more about her. Turning the oven on, I opened the fridge and brought out a small charcuterie board I'd prepared—just a few simple things like olives and a variety of cheeses—and placed it out before rounding the counter to sit on the stool next to hers. I liked sitting there like this, cozied up to the counter, the stools drawing us closer than if we'd sat at the dining table.

"Was it tough? Or was it something you didn't really know about until you were older?" I asked.

"What? Being poor?" Lia laughed and tucked a curl behind her ear, her eyes getting a faraway look as she thought back to her childhood. "For a long time, I don't think I knew any better. I mean, when you're a kid you just...exist. You don't think about money or how food shows up or where clothes come from. It just...arrives. But when my brothers entered the picture is when I really began to understand the depth of what being poor meant. I...well, I had to kind of raise my brothers because my parents were working so much to make ends meet. God, I don't know how they did it."

"Five kids and they both worked? Yeah, I can imagine that was tricky."

"To say the least. If there was no food at home, I'd walk down the street to the corner gas station with money from the emergency stash. It was there I really learned how to budget and stretch food between four growing boys. You'd be amazed how far you can stretch some instant ramen packets. Man, they could eat." Lia shook her head at the memory. "Then, of course, high school is when everyone really starts judging each other. I never had new clothes. Thrift store clothes only and, trust me, the other kids let you know it. Granted, I got pretty good at spotting quality pieces that would stand the test of time, but that didn't always mean I was in fashion with what was popular at the moment."

"Kids can be ruthless. I'm so glad we didn't have to deal

with picking out our clothes. It sounds like a lot of pressure," I said, shifting so I could see more of her lovely face.

"You didn't...oh, did you have uniforms?" Lia asked, and I nodded. "Private school boy."

"Aye, but it's the same with public schools here. Everyone wears a uniform," I explained.

"Really? I didn't know that. Only the fancy schools have uniforms back home," Lia said. "Huh, I wonder how that would have been. Are uniforms expensive? Or are they given to kids in the public schools?"

"I...I honestly don't know," I admitted. Clothing myself as a child had never been something I'd had to think about. Clothes just appeared in my closet, and anything with a hole or a stain disappeared and was replaced with something new by our housekeeper.

"You're a rich boy, aren't you?" Lia gave me a small smile, as though to say she'd forgive me this sin. "Like, aside from the business you own. You grew up with money?"

"Aye, my parents are well off." I stood, uncomfortable with talking about money, but I figured it was only fair. If Lia could talk freely about her lack of it, I had to share what it was like to have an abundance of it. Picking up the lasagna dish, I slid it in the oven, and then topped up our wine glasses before sitting back down. "Very well off, actually. We had a housekeeper, a nanny, a chef, and a gardener. I rarely saw my parents, except at dinnertime, where I was quizzed on my marks at school. We took several holidays a year, in which the nanny accompanied us and babysat me while my parents attended parties and excursions. I never had to think about what something cost until I started my own company. Trust me, it was a rude awakening. While it was a sharp learning curve, I'm happy to say that I didn't make a proper mess of it all, and Common Gin was born."

"Why Common Gin?" Lia turned fully to me, a considering look in her eyes. I couldn't help myself and reached out to twist a tendril of her hair around my finger. Soft. I tugged it lightly and the curl sprung back from my touch. Resilient. Like Lia.

"Why the gin or why the name?"

"Both, I suppose," Lia said.

"Gin because my family business is in whisky. Fancy whisky. For posh people with money. Or the kind of bottle you give on a very special occasion, and you drink from it once a year. It's pretentious and snooty. Granted, whisky is a much-loved part of Scotland's history, and I dearly enjoy a wee dram myself. But when I realized what I wanted to do, I wanted something that was more accessible. A drink that everyone could enjoy easily. No barrier to entry," I explained, my tone soft.

"Oh, Munroe," Lia said, understanding crossing her face. She pursed those kissable lips. "You wanted a friendly drink, didn't you?"

"Aye, I did. The name was just a play on that song...you know the one that sings about living like common people?"

"I do, actually." Lia laughed.

"My whole life I was tucked away like an afterthought. I guess I didn't want to live up in the tower anymore, so to speak."

"You wanted to come slum it with the rest of us," Lia said, tapping her elbow to mine. "Welcome to the gutter."

"Hardly the gutter." I laughed. "You're a celebrated

chef, and I just paid off the loan I took out to start my company. I think we're doing just fine."

"You didn't use your own money for your company?" Lia's eyebrows rose.

"My parents set up a trust for me, which I'll come into when I'm forty. They balked at my choice to go into gin, and tried, desperately, to woo me over to their company. Honestly, I couldn't understand why they were suddenly so interested in what I was doing after a lifetime of all but ignoring me. I suppose it didn't look good for their brand, to have their only son start a lowly gin company. So, instead of groveling, I applied for a business loan and I'm happy to say I finally paid it off."

"Hardly lowly." Lia shook her head. "And good for you. It's not easy to follow your heart. You lose a lot of people along the way."

"I'm not sure I ever really had them," I said before I could hold the thought back. Lia reached out and squeezed my arm, and my skin heated underneath her touch. Our eyes caught, and Lia leaned forward, pressing her lips to mine in the sweetest of kisses.

I wanted to drag her from the stool and carry her into the bedroom and sink into her softness. With Lia, I was home. I wanted, no needed that connection, and everything inside me calmed when her lips were on mine.

The timer dinged, and I pulled back. As much as I wanted to make a move on her, I was reminded that she hadn't eaten that day. I would first take care of her, and then, maybe...well, we'd see how the night went.

"Are you ready for the most enthusiastic Scottish lasagna you've ever had?" I asked, leaning back.

"I cannot tell you how ready I am." Lia laughed, and the sound danced through me.

"We can eat at the table or at the counter," I said, nodding to where I'd put flowers at the small dining table.

"Table it is. Can I help?" Lia asked.

"Absolutely not. Sit."

I managed to not poison her, which I took as a win, when she cleared her plate. We sat, nibbling at the lasagna and the crusty bread, talking about everything and nothing at all. Finally, Lia nudged her plate away and tapped her wine glass to mine.

"Compliments to the chef."

"Really?" I had impressed even myself. It was the first time I'd made a lasagna, so I was proud that it had turned out fairly well.

"Really. Great job, and it really is a treat to have someone else cook for me. I'm so used to doing it all myself."

"That seems to be a theme, doesn't it?" I stood and cleared the plates, glaring at her when she tried to help. "Sit. I still have dessert."

"Oh, you are a man after my own heart."

Pulling out the chocolate sauce from the fridge, I put it on the counter to bring to room temperature as I opened a bottle of champagne and poured us two flutes. I had kept it simple for dessert with strawberries dipped in chocolate. I mean, I had to play to my strengths, right? Handing Lia a glass, I returned to the sink to start the dishes.

"Back to what you were saying...yes, I'll admit, that's a flaw of mine. I find it almost impossible to ask anyone for help. And I can't believe how much of a problem it's becoming here."

"Why here? In what way?" I looked over my shoulder at Lia from where I stood at the sink. She'd stood, but only to lean against a cabinet to talk to me as I cleaned. I liked having her here, it felt cozy to me, and I wondered if normal families hung out like this...washing up after dinner and chatting about their days.

"I can barely get through the day without someone dropping in to offer help. It's...maddening, really." Lia shrugged, an apologetic look on her face. "It shouldn't be, and I know it's a me thing, but...why can't people just trust me to get it done myself?"

"I wouldn't say it's a trust thing more than a community thing," I began, but Lia barreled on.

"Some of it I get. Like, for example, Sophie wants me to buy local where I can. But I thought I would go to a supplier and order my stock. Instead, I've had a butcher stop by. A farmer who sells eggs only. An older woman who makes jams. A bee guy who sells honey. All of which is great. But how am I meant to supply a restaurant when I'm pulling from, like thirty different vendors? And then, it's just...everyone's all up in the restaurant. Offering to print menus. Offering to clean. Moving things around. I can barely turn around without tripping over someone behind me, offering to help. It's...like...why can't people see that I can handle it?" Lia's voice cracked, and I froze for a moment, realizing that we'd touched on a much deeper wound here. Quickly, I dried my hands on a towel and turned to Lia.

"That's not what's happening, Lia," I began, and she stopped me by lifting a trembling chin to me.

"I worked my ass off for Suzette's. It was a dream I hadn't dared to let myself really accept. And I took that restaurant to the top. Only to have it stolen out from under me by a douchebag son. Then I get this great opportunity here...and sure, there's like some really big problems with it. You know, the whole Kelpies and magick stuff. But I like it here. I want to create this restaurant. On my terms. And I'm scared if I let everyone help that it will all just get taken away from me again."

"You want to claim your ownership by doing it all yourself." Reaching out, I ran my hands up and down her arms, only to soothe.

"Exactly."

"Lia...I think you have to understand something about Loren Brae. Perhaps it is small towns in general, but I can only speak for the people here. Everyone is involved in everyone else's business. There will always be gossip. They'll see you at your worst. They'll see you at your best. But the one thing they won't do? Is let you fail. It's a community, don't you see? They're offering to help because they want you to succeed. They want you to win. Nobody here wants to take anything from you. It's family, you see? In fact, Loren Brae is the only real family I've ever had."

"Munroe." Lia's voice cracked, and she brought her hands to my chest. "I'm so sorry. I'm so sorry you didn't know what family is. You're right, I didn't see...not really, how that is what everyone is trying to do here. To be a family to me. I should be more accepting of it."

"It's a gift." My breath slowed, my eyes caught on hers.

Something inside me twisted and broke open. "Not everyone understands that."

"Munroe." Lia stroked my chest, her tone soft, her eyes full of understanding.

"I've a powerful need for you, Lia."

"Why...why don't you show me then?" Lia asked, licking her lips.

I didn't need to be asked twice. My desire for her broke forth, and I picked her up, placing her on the counter, and in one fluid movement pulled her shirt over her head.

"Oh my God, that was...fast." Lia laughed at me, but most importantly, she didn't tell me to stop.

"I don't want your nice top to get dirty. Did you wear that for me?" I asked, trailing a finger down the satin strap of her nude bra. There was nothing fancy about the bra, and yet it was incredibly sexy in its simplicity. Silky fabric covering lush breasts, and already her nipples peaked. Continuing down, I toyed with the button at her waistband.

"I might have," Lia admitted, her skin pinkening at my touch.

"Lift your hips," I ordered, undoing the button and the zip before sliding the jeans carefully down her legs. Crouching, I took my time pulling the fabric off each foot, noting how she squirmed at my touch. I'd been dreaming of this every night, and now I planned to take my time feasting on Lia's gorgeously soft and curvy body.

Graham may give me a hard time about being slow to bed a woman, but when I did, I made damn sure she'd never forget it. Lovemaking was one area where I'd taken my time to learn what women liked, almost as though I was studying for a test, because a woman's pleasure was of utmost importance to me.

Call me a nerd all you want, but the good thing about nerds? When something interested them, they dedicated themselves to studying it until they mastered it. Sure, being shy had held me back in some areas, but it had certainly been a benefit in others. And here? *Here* I could shine.

I took my time standing back up. Lia gasped as I pressed a kiss to her ankle, while lightly stroking the backs of her legs. Slowly, I teased her, trailing hot lips across soft skin, easing my way up to her thighs. Nudging her legs open wider, I lifted my eyes to where she stared down at me, transfixed.

"I like this underwear," I said, tracing a finger over her silk panties that matched her bra. Nude, like the shirt she'd worn. Slowly, I slid a finger across the silk, pleased to see her hips jerk at my touch. "Do you always wear matching sets?"

"I try to." Lia bit her bottom lip as I stroked her through the silk. "It might be a silly indulgence. But it makes me feel...oh..."

"You like when I touch you like this, don't you?" I asked, my eyes on Lia's face as I increased the pressure.

"I, yes...oh that's...nice..." Lia's head dropped back, and I stopped, reaching forward to tilt her chin back down.

"I want your eyes on me, Lia."

"Oh," Lia breathed, her cheeks pink with desire.

"See, the thing about making love...is it's more than just satisfying a need," I said, casually, as I reached for the jar of chocolate sauce. Lia watched me as I opened it and dipped a finger in the chocolate. Putting it aside, I stepped closer, so I pressed against her, hard meeting soft, and I brought my finger to her pretty pink mouth.

"It's kind of like cooking a meal," I whispered, leaning forward and slipping my finger into her mouth. Wet heat surrounded my finger, and I bucked forward, rubbing myself against her panties. "It's about taste. Texture. About feeling with all of your senses." I whispered this into her ear as she sucked my finger, and I bit the delicate lobe, before bringing my lips to her neck. Lia moaned, arching her back, and I chuckled at her neck.

"Do you like the chocolate sauce? I didn't make it myself, so I can't claim credit." She smelled sweet here, like citrus and vanilla, and I took my time inhaling her scent. Imprinting her on my mind. In my heart. Licking slowly down her neck, I blew a hot breath across her skin, and watched as she shivered in response.

"It's...really good. Delicious," Lia gasped after tearing her mouth away from my finger. Angling my head, I threaded one hand into her mass of curls, and pulled her mouth to mine, devouring her lips in a heated kiss. She tasted of chocolate, and my darkest fantasies, and my thoughts blanked for a moment as all I could do was revel in the heat of her mouth. She kissed like she cooked—with dedication, focus, and determination. I wasn't sure who was leading whom at this point, and I no longer cared.

Lia broke the kiss first, gasping for breath as she tugged at my shirt.

"I need this off. I need to touch," Lia ordered.

"Let's both, shall we?" With one hand, I reached around Lia's back and divested her so quickly from her bra that she pulled back and gave me a considering look.

"Do that often?"

"It's not a difficult trick to master." I dropped a light kiss on her lips, secretly pleased that the thought of me with another woman annoyed her, and I pulled my shirt over my head. Then, Lia's hands were on me, running across my chest, and I was distracted by the sheer glory of her luscious breasts. Lia was built like a windy mountain road, a compact short body, with enough dips and curves to make her genuinely a pleasure to touch. I wanted to sink into her softness, and I had to force myself to take a few breaths to pull me back from tipping over the ledge into release.

"I haven't tasted the chocolate sauce yet," I pointed out. "Maybe you'd like to feed it to me?"

"Maybe I would..." Lia grinned, a calculating look in her eyes. Dipping a finger in the sauce, she surprised me by tracing the chocolate across both of her perfect, pink nipples. I hadn't been wrong to think she enjoyed being touched, and this blatant invitation to feast on her glorious breasts made lust jackknife through me. I bent my head to her breasts and swept my tongue across a nipple, enjoying both Lia's gasp of pleasure, as well as the sweet taste of chocolate on her sensitive skin.

"Mmm, this is delicious. Sticky, though. It may take a while," I murmured, and Lia groaned as I took my time. I licked her nipple, making sure to follow the trail of sweet chocolate, refusing to leave any last bit untasted. She bucked against me when I bit lightly, and I grinned at her breast, holding her hips tightly with my hands before she rocked me into oblivion. "Steady there, Lia. We've got time enough, don't we?"

"Munroe. I need...I want..." Lia's breath came in tiny

pants as she writhed in my arms, and I continued my attention at her breasts. Only when her whimpering increased and her legs began to tremble, did I pull back.

"Do you know what pairs nicely with chocolate?" I asked, brushing my thumb across her swollen lip.

"Um...everything?" Lia's eyes were glazed with desire, and my grin widened.

"Off with these," I said, hooking my fingers at her underwear, and she readily obliged, lifting her hips so I could slide them down her legs. Then she sat, bared to me in all her beauty, and I had to count to one hundred in my head to keep focused.

"Champagne," I told Lia. Picking up her glass, I took a healthy sip, holding the champagne in my mouth. Lia's eyes widened as I bent, spreading her open, and put my mouth where I wanted it most.

"Oh. My. God," Lia shouted. She rocked against my mouth, where I let the bubbles of the champagne do their trick, increasing her sensitivity as I neatly pushed her over the edge into pleasure. "Munroe. Munroe. Munroe."

Over and over, she said my name as I continued to savor her, licking and tasting, until I committed every tremble, every sigh, every shout of pleasure to memory. Only when she threaded her hands through my hair, and begged, did I pull back.

"Please, Munroe. Please. I need you," Lia gasped, wild with need.

Without a second thought, I scooped her up and carried her through to my bedroom, kicking the door closed behind me. Easing her onto the bed, I found a condom and got rid of my pants, while Lia trembled on the bed. Gently,

I settled myself between her legs, nudging against her, needing to be inside her as much as I needed my next breath. But first...

"Lia," I said, brushing a soft kiss across her lips, before I met her eyes. Inside them, I saw the answers that I needed, even if I sensed she wasn't ready to admit the truth yet. "I meant it when I said I don't ever want to look at another woman again. You're everything for me." I stopped just short of professing my love for her, knowing I'd scare her away, but I couldn't *not* tell her what she already meant to me.

And when I drove inside her, filling her, it was my name at her lips, a promise to be kept.

And for now, that was more than enough for me.

CHAPTER FIFTEEN

Lia

"I don't know what's wrong with me."

I was on the phone with Savannah, staring out the window at the fading light that shimmered across the waters of Loch Mirren.

"I know what's wrong with you." A horn sounded in the background. "Yeah, screw you too!"

"Trust me, that's all I'm thinking about as well," I said, even though I knew she was screaming at the car. The city sounds were loud in the background, and a part of me missed the hustle and bustle of Boston.

"As you should. From the picture you sent, I'm ready to hop on a plane and fly over to claim my own slice of Scottish yumminess. He's seriously hot, Lia."

"I know he is."

In the week since I'd gone on my first date with

Munroe, any free time that I had outside of prepping the restaurant for the soft opening in a few days, I had spent between the sheets with Munroe. "I think I'm addicted to him."

"Or maybe you're just falling for him. He sounds like a great guy."

"What? *No,* I'm not...it's not like that. I don't have time for a relationship," I protested. "You know how restaurant hours are."

"Maybe in Boston, but you said most things close up early there. It sounds like you'll have a much more flexible schedule," Savannah said.

"Well, it's not that. We're just having fun."

"Uh-huh. Send me an invite to the wedding. Gotta run, walking into shift," Savannah all but sang in my ear before disconnecting the call.

"Whatever," I muttered, putting the phone down on my bed. My stomach growled and I realized that, once again, I'd forgotten to feed myself that day. Instinctively, I reached for my phone to text Munroe to see if he wanted to grab food, and then I stopped myself. It was perfectly fine for us to have time apart. We'd already spent almost every night with each other, and a few stolen moments during the day as well. Frankly, I was surprised I was getting any sleep at all. I couldn't seem to bring myself to stop touching that man.

He may be somewhat reserved in real life, but in private? Munroe hid some delightfully naughty secrets. I'd never been with a partner before that was so invested in my pleasure, and I had to say, it was pretty incredible.

Mind-blowing.

Distracting.

Leg-shaking.

Sighing, I shook my head and checked the time. If I walked fast enough, I'd just make it to the pub before they stopped serving food. There was no time to change, but I didn't really care. Jeans and a T-shirt were my daily uniform anyway, and since the entire village seemed to have taken to stopping by my restaurant to see the progress most days, everyone saw me exactly as I was, flour-covered and all.

A shiver of awareness prickled my skin as I crossed the path that ran along Loch Mirren. Pausing, I cast my eyes out to where a small island, supposedly containing the Stone of Truth, was perfectly situated in the middle of the water. While I'd taken the daily assistance from Brice in my stride, and I was positively best friends with Clyde by now, the Kelpies still worried me. I think, because I'd invested myself so fully in bringing this restaurant to life, I'd allowed the distraction of work to push the hovering threat aside. But their screams continued, in the early morning hours, and most days when I went to the window, I found Sophie and Lachlan pacing the battlement. One of these mornings, I think I needed to go join them. If I was part of the Order, wasn't I meant to protect the town as well?

That was the other thing that bothered me. Once I'd claimed my spot in the Order, I kept waiting for something to happen. I wasn't sure *what*, exactly, I was waiting for, but at the same time, it also felt like everyone was waiting on me. After the excitement of my first spell, one which was quite successful, much to a grateful Catriona's surprise, I hadn't really tried anything else.

Which, I suppose, was my own fault. I'd been so busy

designing the menu, sourcing suppliers, and hiring staff that I'd barely even thought about the spell book. At least I'd found a nice box to keep the book in, which I'd lined with cloth and made sure was tucked away safely. There was so much I still wanted to learn, but between my time with Munroe and the restaurant, by the time my head hit the pillow, I was almost asleep.

Munroe.

What was I going to do with him? This impossibly kind man was starting to consume my thoughts, and I found myself often staring off into space, mid-recipe, and daydreaming about his kiss. His touch. A funny thing he'd told me about aliens or one of his new board games.

And yet I felt helpless to stay away from him. It was balance I needed, and that would have to start with putting some distance between Munroe and me. I mean, the man was busy enough himself, wasn't he? He had an empire to run. I had no idea how he was carving out so much time to spend with me, and a trickle of guilt went through me at the thought of him neglecting work to be with me.

"Lia." I shook myself from my thoughts and turned with a smile on my face. And froze.

Munroe sat at a dinner table by the fireplace with an older couple who reeked of wealth. Based on the gentleman's strong jawline and the woman's disdainful air, these two could only be his parents. My stomach dropped, and I could have kicked myself for not taking more time with my appearance. Munroe's mother, in a Chanel suit jacket, trim slacks, and a double strand of pearls, eyed me like I was something the cat had thrown up. His father glanced at me and then away, quickly dismissing me as a nobody. I suppose I was, to them at least, with my faded work jeans and a T-shirt still dusted with food remnants from the day. All of my feelings of not being good enough from childhood flooded back, and in response, I did what I always did. I lifted my chin and summoned my attitude.

"Munroe," I said, walking stiffly to the table. We hadn't discussed what we would tell people about our...situation and based on the fact that Munroe hadn't told me his parents were coming, I was guessing he wanted to keep us quiet. Which was fine, really, but for some reason, being kept hidden from his life made me feel like I had an itch between my shoulder blades that I couldn't scratch. I stood by the table, frumpy and out of sorts, and pasted my customer service smile on my face.

"Is this a friend of yours?" Munroe's mother asked, her steely gaze sending chills over my skin as she scanned my clothes. An imperceptible sniff was all I needed to know about what she thought of me.

"I work at MacAlpine Castle. I'm the chef at the new restaurant opening up."

"Ah, a cook." Munroe's father nodded as if that made perfect sense. "Are you coming on shift here then?"

"No," I said. "And I said I'm a chef. Not a cook." I rarely called out the distinction, but if his parents wanted to get snooty with me, I'd push back. I refused to downplay my accomplishments for anyone.

"Right." Munroe's father made no apologies. "American then? And you're meant to be serving Scottish food? Interesting choice."

"Dad, knock it off." Munroe stood and pulled out the chair next to them. His mother and I gaped at him with equal amounts of shock. "Lia, please join us. My parents surprised me this evening with a visit. Lia, allow me to introduce my parents, Angus and Charlotte Curaigh. Mum, Dad, this is Lia Blackwood, an esteemed chef that MacAlpine Castle was lucky enough to lure away from Boston. We're also dating, so be nice." With that little bomb, Munroe dropped a kiss on my cheek and almost dragged me into the seat next to him.

A stunned silence fell as his parents regarded me with distaste and, to be honest, I'm sure my expression was about the same when I looked back at them. They reminded me of every rich person who had spoken down to my family at school functions or had been rude to me at the restaurant. Now, let me be clear, I did not equate being rich with being rude. I had some delightful regulars at Suzette's who could have probably bought the restaurant three times over and were about as charming and unassuming as could be. But there was another kind of rich, yes, *that* type of rich, that wanted you to know just how much you didn't live up to their expectations. It was the quintessential "you can't play with us" vibe, like kids kicking you off their team, and that condescending, elitist attitude never sat well with me. It didn't take any money to be kind. There was no way that his parents weren't aware that they were making me uncomfortable, so it was time for Boston Lia to come out.

"Dating?" Charlotte said in the same voice as if she'd said, "Meth?"

"Of course," I said, and winked at her, before throwing an arm casually around Munroe's shoulders. Mind you, it was quite a stretch for me to reach up there, so then I kind of hung awkwardly off him, but now I was committed to this. "Hard not to want a sexy man like this, amirite? I mean, wow." I fanned my face with my other hand. "They sure don't grow 'em like this in Boston. Wicked hot, he is."

Charlotte's lip curled with distaste, and she smoothed the napkin in front of her.

"Yes, well, I suppose you need a lot of money to start up a restaurant," Angus said, his eyes steely as he looked between me and Munroe. "I can imagine that's why you've chosen Munroe."

I've chosen him because he's one of the best men I know.

I opened my mouth to speak, but Munroe held up a hand.

"Whatever this is...stop it. Immediately. You've never had and never will have a say in who I date. Don't try to start now. And, Lia, you don't need to defend yourself to my parents. It's not worth your time. They only hear what they want to anyway," Munroe said, the ice in his gaze matching that of his parents. My resolve crumbled, and all I could do was feel awful for Munroe and what his life must have been like growing up with these two as parents. My family hadn't had money, but we sure had a hell of a lot of love. I never once questioned if my parents cared about me or my future. How Munroe had managed to turn out as warm and loving as he had was a mystery to me now that I'd met his parents.

"That's ridiculous," Charlotte scoffed. "We always listen to you, Munroe. I can't say we understand you all that much though."

"I mean, how could we? Common Gin? What kind of asinine choice is that for a name?" Angus rolled his eyes. "Hardly a proper name for a prestigious company."

This sounded like a fight that I didn't want to be involved in. My stomach growled, reminding me that I still hadn't eaten, and since I hadn't originally been invited to this dinner, I decided it was time for me to make my exit before I made things worse for Munroe and his parents.

"I love your gin," I said, beaming up at Munroe, before pressing a quick kiss to his cheek. I stood. "I see my friends over there, and I need to order my dinner before the chef goes home for the night. Lovely to meet you both. Please, won't you join us at the soft opening of the restaurant in a few days? Munroe can give you the details."

I didn't wait for a response before I made my exit, but if they did come to the opening, I'd show them just what I was made of.

"You survived the Ice Queen," Graham said, sliding a glass of red wine in front of me as I sat down next to where Agnes worked a crossword book.

"Oh, so it's not just me they hate then?" I asked, relief passing through me. "Real quick. Can I order whatever soup is left and a cheese toastie? I'm famished."

"No problem," Graham said, ducking into the back hallway.

"It's a miracle Munroe turned out decent," Agnes said, putting her pencil down and turning to me. "I credit his summers here for showing him what real people can be."

Loren Brae taught me what family is.

Munroe's words drifted back to me, and my heart twisted. He was just crying out for love, wasn't he? The problem was, I wasn't sure that I had enough to give him. I loved what I did for a living, and the restaurant, well, it was my baby. Would I even have enough left to give to someone else? That had always been my issue. I poured my everything into my passion and barely made time for anything else.

"His mother looked like she wanted to eat me alive," I said, giving a dramatic shiver with my shoulders before taking a sip of my wine.

"Doubtful. She only eats air and champagne."

Despite myself, I laughed. The knot in my stomach eased a bit, and I sighed.

"I invited them to the opening."

"Did you now? That's going to be a real treat, isn't it?" Agnes laughed, shaking her head at me. "What were you thinking?"

"I was thinking that I wanted to show them what I was made of. To prove to them that an American can cook Scottish food if she puts enough love into it."

"Och, lass, none of us are doubting you," Graham said, returning to catch the tail end of my conversation. "You've got nothing to prove to them that Munroe hasn't already tried to do himself. Spoiler alert. The both of them are crabbit beasties. Nothing will make them happy. Look at them. All the money in the world and they both look like they're sucking on a mouthful of nettles."

"I don't want Munroe to be embarrassed of me," I admitted.

"He's not. He never could be," Munroe said at my shoulder, and I closed my eyes, shame washing through me that he'd caught my words. "Lia."

"No, it's fine. It's not you, Munroe," I said, keeping my eyes on the wine glass I twirled in my hands. "I get that."

"Lia." Munroe said my name again, and finally, I turned

to meet his eyes. He cupped my chin in his hands. "You don't embarrass me. I'm proud of you. I'm proud of what you're building here. And I'd shout it from the rooftops that you're my woman if you'd let me. We just haven't had that talk yet."

"And why not?" Agnes put in when I was too stunned to speak.

"Surely you can both admit you have a liking for each other," Graham added. I tore my eyes away from Munroe's to see both Agnes and Graham leaning on the bar, as invested in the outcome of this conversation as I was. "This is what you get for moving too slow, Munroe."

"Lia needs time. I'm giving it to her," Munroe shot back.

I did?

"So you can sneak around with her at night, but you can't claim her in the open?" Agnes asked.

Wait, claim me? I didn't need claiming.

Did I? My cheeks heated as I thought about how Munroe had whispered to me, repeatedly, that I was his, while I'd broken to pieces under his touch.

"See? She's blushing," Graham pointed out, and my skin flamed brighter.

"It's not because...he's not...he doesn't have to..." I was flustered that they were discussing me as though I didn't have a say in this.

"I was planning to ask her properly when I took her to dinner tonight. I even ordered flowers from Shona."

"Och, she does good work, doesn't she?" Agnes patted Munroe's arm in approval. "I think she popped around to the castle to see if Lia needed her services for the table settings, didn't she, Lia?"

"She did," I said faintly, my mind whirling at Munroe's words. What had he meant to ask me?

"You can't go wrong there, Lia. Solid choice," Graham agreed. "She did the flowers for my cousin's wedding. Stunning, really."

"Och, I remember that. Didn't she add an artichoke in the bouquet? Since it was your cousin's favorite? They looked amazing."

"That's right. It was class, wasn't it? I never thought to use vegetables in a table display before," Graham agreed. He winked at me, and that's when I realized they were just winding me up. Just like my brothers back home would. Understanding, along with warmth, bloomed in me, pushing out the worst of my nerves. Munroe had been trying to tell me that the people of Loren Brae could be my family, my community, my friends...if I just accepted their weird way of inserting themselves into my life. Turning, I glanced up at Munroe who looked ready to flip a table in frustration.

"Ask me now," I demanded.

"What? But the flowers...and I had music," Munroe protested.

"Ask her now, mate. Go on then," Graham said, and I grinned, despite the nerves fluttering in my stomach.

"Away and shite, Graham," Munroe ordered, and Graham faded a few steps back. "Lia, we don't have to have this talk now."

"I think we do, Munroe," I said, refusing to look back at the table to see if his parents still sat there. "Because otherwise I'm going to make a million excuses to myself about why this, *we*, wouldn't work."

"Right, well, we can't be having that, can we?" Munroe stepped closer, so his broad shoulders overshadowed me, and he gently tilted my chin up with one hand. "Cecilia Blackwood, since the day you first walked into this pub, there's been no other. You've eradicated the memories of any other women from my mind and made it impossible for me to ever desire another. You are, quite literally, my living, walking, breathing, fantasy come to life. Watching you claim your power was one of the most beautiful things I've ever had the honor of experiencing. I would be honored if you'd allow me to accompany you on your journey here, and would love to claim, yes claim, you as my girlfriend."

Well, shit. How could any sensible woman say no to such a beautiful request? I was actually getting a little misty-eyed.

"What, no proposal mate?"

"Bloody hell, Graham," Agnes hissed behind me. "You're ruining the moment."

"Am I? It's not like he's asking the lass to marry him."

"Like I'd ask her to marry me with this clarty bastard around," Munroe said, not taking his eyes off me.

Laughter bubbled up, alongside a delicious sliver of happiness. I didn't need, or want marriage, at least not any time soon. Being with Munroe and exploring who we were together, here in this place, was more than enough for me.

"Aye," I said, trying out my Scots. "I'd be honored to be your girlfriend, Munroe."

Relief swept across Munroe's face, and I realized just how nervous he'd been for my response. I suppose I had been keeping my walls up with him. Leaning down, Munroe brushed the sweetest of kisses across my lips.

"Did ye hear that then, Graham? Keep your grubby mitts off my woman," Munroe growled. I should have protested, but something about his protective instincts really turned me on.

"You're choosing the wrong man," Graham sighed, dramatically, and he pulled my hand to his lips while Munroe snarled at him. "If you change your mind though..."

"Cheeky bastard." I laughed and pulled my hand back, making a big show of wiping it off with a napkin.

"I am at that," Graham grinned. "It's part of my charm."

"Charm? *You* call that charm. I'd call it annoying," Agnes argued.

I laughed and leaned into Munroe, wrapping my arms around his waist and resting my head against his chest. My man. My new life.

Things were going to be just fine.

I just needed to get through the soft opening of the restaurant, and everything would be smooth sailing.

CHAPTER SIXTEEN

Lia

"Do you think he'll talk to me?" Agnes asked a few days later as I unpacked the last of my deliveries for the soft opening later that night.

"I have no idea. I haven't actually seen him since the first night. But he's around. I think he's just shy," I said, my mind on other things. Nerves hummed through me, like a plucked guitar string, and anticipation fueled my focus. Tonight was the soft opening of the MacAlpine Castle Restaurant and, with the number of people attending, it might as well be opening night. I'd labored over the menu but was pleased with my final choices.

"Brice," Agnes called, wandering into the banquet hall, and I left her to it. Brice would show himself or he wouldn't, but thus far, he'd proved to be an invaluable helper, often anticipating my needs ahead of time, and was an absolute whiz at organization. He'd started leaving me certain ingredients, and I'd come to realize that the little man had a sweet tooth. Each night, before I left, I'd talk to him while I cleaned up, telling him about what I was planning to cook or how excited I was for the restaurant. He never answered, not really, but I knew he was there. In an odd way, it had become comforting instead of nerve-wracking to have him near, and aside from the batter-throwing incident, I hadn't seen any of this mischievous side that Agnes had warned me about. I dearly hoped it would stay that way. I'd explained, several times, how important tonight was and that there would be a lot of people coming into the restaurant, so Brice would have to get used to sharing his space. There wasn't much else to be done about that, as nothing in culinary school had trained me for appeasing a kitchen goblin.

"Knock, knock." Shona, who ran a local garden center and was a flower enthusiast, popped her head in the door. She was young, younger than me at least, with pink cheeks, wispy blond hair, and brilliant blue eyes. A nice woman, with a shy smile always hovering at her lips, I'd taken to her immediately. "I have your flowers."

"Ah, perfect. Agnes is here to help you set them out if you don't mind. I've got too much to prep at the moment. I want to make sure everything goes perfectly tonight. Oh, were you able to get the fresh herbs I had ordered? I wish we could get a garden going here. It would be nice to grow our own produce." Shona had told me that she didn't just grow flowers, in fact they were just a side hobby of hers, and she'd dreamt of one day opening her own farm-to-table market stall. For now, she delivered her produce each week to various vendors around the area, and I made a mental note to see about using her services for the restaurant here as we grew. Tourism, and the lack thereof, was something that Sophie was working hard on changing with her new marketing campaign, and I suspected that once the threat of the Kelpies was subdued, we'd be doing a bustling business. In the meantime, gardens took a while to plan and grow, so I'd bring the project to Shona at another time.

"Let me know. I definitely have some ideas of what you could do. Depending on your menu, of course." Shona leaned one hip on my prep table. "Mind if I take a look?"

"Of course, though the menus are already printed for tonight, so I can't change anything." Together, we bent over the list of dishes that I'd settled on. While it wouldn't be our full menu, because I was still in the process of hiring staff, I'd decided to showcase the idea of what I planned to do with the menu moving forward.

"Right, so you've nailed the traditional dishes," Shona murmured, and her face brightened. "Oh, cool! I see what you're doing. It's like if Scottish food had an identity crisis."

I laughed, amused at her take on it.

"Scottish fusion, essentially."

I'd taken four of the classics—haggis with neeps & tatties, Cullen Skink, Scotch pie, and venison, which I would prepare in the usual way, and added my own twist for the variations. For the haggis dish, I'd created haggis samosas, using the savory meat, along with peas and potatoes, as filling in crispy dough wrappers. I changed the flavor profile by adding coriander, garlic, chilies, and cumin. The dipping sauce was a teriyaki aioli, and I was particularly pleased with how the flavors played well together.

For the venison, I'd decided to go with a Mexican-inspired flair and pulled from my love of street tacos. There, I offered both vegetarian and venison versions of three flour tacos, with black beans or shredded meat, with chipotle, cinnamon, ancho chili powder, agave, and a squeeze of lime. I'd whipped up a refreshing pico de gallo as a topping and was delighted with the final results.

Cullen Skink is a type of chunky smoked fish soup, similar to what we in Boston would call a chowder. As an homage to my roots, I altered the dish slightly to make my famous New England Clam Chowder but replaced the clams with fish. The secret to my delicious chowder? I smoked the thick-cut bacon and used decadent heavy cream in the broth. Because I liked a kick, I always added a hint of red pepper flakes to the soup, and my diners had loved it. Luckily enough, the fish worked just the same as the clams, and I hadn't had to make any adjustments to my favorite recipe.

And finally—my personal piece de resistance—the Scotch pie. Honestly, there were so many variations that I could take with the pie, that I'd tried out several recipes before landing on the version I'd picked for this evening. Hilda and Archie had argued hotly over which dish should win, and eventually I'd deferred to Hilda's top choice.

A traditional Scotch pie is usually made with minced lamb, onion, mace, and a few other spices to add flavor. Often served with mashed potatoes or beans on top, it was an easy grab-and-go type meal for most people. A pie was a pie, as far as I was concerned, so it really came down to what type of filling I wanted to add. Since I'd touched on Asian,

American, and Mexican food—and based on cooking from the heart—I chose torta rustica, an Italian rustic pie.

This dish was entirely vegetarian, with a ricotta and spinach filling as the base. For additional flavor, I added sun-dried tomatoes, minced artichoke hearts, and roasted red peppers. Knowing Sophie's love for cheese, I'd sourced some delightful pecorino romano and mozzarella to add depth to the filling. For those who enjoyed an additional kick, I'd made an olio di peperoncino to dribble across the crust. For one of the monthly themed weekends, I planned to go full Italian, but for now, this was a way to incorporate my mother into my cooking.

All in all, I felt that I had a fresh, fun twist on traditional dishes that wouldn't take people too far outside their comfort zones. I also had a zesty side salad, an elegant leek soup, and two dessert offerings: cinnamon-flavored Scottish tablet, and Cranachan, a dessert featuring raspberry, whisky, and cream.

"This is so fun, and it all sounds delicious. It's nice to have something different here," Shona said, smiling up at me. "I honestly can't decide which dish I'll get."

"Well, if all goes well, you'll have plenty of time to try them all."

"Even better. Agnes, can I get your help with the flowers?" Shona looked up as Agnes returned.

"Of course." Agnes shot me a look and gave me a little shake of her head before shrugging her shoulders. I guess Brice had not made himself known.

"I can spare ten minutes to help too," I said, dusting my hands off on a towel and stepping outside to where Shona's van was parked. The women chattered around me as my mind was on thoughts of tonight.

Munroe was coming, and he was bringing investors with him. Apparently, when wind of his new distillery had gotten out, a few major players had asked about joining up with him and creating something much larger than just a distillery on the land he was close to signing on. We'd spoken about it, at great length the night before, and I had felt really honored when Munroe had taken the time to listen to my opinions. While maybe I didn't know the ins and outs of running a big business, I did know what common people liked. And some of what these investors were floating past him did not, to me, feel like what was on brand with Munroe's company. They were talking about a VIP gin experience, where people could travel over and stay at a five-star hotel and get certified in gin making. That kind of thing. It was a far cry from Munroe's home gin-flavoring kits, and I wondered what else the investors would try to entice him with. They'd been introduced to him by the real estate agent, and from my understanding, the property with the auld mill was the frontrunner for the location. Munroe hadn't made that part known yet, swearing me to secrecy, as he knew that such a choice in a small town would bring too many opinions for him to make a clear decision.

A part of me wished he wasn't bringing fancy people to dinner tonight, as I really wanted the soft opening to be just friends, but the entire event had grown past what I wanted the minute that Hilda and Archie had started inviting people. And they were all so helpful, it was hard for me to say no in the face of their enthusiasm.

"This...God, this feels magical, doesn't it?" I said,

holding a hand to my stomach as I stared at the newly decorated space. What had once been a dusty, cavernous hall had been transformed into an intimate and welcoming space.

Obviously, the guests wouldn't be entering through the kitchen, so Munroe's team of tradesmen had helped me create a beautiful reception lounge on the other side of the hall. Two large double doors—large as in at least fifteen feet tall–were propped open to encourage the light breeze. To buffer the space, and along with Shona's help, we'd created two walls of greenery on both ends of the hall. The first wall separated the lounge area from the restaurant, and the second wall hid the door to the kitchen and allowed a space for the servers to prep silverware, fold napkins, and take a moment to catch their breath but not be underfoot in the kitchen.

The day after the men had cleared out much of the miscellaneous furniture, I'd sat down on the bare floor in the middle of the hall and had really looked at the space. Although I'd already had the instinct to leave the room uncluttered and open to the natural beauty of the rough stone walls and thick wood beams, giving myself time to sit quietly in the space had solidified that decision. Now, the greenery added a lovely element to the stone and the wood, and we'd strung teeny-tiny, delicate fairy lights among the leaves, giving the room a soft glow. Each table had candles, and simple, yet elegant, vases holding thistles with a mixture of greens. The whole space was earthy, elemental, and not too fussy. It was a place where anyone would feel comfortable dining, and the backdrop would allow my food to shine.

Pleased, I checked the time. My staff would be arriving

shortly and once we started prep, I wouldn't likely look up from work again for hours. Anticipation shivered inside me, along with what I now realized was likely my power. I could do this. No, I *would* do this, and it would be magickal. In every manner possible.

"Ladies, thank you. This place looks incredible," I said, raising my hands in the air as Shona and Agnes finished prepping the tables. "I have to—"

"Take a moment to appreciate everything you've accomplished?" Munroe's words behind me caused a different, and very appreciative hum, to tremble through me. My ladyparts were very happy these days.

As was I.

Although we were still so new as a couple, I could genuinely say that Munroe was turning out to be a person that I hadn't known I'd needed in my life. Delightfully nerdy, innately shy, and decadently naughty in the bedroom, the contrast of who Munroe was as a person was keeping me intrigued, enlightened, and satiated. I was becoming more comfortable with him, and I thought we were starting to establish an easy rhythm between both of our hectic work schedules.

"Congratulations, Lia," Sophie said, and I turned to find her, with Lachlan, Munroe, Hilda, and Archie clustered around her. Lachlan held a large vase of flowers and Munroe had a small giftbox in his hand. "We're all so proud of you, and we can't wait to taste everything you've created tonight. I know we still have a ways to go on our journey together, but at the very least, this is one challenge you've well accomplished." I understood that Sophie was tempering her words because Shona was present. The challenges for the Stone of Truth still weighed on me. We'd determined that the gold band that had appeared in my knife after creating a spell for Catriona had been a challenge passed, but since then, no other gold bands had appeared. I had to pass three, and though I'd been consumed with getting the restaurant up and running, the challenges were never far from my mind. In fact, I'd even tried a few other quick spells from the book, for example a tea to ease a headache, but no gold band had appeared in my knife. I was guessing the Stone required more than me just dabbling in magick, but I couldn't just walk around Loren Brae asking if someone needed me to cook something to heal them, could I? While patience wasn't a strong suit of mine, Hilda had cautioned me to be prepared, but judicious in my use of magick.

Therefore, the challenges had fallen to the side while I'd readied the restaurant. Catriona wandered in from the kitchen and joined them.

"You guys didn't have to do this," I said, walking toward the group.

"Flowers are from your family," Archie said.

"They are?" I gasped, my heart twisting. It was hard for me to not have them here for this moment, to share in something so important to me. While I'd never had an opportunity of a soft opening at Suzette's, I had been able to cook for them there, free of charge, as a birthday gift from Suzette to me. It had been one of the best nights of my life, showcasing for my family what I could create, and I still remembered the awe on their faces as they'd looked around the fancy restaurant that I helmed. Reaching, I tapped the thistle locket my mother had given me. *They were with me*, and I made a mental note to call them after the night was done to tell them everything. "That's so sweet of them."

"Your mother is lovely," Hilda said, coming over to give me a quick hug. "We had a grand chat on the phone while I helped her pick out the flowers. I do hope we'll get them out here to visit at some point."

"I do as well," I said, though I knew it would be tricky for them financially. "Maybe one day they'll be able to swing it."

"There's time enough for that." Hilda patted my arm.

I caught Munroe pressing a kiss to Catriona's cheek and narrowed my eyes at the flirting granny. She grinned at me and gave me a wink.

"Catriona, we discussed this," I said, professing annoyance as I moved to stand in front of them.

"As I said, I can't help it if he flirts with me." Catriona shrugged and fluffed her short hair. "You'll have to have that talk with your young man."

"What's this about?" Munroe looked between the two of us.

"Catriona is a hussy, that's what," I said, raising an eyebrow at the woman. "She's trying to steal my man."

"And I will, at that, if you don't keep him happy." With that, Catriona blew me a kiss and walked back to the kitchen. "The dough's prepped and in the pantry. I'll get the ovens started in time for first service."

"Perfect, thanks." Hilda hadn't been wrong. Catriona's bread, and other baked goods, had turned out to be mouth-wateringly good. Once I'd been able to ease the pain with her arthritis, she'd been happily back to baking every day. She was a welcome addition to my kitchen.

So long as she didn't steal my man.

"Stop flirting with Catriona, or she's going to steal you out from under me," I ordered Munroe, a mock look of outrage on my face.

"Understood," Munroe said, schooling his face into a serious look. "I realize how poorly I've acted. Can you forgive me?"

"Maybe." I sniffed, tilting my head at the box in his hands. "If you show me what's in the box."

"It's a gift. For your first night," Munroe said. The box was small, wrapped in gold foil paper, and had a delicate gossamer ribbon tied around the edges.

"You don't have to get me gifts, Munroe," I said, admiring the pretty packaging. Tracing my finger along the paper, I looked up at him. "You know that, right?"

"Och, Lia. What kind of man would I be if I didn't buy a bonnie lass a trinket or two?" Munroe thickened his accent and winked at me. I didn't care that he was teasing a bit, as the brogue did delightful things for my baser self. I could feel my cheeks warming, so I bent my head to carefully unwrap the box while Lachlan found a space for my vase of flowers. I handed the paper to Munroe and carefully eased the top of the velvet jeweler's box open, my heart hammering in my chest. When I saw the contents, my mouth dropped open.

And then I threw my head back and laughed.

"Oh, I'm so nosey. What is it?" Sophie demanded.

"It's a grasshopper," I said, delight filling me, as I traced the emerald and diamond grasshopper pendant. Strung on a long sturdy gold link chain, the grasshopper was intricately detailed, covered in tiny emeralds, with two bright diamond eyes that glittered in the light. It was ridiculous.

And perfect.

Just like Munroe.

Throwing my arms around his neck, I pulled him in for a deep kiss, not caring that everyone was watching.

"Right, we need to stop, or I'll embarrass myself," Munroe said, pulling back to whisper at my lips.

"It's perfect, thank you." I stepped back, and Munroe helped me pull the chain over my head and the pendant nestled at my breasts. The necklace was the perfect length, because it didn't interfere with the thistle locket my mother had given me, and I could wear it under my shirt while cooking.

"I don't get it," Sophie said to Hilda, who just shrugged.

"Didn't I tell you the story of how I quit my job in Boston?" I turned to the group, and they shook their heads.

"Well, now, you'll love this. Walk with me. I'll tell you while I start prep."

CHAPTER SEVENTEEN

Munroe

Nothing pleased me more than seeing Lia in her element. Knowing she wore my necklace under her shirt was doing strange things to me, like she was happy to admit she was mine, and I wondered if this was how people felt when their person wore a wedding band.

I'd returned to the cottage after Lia had started her food prep, knowing she didn't need or want the distraction. After she'd assured me, for the tenth time, that there was nothing else I could do to help, I'd left to get some work done before the dinner. I still needed to look over the paperwork for the new distillery, and I had a mound of unanswered emails from Cassidy who was beginning to threaten to look for another job if I didn't attend to the more pressing issues.

This was a problem I'd created, I realized, as I worked

my way through my inbox. Because I'd dedicated my whole life to building Common Gin, at the expense of my social life, I'd trained my employees to expect me to be readily available. And now, for the first time, I wasn't. For once, I was using my free time to get to know Lia and invest in myself and my personal life. The problem when you changed the pattern though, is that other people needed to catch up. If I wanted to enforce more boundaries between my work and personal life, then I needed to create a better framework for me to do so.

Which meant I'd likely need to promote Cassidy and give her an opportunity to hire more help. It was an ideal solution, one which I'd flirted with before, but hadn't really needed to pull the trigger. I'd have to hammer out some details with her, and see if she was up for more responsibility, but I trusted Cassidy to rise to the occasion. Firing off a meeting request for next week, I grinned as I typed the subject line: *To discuss Cassidy's promotion.*

Two seconds later my email dinged in response.

This is how you tell me you want to promote me? Through a meeting request?

You've mentioned that you want me to be more efficient, I wrote back, a grin on my face.

My only response was a notification that the meeting was accepted, and I laughed. Cassidy hated unnecessary emails as much as I did. Pleased with the direction that was headed, I bent my head to the file of paperwork with the historical deeds to the auld mill land. The file held a mix of papers, maps, and printouts. Many with conflicting information, which wasn't highly unusual for plots of land that had been passed down for centuries. It was just following the thread, I told myself, and pinched my nose as I tried to make sense of it all.

My telephone pinged with a text message.

Investors need to reschedule. Can we meet in the afternoon?

That actually worked just fine for me. I'd been a bit annoyed that the real estate agent had pushed for the soft opening as a way to impress the investors, because I hadn't wanted to work on Lia's big night. They'd been insistent, so I had acquiesced, and now I was being let off the hook. I stood and stretched, needing to take a break from the paperwork, and walked out into the back garden. The cottage was set against a small burn, which made a lovely trickling sound as the water rushed by, and birds swooped to its bank to peck at the grass.

Did I really need or want investors? Common Gin had grown well on its own, without any outside investments, and I'd taken great pride in paying off my business loan. But this? This could be a leveling-up moment. When the opportunity had presented itself last week, I knew I had to at least entertain their offer. If I worked with investors, Common Gin might be able to go global in a way that I couldn't achieve on my own. What they were offering was more than just me opening another distillery in little Loren Brae, it was an opportunity to become a household name worldwide. This would be the penultimate step in my career and could potentially far exceed what my parents had achieved with their whisky. While their brand was one of prestige, you had to be educated in the history of whisky to truly appreciate it, which made their market narrower than mine. With this step, I could finally show them that I'd known what I was doing all along. That I was good enough. That I was *better* than them.

That was the crux of it all along, wasn't it? For some reason, I was beginning to understand that I no longer truly needed their approval. Somewhere along the way, that little boy's desire for their love had turned to anger, and that anger had fueled the need to show them up. At times, it had been the only thing keeping me going in getting Common Gin to the success it now had. The thing was, now that I had it all? I wasn't sure I wanted to be angry anymore. I didn't need it to fuel me. Maybe it was because I'd realized that I genuinely loved what I did for a living, and with that, I didn't need any other justification for me to work hard.

I rubbed at a spot at my chest, my thoughts tumbling around, as I thought about Loren Brae, about what Lia was building here, and what *I* wanted to build here. I thought about what my life would look like if I took Common Gin global. The demands on my time would triple. It was hard to say if it would be worth it or not. Not when I was also growing something here.

A grasshopper leapt from the ground and pinged off my shin before landing a few feet away from me on the patio. We regarded each other solemnly for a moment before it bounced wildly to the left and back into the grass.

Epiphany by way of a grasshopper.

That was certainly a new one.

My phone rang, drawing me back inside, and I steeled myself when I saw my mother's name on the screen.

"Mother."

"Munroe. You'll accompany us for dinner tonight at the castle."

There was no *hello* or asking how I was doing. It was always the same with them. They ordered, and I followed. However, in this case, it might cause more issues if I went to Lia's dinner and didn't sit with them. I didn't want to cause Lia any distress on her big night, and at the very least, if I was at their table, I could run interference if they were difficult with the waiter.

"Can't wait!" I said, infusing cheerfulness into my voice.

"We'll meet you there at six."

With that, she hung up, and I scrubbed my hands over my face. Glancing at the time, I reasoned I could get another solid hour's worth of work in before I had to get ready. Setting a timer, in case I lost track, I dug into the pile of paperwork in front of me so I could have a clear head for the evening. I couldn't wait to see Lia shine tonight.

Later, I pulled up to the castle, pleased to see cars already arriving. The soft opening had been the talk of Loren Brae and I hoped everything went perfectly and exactly as Lia wanted. Driving around the private side of the castle, I parked my car by Lachlan's and got out, a flurry of barking greeting me.

"Well, now, aren't you a fine gentleman then?" I asked, bending to reach a hand out to Sir Buster, done up in his kilt. "We're matching this evening, good sir."

I'd dressed up in my kilt, as Lachlan and Graham would be wearing theirs, and it appeared Sir Buster had been ordered to do so as well. Lady Lola followed, a tartan bow at her neck, which she immediately ruined by flopping over on her back when she saw me.

"Hilda's going to be mad at you for messing up your

bow," I lectured Lola as I scratched the happy puppy's stomach.

"She already is. Every time I turn around, she's trying to tear the bow off," Hilda said as she approached with a disapproving look on her face. She wore an elegant black dress, with a pretty thistle pin at her collar.

"Don't you look nice," I said, dropping a kiss to her cheek.

"You're looking quite smart yourself," Hilda said, holding me back and looking me up and down. "I like that tartan."

"Thanks, we lucked out with our colors." Not all clan tartans were a pleasing pattern, but the Curaigh tartan sported black, red, and gray. "I just wanted to pop my head in and wish Lia good luck. Or is it too busy?"

"No, I think that would be grand. Walk me around? Archie's already over there fussing with something or other."

"Happy to." I held out my arm, and we strolled along the path that wound around the side of the castle, the dogs following at our heels. "I'm meeting my parents here."

"Hmm." Hilda sniffed, and I grinned.

"Not a fan?"

"Well, now, I don't wish to speak ill of others, so I won't be saying anything about that." Hilda nodded across to where Loch Mirren reflected the early evening light on its still waters. "Kelpies have been acting up again. Maybe it's because your parents are here."

"Wouldn't that be something?" I pursed my lips. "Run them right out of town, that's for sure."

"We'd all be grateful for it. Miserable people." Hilda

clamped her lips together. "Right, enough about that. On you go. I'm going to wrangle these beasties into their best behavior to greet the guests. Don't hang your hat on your parents' opinions, Munroe. You're better than that."

I'd already come to that conclusion earlier that day, but it was nice to hear it, nonetheless. A clatter of dishes and hurried voices caught my attention, and I peeked my head into the open doorway of the kitchen. To the untrained eye, the kitchen might seem chaotic, but very quickly I picked up the rhythm. There were two other chefs prepping ingredients, Catriona was putting a tray of scones into a cooling rack, and servers were breezing through carrying trays of plates.

"Oh. My. God." At Lia's words, the whole kitchen stopped and turned to see what she was looking at.

It was me, apparently.

"I'm sorry," I said, my shyness kicking in. "I didn't mean to interrupt. I just wanted to wish you good luck."

"You're in a kilt." Lia said the words faintly as she drifted toward me like she was drugged, her eyes fixated on my waist. I'm not going to lie, I was grateful for my sporran because a dead man would respond to the way she was staring at me right now.

"Aye, lassie. That's the traditional dress of a Scotsman," I said, deepening my brogue, as I realized she hadn't seen me in my kilt before.

"I had no idea," Lia whispered, reaching out to press a hand against my chest. "I truly had no idea it would affect me like this."

"And I'm deeply interested in hearing more about what it does to you, darling," I said.

"Do we have time?" Lia whispered, glancing over her shoulder at the bustling kitchen, and I threw my head back and laughed.

"No, *no,* we do not. Save those dirty thoughts for later. I'll keep the kilt on."

"Oh, thank God," Lia breathed. I brushed a soft kiss over her lips, conscious of the other people in the room.

"Good luck tonight. Oh, I'm not bringing the investors. We're meeting tomorrow."

"Oh good, phew. Then you can just relax and have fun." A relieved look crossed Lia's face as she stepped back.

"Not quite. My parents are here."

"Right." Lia took a deep breath. She looked so pretty, a soft sheen on her face from the heat of the kitchen, her riotous hair braided neatly back. "That's good. I like having someone out there to prove myself to. I'll cook like a demon."

"No," I said, raising a hand to stop Lia before the demands of the kitchen drew her back in. "You don't have to prove yourself to them, Lia. They're not worth it."

"I know." Lia's grin was lightning fast and just a bit wicked. "But I like a challenge."

If anyone was up for tackling the Ice Queen, it was my beautiful Kitchen Witch. I wondered if Lia would use any spells tonight or if it would all be normal cooking. We'd spoken of it, just a bit, and she'd told me how she needed more time with her spells book to read about what her ancestors used to do. The book itself seemed an interesting mix between actual recipes, healing tonics, and spell work. She was lucky to have it, and my nerdy heart deeply wanted to spend a day devouring the pages and learning more about magick. But, this was for her, and I wanted to wait until she felt more comfortable with sharing before I asked if I could also read the book.

"Munroe."

Steeling myself, I pasted a smile on my face as I turned toward my parents. Resignation turned to delight. "Robyn?"

"It's good to see you," Robyn said, standing at my parents' side. A childhood friend, it had been ages since I'd last seen her. She'd grown into a slim woman, with a short cap of brown hair, deep-set brown eyes, and was dressed in fitted black pants and a tailored suitcoat. Slinky necklaces glimmered at her neck, and a sparkle of diamonds winked at her ears. She looked chic, effortlessly elegant, and worlds away from the girl I used to climb trees with. We hugged.

"What are you doing here?" I asked, surprised to see her so far from Edinburgh.

"Your parents invited me," Robyn said, an odd look darting through her eyes before she turned to my beaming mother.

"Yes, well, we felt it was time to introduce you to more suitable prospects," Mum said, sliding her arm through Robyn's and trailing her toward the entrance. Shock filled me, and I turned to my father.

"Surely you're having a laugh? I told you that I was dating Lia."

"Dating isn't marriage, is it? You're still free to look around." Dad shrugged and straightened the lapels of his coat. "Did you know that Tommaso Bianchi is here? Surprising, really. Given the nature of the restaurant and all."

Tommaso Bianchi was an Italian business magnate who spent part of his time in Scotland every year. He had interests in everything from whisky to wine, and loved taking on new projects as much as he did a new girlfriend.

"Given the nature of the..." I shook my head as I followed my father to the opened doors of the restaurant. "First of all, you haven't even eaten here yet. And, second, this is a restaurant in a *castle*. With a celebrated chef running it. Surely even you can't turn up your nose at this."

"You're always so fussy, Munroe. Honestly, I don't know what the big deal is. We came to the opening, didn't we? You should be happy we're even here." With that, my father crossed the front lounge to where my mother and Robyn stood by the bar.

Happy was the last thing I felt when I looked at my parents as they sized up the restaurant. All I knew is that I would do anything to protect Lia from them.

"Want me to show them the dungeons? I can lock them away for the night."

I turned to find Lachlan and Graham, both done up in their kilts, standing behind me.

"I might just take you up on that."

"Who is the woman?" Graham being Graham, asked.

"Robyn. I grew up with her. She's old money and, from what I remember, actually really nice. My parents have decided she's a better match for me than Lia."

"Dungeons it is." Lachlan started forward, and I grabbed his arm.

"No, don't make a scene. I can handle this."

"Careful, lad. You don't want Lia coming out and

thinking you're a part of this." Lachlan nodded to the group.

"How could she? I'm besotted with her."

"You're walking a fine line, is all."

"Aside from kicking them out, they've given me no choice, have they?" I sighed as they waved to me, the maître d standing expectantly by their sides.

"If you need me to take Robyn off your hands..." Graham suggested, and I grinned at him.

"I might actually take you up on that."

"Just say the word, lad."

I tried not to let my annoyance show as we were led to our seats, though Robyn did shoot me a few considering looks. What was I supposed to say to my old friend? Go home? No. I would make nice and then when I had a moment, I'd explain to her that the chef was my girlfriend.

"This place is really pretty," Robyn said as I held out a chair for her.

It was, and I couldn't be prouder of Lia, seeing the restaurant for the first time in all its glory. Chatter filled the hall, but the large greenery walls softened the sound, and the lighting danced through the leaves and against the wood beams that crossed the ceiling. Candles were scattered along the walls on various points where the stone walls created natural ledges, and the entire atmosphere was both rustic and elegant. Most of the patrons wore happy smiles, and I greeted more than one person that I knew. This was how it would be, I realized, if I stayed here. Greeting friends, gathering at Lia's wonderful restaurant, and creating places for the community to enjoy.

"It's not bad," Mum agreed, looking around the room

for anyone of importance. "Although the table settings could use an upgrade."

"I like the flowers," Robyn inserted before I could say anything. "The mixture of thistles with greenery is really pretty. Just the right touch for the space."

"I think so too," I said, with a glare for my mother. At that moment, a server arrived at our table with a basket of warm bread, a variety of dipping oils, and took our drinks orders. Once that had been sorted, my father leaned in to speak to my mother, and I took the opportunity to turn to Robyn.

"I apologize for whatever my parents have dragged you into. To be clear, this is my girlfriend's restaurant. She is the head chef."

"Oh, Munroe. You don't have to worry about that..." Robyn reached out and squeezed my hand. At that moment, Lia came out of the kitchen, her eyes immediately zeroing in on where I leaned into Robyn with her holding my hand. I froze, unsure if I would look more guilty pulling my hand away or acting like this was nothing, and by the time I came to a decision, Lia's gaze was already dancing past us to the crowded room.

"Thank you all for coming tonight," Lia said when the restaurant quieted down after someone had dinged a glass. "I'm honored to cook my food for you this evening. We're creating something very special here, and I'm delighted you could be the first to join us. As you'll see from the menu, not only are we offering some traditional favorites, but I've also had fun with creating a twist on those same favorites. Feel free to choose as many as you like, as for tonight, we'll serve the dishes tapas style so you can have a taste of everything. Enjoy!"

Applause broke out, and when Lia looked back at me once more, I blew her a kiss and then held my hands to my heart. A smile broke out on her face, and I hope I had assuaged any worry she may have over Robyn before she ducked behind the greenery wall and went back to her kitchen. There was nothing else I could do at this moment, as I knew I'd only be a distraction if I tried to talk to her now.

Soon, dishes were whisked out by the servers, and I couldn't help but eavesdrop on other tables and what they were saying about the food. As this was the first time that Lia had cooked for me, joy flooded me when I finally tasted her food.

It wasn't *just* good.

These dishes were *excellent*.

There was no way even my parents could find fault with it. Instead of going exceedingly fancy with the food, something I was certain Lia would be capable of if she so chose, she'd taken simple food and elevated it with an elegant and artful twist. My heart was almost bursting out of my chest with pride for her.

"I could eat the entire bread basket myself," Robyn observed. "Let alone all of these dishes. I mean...tacos? A woman after my own heart."

"Robyn, how is work these days? You're with the National Museum of Scotland, correct?"

"Actually, I've moved to an art gallery on Princes Street. More modern than antiquities, but I'm finding the twist to be quite engaging. In fact, I sold my first two paintings just this week."

"Congratulations," I said, tapping my glass to hers just as someone appeared at my side.

"Tommaso, it's grand to see you outside of the club." My father stood and shook the Italian investor's hand. I stood as well. Tommaso Bianchi was short, with perpetually tanned skin, a well-fitted Italian suit, and a silk pocket square. A hefty gold watch glinted at his wrist, and two thick gold rings were on each hand.

"Good to see you again," Tommaso said, smiling a greeting at Robyn and my mother.

"We're surprised to see you out this way," Mum said, dimpling up at him.

"I've some interests in the area. And I'm never one to pass up the opening of a new restaurant." Tommaso patted his belly and laughed.

"Yes, the food is serviceable, I suppose." Coming from my mother, that was a high compliment.

At that moment, Lia appeared, and I was certain she'd caught the tail end of my mother's comment.

"Ah, the chef!" Tommaso rounded the table and clasped Lia's hands in his own, before kissing each of her cheeks. "Belissima! Perfecta!"

"Grazie. Ti è piaciuto il cibo?" Lia spoke in Italian to Tommaso, much to his delight, and my mother's deep annoyance. My grin widened as I watched Lia woo the richest man in the room.

"Sei Italiano? Devi sposarmi." Tommaso brought her hands to his chest, and I narrowed my eyes. I wasn't entirely sure what he was saying, but I knew when a man was hitting on my woman.

"She's spoken for," I said, and Tommaso turned to me with a knowing look in his eyes.

"Ah, so it's like that? Smart man," Tommaso said.

"Sono Italiano e scozzese. E sì, è il mio ragazzo." Lia smiled.

"Se mai vorrai lasciarlo..." Tommaso sighed when Lia shook her head. Turning, he addressed the table.

"It appears that your beautiful chef is refusing to run away with me. Unfortunately. One of the best torta rusticas I've ever had." Tommaso brought his fingers to his lips and made a kissing noise. Someone called his name and he turned, waving a goodbye to us, as he made his rounds.

"Well, you certainly charmed him. I didn't know you spoke Italian," Mum said to Lia, and she just looked at me, half torn between confusion and laughter.

"How would you, Mum? You've barely met her," I pointed out. Lia cleared her throat.

"I hope you all enjoyed your meal tonight and saved room for a light dessert."

"It was exquisite, Lia." I was still standing from when Tommaso had shaken our hands, and I rounded the table to brush a soft kiss on her lips. It was all I was comfortable doing with the entire restaurant full of people watching me, but I wanted her to know that I was showing the world that she was mine and that Robyn was nothing to me no matter what my mother was trying to pull.

"You like?" Lia asked, smiling shyly up at me.

"Incredible. I'm embarrassed I even attempted to cook for you after tasting what you can create."

"Don't be. Your lasagna was perfect." Lia laughed and squeezed my hand. "I have to make my rounds, but I'll see you later?"

"You couldn't tear me away."

"I hope you enjoyed your dinner," Lia said to the table, and my parents being who they were, just nodded stiffly. Would it kill them to show approval once in a while? It was like they made a game of who could find more things to critique. *What a horrible way to move through life.*

"It was fantastic," Robyn spoke up when my parents didn't. "And the bread..."

"That's Catriona. She's incredible. I'll pass on your compliments." With that, Lia moved to the next table, and I glared at my parents as I sat back down.

"Would it have been so hard to be nice?" I demanded as the desserts were served.

"Our behavior was perfectly acceptable. Unlike yours at the moment. Particularly in front of our charming guest. Now, Robyn...are you seeing anyone? Your parents mentioned you were still single. As you know, Munroe is a successful businessman, and you two used to be such dear friends."

I was saved from throttling my mother when all hell broke loose.

One moment, the cranachan was plated neatly in front of my mother, and the next, it was as though it had exploded. Whipped cream dripped from her shocked face, raspberries matted her hair, and her hands were frozen in mid-air as though she had no idea what to do. I certainly didn't, as I was torn between laughter and confusion, when the same fate landed on me.

Gasping, I wiped whipped cream from my eyes to see everyone at our table, and *just* our table, covered in dessert while the rest of the restaurant looked on in shock.

My stomach twisted.

Brice.

"What the hell?" my dad thundered and started to rise. I knew he was going to make a scene, and the last thing Lia needed was for everyone to think this restaurant was haunted. Even though it was.

"And that's for being rude to my girlfriend." I stood as well and tossed the rest of my dessert in my father's face, to make it look like I'd been the one to start the fight. Admittedly, I did take some joy from throwing food at him, but this was not the time to examine that feeling.

"Munroe," my father seethed, coming nose to nose with me. "Have you lost your goddamned mind?"

"Was it really..." Robyn asked, looking with confusion between me and the table, whipped cream dripping down her hair.

"Go on then," I whispered to my father, meeting his steely gaze. "Show the world who you are." I waited, my adrenaline kicking in, and wondered if he would throw the first punch.

"You're not worth it," Dad said, instead, and turning he collected his coat and my mother before dragging her across the silent room.

Clapping started from across the restaurant.

"Brava!" Tommaso called. "I do love dinner entertainment, no?"

The restaurant exploded in applause, and I took a mock bow, thankful for the Italian's quick thinking. I was too embarrassed to have come up with that response, and he very likely saved Lia's restaurant opening.

"Why don't you two come with me and get cleaned up?" Hilda had appeared at the side of our table.

"Shall we?" I asked Robyn who looked more than a little stunned by the debacle.

"Oh, we shall. I have questions," Robyn began, and I hooked her arm before pulling her up and through the restaurant.

"I'm sure you do. One thing at a time, lass. Let's get you sorted, and we can have a whisky and a nice long chat."

The cheerful din of the restaurant followed me as I walked into the cool night air and steadied my breathing. Fingers crossed that the rest of the night would go smoothly, and hopefully Brice wouldn't cause any more drama. It was clearly a targeted attack, and I realized now just how protective the broonie must be of Lia.

I couldn't blame him either. He'd basically acted upon every emotion I'd ever had regarding my parents.

I wasn't sure what the fallout would be with them, and frankly, I couldn't say that I cared all that much. Perhaps this was just how it needed to be.

"At least it tastes good," Robyn mused as we wandered to a private side of the castle, and I threw my head back and laughed.

"Aye, a silver lining, I suppose."

CHAPTER EIGHTEEN

Lia

I didn't hear about the incident until we were closing up and I was shooing out the servers to go home and relax. I needed a moment alone, in my kitchen, to settle my nerves.

And to have a talk with Brice, it seemed.

My phone pinged and I pulled it from my pocket to see a text message from my dad. Opening it up, I smiled as a photo came through of my entire family smiling around a sign that read: *Congratulations, Lia!* Laughter quickly turned to tears, and I walked out into the empty restaurant and dropped into a chair.

I'd *so* wanted for tonight to be perfect.

Instead, my boyfriend's parents had brought a woman they found to be more suitable than I was, and then my kitchen elf had thrown food in their faces. It was an all-around mess, and knowing the type of people that Munroe's parents were, it wasn't something I'd live down. In fact, I was certain they'd be badmouthing my restaurant to all of their rich friends. Worry filled me for the future of what I was trying to create here.

A soft chattering caught my attention, and I wiped my tears to look up and see mournful eyes peering at me from under a table. Brice never showed himself, so I had to assume he was feeling bad.

"I'm not sure what your motive was, buddy, but what happened tonight wasn't great."

His eyes filled.

"I'm not mad, I promise." I held up my hands. "I suspect you were trying to protect me. I agree, Munroe's parents are jerks. But Munroe isn't. You know that. He's one of the good ones. Remember how he always asks if you've been fed or how you are doing?"

The eyes nodded from the darkness beneath the table.

"Well, just remember that for the future, okay? We *like* Munroe. And I really need this restaurant to be a success. Or we...*I* won't be here anymore."

Brice's eyes widened.

"Exactly. I really appreciate all your help around here, but you have to trust me to handle certain situations, okay?"

"Aye."

It was the first time the little guy had really spoken to me, at least clearly, and I took that as a good sign. Sighing, I stood and stretched.

"Let's put this behind us. I left you a full meal in the

pantry, okay? I'm heading out to get some rest, but I'll see you tomorrow."

There wasn't much else to be said. I had a magickal kitchen goblin that could prove to be a liability if I couldn't figure out how to rein him in. Picking up my spells book, I put it in my purse and closed the kitchen behind me, the adrenaline from the day long worn off. I wanted a hot shower and not to speak to anyone for a few hours.

Instead, I was immediately confronted with Munroe cuddling his perfect dinner companion in the parking lot in front of me. Would the hits keep coming? Rage flashed through me, and I veered from the direction of the castle and stomped out to the parking lot. It looked like we were going to do this now then. I hadn't really thought that Munroe would succumb to something like this, but maybe the broonie had pushed him over the edge. Maybe the elegant woman his parents had chosen for him was a far better fit than I was. Who was I to say? I hadn't known him all that long, and maybe I was just a fool. I skidded to a stop, ready to let them both have it, when the woman lifted her head from Munroe's chest, and I saw tears dripping down her face.

Instantly contrite, I stepped forward.

"What's wrong?" I asked, softly, and Munroe turned, a worried expression on his face.

"It's not what it looks like..." Munroe began, but the woman stopped him, stepping back and wiping her cheeks with her palms. She wore a baggy sweatshirt, which meant her nice jacket had probably been soiled by Brice, and she gave me a tremulous smile.

"It's not, I promise you. In fact, that's what I'm crying about."

"Robyn has some personal issues going on," Munroe said, coming to stand next to me and put his hand on my arm. "I've known her since I was a wee lad. I promise you, it's not—"

"I get it," I said, raising a hand to stop him. The rage that had flitted through me ever so briefly left as quickly as it had come. I'd been correct about Munroe. He was far too nice to pull something like that on me. It wasn't in his nature to deliberately hurt others. After meeting his parents, I realized that trait likely came from a lifetime of getting hurt himself.

"Munroe's protecting me, but I'll second what he said. It's really not what it looks like. In fact, it's *so* far from what it looks like." Robyn huffed out a small laugh. "I'm gay. And my parents are best friends with his and, well, I'm their only child, and so I think they were hoping there would be a love match between the families."

"And your parents don't know?" I guessed, sadness filling me.

"I haven't worked up the courage to tell them." Robyn shook her head and rolled her eyes. "God, you'd think after all these years, I could just stand up to them and show them who I was. No matter the outcome, it has to be better than hiding."

"I'm sorry," I said. I couldn't imagine how difficult it had to be to live under the weight of potential consequences from a family that wouldn't accept you.

"Normally, it's fine. But they've been making more noises about grandkids. And the family bloodline. And well, this just kind of brought it all to a head. I'm going to have to say something, or they'll keep pushing this, won't they?" Robyn looked up at Munroe.

"I can go with you when you tell them. If that will help?" Munroe, ever the gentleman, asked.

"No, God no. Could you imagine my father trying to hide his embarrassment in front of an outsider?"

"What if he accepts you? Are they...as difficult as Munroe's parents?" I'd wanted to say awful, but I caught myself in time.

"Well, they're best friends. So, definitely a lot of similarities. I'm sorry. This is your big night, and here I am crying on your boyfriend." Robyn gave me a watery smile, and a thought occurred to me.

"You know, you never did get dessert. And we're certainly not going to let you drive home in this condition. Come to the kitchen with me. Nothing makes things better like a cup of tea and some sweets." I all but dragged Robyn back to my kitchen, flipping the lights on and pushing her onto a stool at the prep table as I did. Munroe followed, a curious look in his eyes, as I pulled out my book of spells and began to page through it.

"Robyn, what did Munroe tell you about what happened tonight?"

"He said the castle was haunted."

"Not entirely wrong, but in this case, that isn't what happened." I leveled a look at the woman while Munroe rounded the table to my side.

"Lia...you don't have to explain anything. Robyn's cool. She's one of the good ones."

"I get that, but I'm also not afraid to tell my own truth

either." I met Robyn's eyes and saw the spark of approval there. "So, in speaking about sharing our truths. I'm a Kitchen Witch, and the antics you saw tonight were due to a broonie who lives here."

Robyn's mouth dropped open, and she glanced between the two of us. Likely to see if we were having a joke at her expense.

"And, with that being said, I'd like to do a spell for you. I'm torn though. Is it courage you need or protection?" I tapped a finger at my lips, and Robyn's face bloomed in a smile.

"If I get a say? I'd pick courage. I don't need protection from my parents. I'm strong enough to come out standing on my own two feet whatever may happen."

"If you really feel that way, what's stopping you from saying anything?" I asked, likely more bluntly than needed, but I'd had a long day, okay?

"Courage." Robyn laughed. "And I don't know...I'm just not ready to break their hearts, I suppose."

"But you're breaking your own in the meantime," Munroe said softly, and my heart trembled at his words. *This man*. This impossibly lovely and decent man. How did I luck out to have him be interested in me?

"I am." Robyn's face fell. "I've met someone. I think...I think she's the one. And she's being patient with me, but I hate having to hide her like she's a dirty little secret. She's not. She's wonderful. She's everything."

"A tea, a tincture, or a soup?" I asked, studying the recipe for courage.

"Tea, I think. Since we were going to have a cup anyway. Oh, wow. Is this...like am I going to have magick now?"

Robyn patted her hands on her cheeks, an excited flush crossing her face.

"No, at least I don't believe that's how it works. I'm the one who carries the magick, and you'll be the beneficiary. Right, let's have a look." Pursing my lips, I studied the ingredients list before walking over to the spice cabinet. Mustard seed, black tea leaves, and thyme. It didn't call for much, and to me, that made sense. When courage was needed, who had time to build a massive spell? It made me think of the history of this book, and other times through the years when courage might have been called for. Had Kitchen Witches of yore brewed this same tea for their men going into battle? Simplicity certainly made sense on such an occasion. I imagined a woman, bent over a boiling pot of water in a small cottage, rain raging outside while she worked, knowing she'd have to say goodbye to her love. It was enough to make me weepy all over again, and I forced myself to bring my thoughts back to the present. It had been a long day, and clearly exhaustion was making me a touch maudlin.

Following the instructions, I ground the spices together in a clockwise motion while they watched me, solemn looks on their faces. I hadn't yet tried my magick in front of anyone, so I sincerely hoped this wouldn't backfire. However, I was too tired after my day to care all that deeply. Either this would work, or it wouldn't, but at the very least —I was trying to help. My tea kettle whistled, and I turned to pick it up from the stove.

"Munroe, can you get a candle and lighter from the service prep area?"

"Nae bother, hen," Munroe said with a wink and disappeared while I poured hot water into a mug and added the tea in a little mesh bag. When Munroe returned, with a chunky white candle in hand, I pointed to the drawing in the book.

"I need you to carve these into the candle," I instructed Robyn, handing her a knife.

"Me? But...what if I do it wrong?"

"You can't go wrong if your intention is pure."

Robyn studied the drawing of a diamond shape with three straight lines coming from the bottom and dutifully inscribed it on the side of the candle.

"Now..." I pushed the mug in front of her and handed her the lighter. "Light the flame while I recite the spell and then you'll drink the tea."

"Do I have to chug it? It's still quite hot," Robyn pointed out, and my lips quirked.

"I think you'll be fine to finish it with dessert."

"That's grand. Right, let's get on with it, shall we?" Robyn clasped her hands in front of her and stared at me, as though she was waiting for a punishment.

"Relax," I advised her, nudging the tea in front of her. "This is good magick. Light to light." With that, Robyn lit the flame and I reached for that space inside me where my magick danced and flowed. Grabbing a tendril of it, I pulled it through my body and placed a finger on the handle of the mug, and another finger on the side of the candle.

"Fire, we ask of you to burn fear away,
A tea to give strength to a nervous heart,
And grant bravery in her life each day,
Along with the courage to tear doubt apart.
Follow your path to have your say."

A soft wash of light, like the smallest of sparklers being lit and immediately extinguished, glowed in the cup of tea before disappearing. Robyn's eyes widened, and she looked from the cup of tea up to me.

"Go on," I said, a small smile on my face.

Robyn took a sip of the tea, cautious at first, and then a long gulp of it. I waited, until she gave me a small nod of approval.

"I can't quite say how I feel yet, but the tea is actually delicious."

"Is it? I wasn't sure on that flavor profile. Well, shall we get the dessert?" I turned and pulled up short when I saw three dishes of cranachan had been placed behind us. Brice must be feeling bad if he was willing to do that when we were in the room. I'd been too focused on my spell to hear anything.

"Oh my...was that the broonie who did that?" Robyn's voice was hushed, and she looked between the food and me. "Or was that your spell?"

"The spell was for courage," I said, my smile widening as I picked up the bowls and placed them in front of Munroe and Robyn. "Not for dessert. Although I'm glad to have it, I'll tell you that. I didn't get a taste of this tonight."

We lingered at the prep table, talking about the highs and lows of the night, spooning delicious cream and berries into our mouths while Robyn finished her tea. Once done, she shook herself, like a dog shaking off the rain, and stood.

"I feel...I feel good, Lia. Like, really good. Maybe it was being able to talk to friends about this or maybe it was your magick tea, but either way, I think...I think I do feel confident enough to have this conversation with my parents. It might just be time to start living an authentic life."

"It's the only life you have," I agreed. "Go forth and be strong and all that."

"And all that?" Munroe laughed and walking forward, he gave Robyn a tight hug. It didn't bother me now, knowing what I did about their friendship, and I accepted a grateful hug from her as well. Once she left, I sighed and slumped against the table.

"I'm dead on my feet."

"You did good tonight, Lia. In so many ways." Munroe rounded the table and to my surprise, he lifted me up like he was carrying a bride over the threshold.

"Munroe! You don't have to carry me. I'm used to long days on my feet. I'll be fine."

"I am nothing if not your humble chariot," Munroe said, stopping at the doors to pull them shut behind us.

"But the dessert dishes..."

"Wheesht, lass. The broonie will take care of it. Brice knows he has some apologizing to do to you, I'm sure."

I snuggled into Munroe, leaning my head against his chest so that his voice rumbled against my ear. He was like a big, warm teddy bear.

And when the Kelpies shrieked in the night, startling me from the edge of sleep, his grip only tightened around me.

"I've got you, Lia. Go on and rest."

I didn't know if I could fall asleep again after the otherworldly screams that ripped through the cool night air. I searched the loch, but no water horses appeared, at least from what I could see in the murky light. But they'd made themselves well known. It seemed like they were screaming earlier and earlier each night, and I wondered if I wasn't living up to my end of the bargain. What would happen if I didn't complete my challenges? Would someone else get hurt like Lachlan's mum had?

To my surprise, Munroe carried me all the way upstairs to my apartment, navigating the winding halls easily, and Clyde must have sensed my exhaustion because he didn't even try and prank us. Once inside, Munroe looked at the doors leading off the main room.

"Which way?"

"I need to shower." I hated to. I was dead on my feet, but it was important to rinse off the kitchen grime at the end of a long day.

"Funnily enough, so do I," Munroe said, reminding me that he, too, had been caught up in Brice's path of destruction.

"I doubt we'll fit," I said, stifling a yawn, as I kicked my jeans off and pulled my shirt over my head. I was too tired to care about what I looked like, but judging from where Munroe's kilt tented, I could see he didn't care. "Munroe, can you promise me something?"

Munroe stopped where he was unbuckling his kilt.

"Of course, Lia. Anything."

"Maybe not tonight, but sometime soon, can you put that exact outfit back on so I can live out all of my fantasies of being ravished by a hot highlander?"

"Aye, lassie," Munroe said, slipping the kilt off and hanging it over a towel rail. My mouth fell open.

"Wait, were you really naked under there all night?"

"Aye, lassie," Munroe said again, coming to cage me

with his arms and walking me back to the shower, his voice a warm timbre at my neck.

"Oh my God. I think I'm glad that I didn't know that. Or did I know that? At the very least I'm glad I didn't think about it. I wouldn't have been able to get anything done." I shivered at Munroe's mouth at my neck. Reaching over me, he slid the shower door open and flipped the handle to turn the water on. Turning me in his arms, he pushed me lightly forward until the warm water hit my breasts, and then joined me. It felt like being cocooned by a large bear. I shuddered as he pulled my back to his front, his hard length nudging me from the back, and reached up to angle the spray so it could soak us both.

"Do you want to wash your hair tonight?" Munroe asked, absentmindedly nibbling at my ear.

"No, I don't feel like going to bed with wet hair, and I'm too tired to dry it."

"Noted," Munroe said. Without another word, he reached around me and picked up the bar of lavender-scented soap and trailed it lightly across my breasts. I arched back into him, moaning as he circled my nipples lightly with the bar, his other hand coming around to stroke me gently at the front. My hips bucked at his touch, and he slipped a hand between my folds to find me already ready for him.

"Munroe," I gasped, reaching backward to hook an arm around the back of his neck. "That feels so good. *You* feel so good."

"Open for me, Lia," Munroe instructed, and I did so, gasping when his fingers found me. Gently, he circled me, his large palm bringing me to the brink of pleasure. "Go on, darling. Let go for me."

His words undid me, and I let myself fall over the edge as desire rocketed through my body. Turning in his arms, I stood on my tiptoes and licked into his mouth. He tasted of whisky and raspberries, and I wanted to stay here, locked in this moment forever. Grabbing my waist, Munroe hitched me up until my legs wound around him and he entered me in one smooth thrust, my back to the shower wall, claiming me as his own. I collapsed, clinging to him as he rode me to another sharp crescendo of pleasure, his lips fevered on mine.

"I'm so proud of you, Lia. My woman. My beautiful magickal woman. You're mine."

Over and over, he repeated the words, like a mantra, until I could almost believe that I had a future with this man.

And maybe, just maybe, I did.

CHAPTER NINETEEN

Lia

"I've got to crack on," Munroe said, after we'd enjoyed a cup of coffee in bed together. "I have that meeting with the investors later this afternoon, but I'll stop by on my way to check in."

"You don't have to do that," I said, nerves kicking up in my stomach about how much I actually did want him to do that. I had plenty to do today to make sure there wasn't too much damage control needed after last night and to prepare for our actual grand opening in a few weeks. What I needed to do was focus and get this restaurant off the ground.

My restaurant.

I'd spoken at length with Sophie about how upsetting it had been to have my dream at Suzette's ripped out from under me when the ownership changed hands. We were in the process of hammering out an agreement where I could buy my way into partial ownership of the restaurant here. It would need to be over time, as I only had so much of my savings I could contribute now, but at the very least, the idea that I could own actual stakes in the restaurant was deeply appealing to me. I wasn't sure that I could handle losing another restaurant that I loved.

And I did.

I loved it here. I loved the eccentric people, the nosy neighbors, and even the cantankerous Sir Buster. I even loved...my eyes landed on Munroe, looking gorgeous and too good to be true at the end of the bed. He'd put his kilt back on, and it took everything in my power not to crawl across the bed and drag him back to the mattress with me. But I knew today was important to him, so I ordered my ladyparts to settle down. They'd already been well serviced both last night and this morning.

"I know you don't have to, but you can wish me luck before I go to my meeting."

"It's a big deal, isn't it?" I ran my finger across a wrinkle in the bed sheet, smoothing it repeatedly as I considered how significant Munroe's business actually was. Here I was obsessing over my restaurant when he had multiple distilleries all over Scotland and international investors wooing him. When it was just us, like this, it was easy to forget our differences.

"It could be a big deal. Life-changing, actually. I do find it fascinating that they tracked me down to Loren Brae, which means they're already showing their hand on how interested they are in the brand."

"That's great, Munroe. Really great. I'm proud of you."

I pasted a smile on my face and tilted my head when an odd look crossed his face.

"It is. I just..." Munroe laughed and shook his head, crossing his arms over his chest as he turned to gaze out the window and over Loch Mirren. The Kelpies had woken us twice the night before, and each time, Lachlan had waved us back to bed from where we'd gone to the window. I wasn't sure what they were doing to subdue the Kelpies, but it looked like they were working overtime. "I don't know if I want it."

"What? Of course you do," I exclaimed. "You could take Common Gin global. That's a huge deal." I still didn't think I could fully wrap my head around just how wealthy Munroe was, or could be, if he took this deal. It was astounding, really. It would set him up for life, I was sure of it. Why wouldn't he take the deal?

"Aye. Of course, you're right." Munroe studied me with an odd look in his eyes, and I wished I understood the undercurrents here. His phone pinged with a message, and the moment broke. "That's me off then. I'll see you later."

After a lingering kiss, Munroe strode from the room, and I was left with a disquieting feeling in my stomach. Perhaps it was just nerves over the incident at the restaurant yesterday, but either way, my thoughts were swirling around in my brain like a blender on high.

I did what I always did when I was feeling out of sorts —I went to my kitchen. There, I had control. There I could be me.

Brice had indeed felt contrite, I noted, as I opened the kitchen doors and flipped on the lights. The place was spotless and ingredients for breakfast were already laid out.

Smiling, I turned on some music and started the coffee, before popping my head into the banquet hall.

"Brice, I'm here. If you're hungry, just let me know." I'd already checked the storage room, and he'd devoured the meal I'd left for him, so I'd make extra breakfast this morning. While I was unhappy with his behavior the night before, I couldn't quite bring myself to do the ritual of ridding my kitchen of him. The odd little guy had grown on me, and to be honest, there was a part of me that thrilled at having a magickal being in my kitchen. I mean, how cool was that? In fact, now that I had a brief moment to myself, I was going to take that time to read more of my spells book. I still couldn't get over that I was descended from a long line of Kitchen Witches. I'd gone from Lia, chef extraordinaire in Boston, to Kitchen Witch Lia of Scotland. Granted, I was still a chef here, but knowing that I was wanted, no...needed, to contribute to the greater good of Loren Brae, well, it was a heady prospect.

I was building something here that I could be proud of.

I just had to figure out how to hold on to it. My heart, quite simply, couldn't take it if I lost what I was building here.

After I'd made a simple bowl of oatmeal, or porridge as they called it in Scotland, I added some fresh blueberries and cinnamon, left a bowl for Brice in the pantry, and pulled a stool to a ledge by the window in the kitchen. There, I could enjoy my coffee while looking out over the castle's expansive gardens, while I paged through the spells book.

"The divine feminine," I murmured. The book was pretty incredible. Not only did it contain page after page of recipes and spells, all with notations added over the years, but it also had random journal entries from the various owners. I smiled as I read about babies being born, weddings, and even in one particular instance, a battle being won. But this entry caught my attention, as it related to the Order of Caledonia, and, to my delight, was written by my great-grandmother. "'The Order of Caledonia is at its most powerful when comprised of women, as the divine feminine power fuels the protective magick surrounding Clach na Fìrinn. We are all witches, be it a Kitchen Witch, a Knight, or even a Gardener. The power of the divine flows through us, and together, we create a thriving and magickal community for our people to flourish.'"

I was shocked to discover a listing of some previous members of the Order, and their roles. As indicated, it hadn't always been an Order of just women, but it did indicate that the best years of Loren Brae were when it was protected by women. I found it fascinating that the Order wasn't made up of a bunch of men acting as soldiers. Instead, it had been formed by mystical women protecting something that had the power to destroy the world. It made sense, I supposed, that a magickal *truth stone* would need magick to defend it.

Even little broonies played a part.

I made a note to speak to Agnes about the book, knowing she had an encyclopedic knowledge of Loren Brae's history, and this information would delight her. I stood and walked to the open doors to look across the garden to the calm waters of Loch Mirren. The tiny island in the middle was just a speck of green from where I stood.

I took a deep breath, and then another, inhaling the earthy dampness that clung to the air in Scotland.

I am magick.

I am powerful.

I am the divine feminine.

Joy flooded through me at my thoughts, even though I couldn't help but laugh softly. I sounded a bit like my yoga instructor back home, who insisted we were all divine goddesses channeling energy from the moon. Wouldn't she get a kick out of this if I told her that she'd been right all along?

"Caw!"

I started as three crows landed at my feet, tilting their heads back and forth at me, as though they expected something from me. Was this what happened with witches? Was I going to have crows following me where I walked now? Amused, and uncertain of how to approach them, I tilted my head back at them.

"Good morning?" I asked.

The crows danced around my feet in a circle —*performing for me?*—and surprise filled me when they dropped something at my toes.

"What is this?" I bent down and picked up a small, tarnished spoon. "Did you bring me a spoon?"

"It looks like you've been accepted into the pack." I turned at Sophie's voice.

"Are these your crows?" I asked, turning the spoon in my hand. "Thank you, ladies, er gentlemen. I'm not sure which you are but thank you for your gift."

The crows fluttered about my feet and seemed pleased with my response. Granted, I wasn't sure how to gauge the happiness of a bird, but if they weren't trying to peck my eyes out, I had to assume they were, at the very least, content.

"Can I feed them?" I asked, immediately defaulting to my de facto way of making friends. "What do they like?"

"Crows eat a lot of things, I've learned. But if you have any berries or nuts, that will make them happy."

I stepped back inside to find a bowl of peanuts in their shells and a bowl of blueberries on the prep table. Brice must like the crows.

"Well, that was easy enough." I returned outside with the bowls to find Sophie cooing to the birds. "Breakfast for you."

"Oh, Moe, stop bugging Larry," Sophie lectured, nudging one of the birds away from the other when he jostled his buddy to get close to the bowl. "Maybe just scatter the food?"

"Sure," I said with a grin and tossed the contents of the bowls away from where we stood. The birds flew after their meal, and Sophie followed me inside.

"Coffee?"

"Please," Sophie said, plopping onto the stool while I poured her a cup. "Quite a night last night."

"I know," I said, my stomach twisting. I'd been waiting to have this conversation. Although we were close in age, Sophie was still my employer. As owner of MacAlpine Castle, she had final say in all major decisions here. Once again, I was reminded how foolish I might be to think that I could build a future here that could potentially be taken from me at any moment. Nerves kicked up, and I began prepping my table for the day.

My knife.

"Sophie!" I gasped, lifting my knife to angle the handle toward her. "Look."

A second gold band shimmered next to the first that had appeared in the handle.

"You must have passed a second challenge. Oh, Lia. That's fantastic news. I swear, the Kelpies have been increasingly difficult lately. I'm barely getting sleep as it is."

Only then did I really look at Sophie and see the dark circles that ringed her pretty eyes.

"What are you doing to stop them? From being worse, that is?"

"My power comes in my voice. I have to order them back, each night, and reassure them that we're protecting the Stone. It's a constant battle, and it will be until the Order is fulfilled. This is great news, though," Sophie said, beaming at the knife.

"I found some information in my spells book. It seems to indicate that the Order is strongest if it is all women."

"Ah magick." Sophie laughed. "Gotta love the ultimate feminist power, huh?"

"I'm sorry about last night," I burst out, needing to get the conversation over. I had to know if she was going to fire me for not being able to control the broonie.

"What? Why? It was an incredible success." Confusion crossed Sophie's face. "Are you talking about Munroe's parents? They got what was coming to them as far as I am concerned."

"But...but..." I waved my hands in the air. "It was a total spectacle. Everyone was looking. They could have seen Brice."

"Ah well, that's not really a problem." Sophie shrugged.

"It's not?" I scrunched my nose up. I could not, for a moment, fathom a magickal kitchen elf not being a problem back at Suzette's.

"Listen, I can speak freely because it's just you and me. The Scots are, well, I should say *my* Scots, are pretty open-minded. They've been living with magick and myths for a really long time. They've seen enough to understand that there's more to this world than we can fully grasp. And last night? Almost everyone there was from Loren Brae. Even if Brice had jumped on the table and done a jig, they wouldn't have been upset. The Scots are, well, somewhat unflappable, I guess? It's an unnerving and endearing trait. You don't have anything to worry about, at least from my end. It's Munroe's parents that you'll need to concern yourself with."

"Yeah, they're not a big fan of mine."

"So I gathered. Do you think that's why you got the second gold band? You weathered the storm?"

"I..." I didn't want to betray Robyn's confidence, so instead I just shrugged. "I did perform a spell last night, but I don't want to break someone's trust."

"Ah, my curiosity is piqued. Fair enough, though. As your Knight, I must respect a code of honor." Sophie gave me a dramatic bow before walking back to the door. There, she paused. "Last night was great. And if it's any indication of what you can do here, the restaurant's going to be hugely successful. My spreadsheets even say so."

"Well, in that case..." I laughed. "Thanks for believing in me. It means a lot."

"It's not me that needs to believe in you," Sophie said. "You proved yourself long before you got to Loren Brae."

With that, Sophie left, and I let her words roll around in my head as I made notes about what I wanted to discuss with the staff about the night before. I had proven myself, hadn't I? *What was it that made it so hard for me to step back and congratulate myself on a job well done?* I was always so busy working toward my next goal that I never really stopped to bask in my achievements of the moment. Perhaps it was just the nature of how I'd grown up, always busy, always trying to make ends meet, never accepting help. At the very least, I'd learned that I could always rely upon myself.

The morning drifted by in a relatively calm manner after the chaos of the day before. Both Hilda and Archie dropped by to congratulate me, along with the dogs sniffing around for treats. I had planned for today to be a down day, so I could spend my time making notes and assessing what changes I'd want to make to the menu, if any at all, as well as any areas of improvement that were needed. For example, I already knew that we would need to reconfigure the lounge space where the diners had converged on the bar. Too many people standing in a narrow space had created a bit of a cluster at the entrance. There were various details that could make the entire experience run more smoothly, and I happily committed myself to writing down my observations. Next up, I'd bring the staff in and get their feedback as well, which in turn would help to contribute to what would, ideally, be a seamless dining experience for both the diners and the employees who would work here.

"Hey, beautiful."

I looked up from my notebook to see Munroe standing at the door in a slick suit that fitted his broad shoulders precisely. Although I liked the kilt better, he was still heart-stoppingly gorgeous in this suit, and while my ladyparts stood up and paid attention, I couldn't help but feel a bit frumpy in my jeans and T-shirt.

"You look nice," I said as I crossed the room. Munroe cupped my face in his hands and brushed the softest of kisses across my lips. My heart sighed.

"I have something for you," Munroe said, and he put his laptop bag down on the table. "Come here."

"Munroe. You don't have to buy me gifts," I said, uneasiness flitting through my stomach. Every time he brought me a gift, I was reminded that I couldn't afford to do the same for him.

"But I like to," Munroe said. He put an arm around my shoulders and walked me outside to a shiny, new bicycle, with a pretty tartan bow wrapped around the handlebars. A bright teal color, it had a basket on the back for carrying supplies, and a cute bell on the front.

This was *so* like Munroe. I'd never even mentioned my lack of transportation, as I had my own two feet. And yet, he'd seen the issue and had quietly done something about it. Frankly, I was surprised he'd restrained himself from buying me a car. Frustration filled me.

"Munroe, thank you for thinking of me," I began, refusing to walk forward and admire the pretty bike. Instead, I put my hands behind my back. "Truly. I appreciate it, but I can take care of myself."

"But you don't have any way to get around. I thought this would be a nice option for you. I even got a matching one, in a manly color, of course, so we can ride together if we feel like it."

My stomach twisted, and I shifted on my feet, uncertain how to accept this gift. It was incredibly sweet of him, *but...*

"Thank you for getting this for me," I said, looking up at him. "How much was it? I can reimburse you."

"No, Lia. It's a gift." A stubborn look crossed Munroe's face, which I ignored, and went to get my purse.

"I'm not sure how much I have on me here, but if you just tell me how much I owe you, I'll be happy to pay for it," I said. The words hung heavy on my tongue, and I knew that I was doing something wrong, and yet I couldn't stop myself from trying to pay for the bike. It was too much, and it made me uncomfortable. Already, Munroe had bought me the pretty cutting board and the sparkly grasshopper pendant, what would be next? I wondered if he thought he had to buy my love.

Love.

Huh, that was also an uncomfortable, and yet not entirely unwelcome, thought.

Turning, I winced at Munroe's expression. Hurt filled his eyes, and I opened my mouth to try and explain myself —that I needed to be able to take care of myself, that I couldn't have my future ripped away from me again because of someone else's choices, that I needed to know I could support myself—but before I could say anything, the kitchen erupted in chaos.

Metal mixing bowls flew from the shelves, narrowly missing my head, as the spice cabinet shifted and wobbled. A ceramic platter launched at my head and shattered on the wall behind me, and Munroe ducked a flying stool as he dove for me, pulling me to his body to protect me from the onslaught of flying utensils.

"Brice!" I shrieked, my face pressed into Munroe's chest. "Stop! Stop it!"

Instantly, the chaos stopped, and Munroe pulled me outside before dropping his hands from around me and storming back into the kitchen.

"Oh, shit."

"Brice, you clarty bastard. Show yourself," Munroe thundered, and I raced after him to find him in the pantry, knife in hand, towering over where Brice cowered in a dark corner.

"Munroe, no." I schooled my tone, trying to bring the tension down, and eased forward.

"He almost hurt you," Munroe said, the knife raised in his hand. "You could have been killed."

"But he didn't. He *didn't*," I said, reaching up to gently tug Munroe's arm. It didn't move, not even an inch. "Munroe. I'm safe. Listen to me. I'm just fine. I'm sure Brice wouldn't mean to actually hurt me. It was just an accident is all." Sweat broke out across my brow, and the seconds ticked by as I waited for Munroe to come to his senses. I truly didn't know what I would do if he actually tried to hurt Brice. In fact, I wasn't sure what the broonie would do either, if he knew his life to be in danger.

"You will *not* hurt her. Understood?" Munroe barked at Brice.

The broonie's small body trembled, but he lifted a head and nodded, his eyes watery with tears. My heart twisted.

"If I even think, for a second, that she is in danger—I'm coming after you. This is your one and only warning."

With that, Munroe dropped his hand and pulled me from the pantry, slamming the door behind him.

"Munroe, you can't threaten him like that," I said, my nerves pulled tight. Frustration filled me, and I don't know if it was from the gift, or the mess that my kitchen was now in, but I rounded on Munroe. "He's little. You scared him."

"I...*I* scared him?" Munroe pointed a finger at his chest and then at the destroyed kitchen. "He threw a platter at your head. You could have gotten a concussion. Or worse. And you're mad at me?"

"I'm not...it's just..." I waved my hands in the air, unable to articulate all the emotions bouncing around inside of me. It was too much. Munroe's gift, his need to take care of me, the broonie using magick at a whim... My brain basically short-circuited and shut down, so I just gaped at Munroe, unable to speak.

An alarm sounded from Munroe's bag, and he pinched his nose.

"I have to go to my meeting. I'll be back to help clean this up afterward. We'll talk then."

"Munroe, it's fine, I can clean..." I stopped when he snapped his fingers in the air.

"Not another word, Lia. I'm this close to losing it."

I raised my eyes at the ever-unflappable Munroe, surprised to see that he did, indeed, have a temper. Without another word, he grabbed his laptop bag and stormed from the kitchen while I stood in the middle of the shattered mess. Picking up the stool that had fallen over, I dropped onto it and cradled my head in my hand as tears welled.

Maybe I was in over my head.

This might all be too much. The restaurant, the

magick, the broonie, the Kelpies...all of it. What was I even doing here? I couldn't even control my own little kitchen elf. How the hell was I even going to help Sophie with the Kelpies?

Two pieces of paper fluttered onto the table in front of me and I looked up, wiping my eyes, as Brice popped his little head out from behind where the spice cabinet had moved from the wall. He lifted his chin, urging me to look at the paper he'd dropped in front of me while I was crying.

"What is this?" I said, wiping my eyes before picking up the papers in front of me. "Tommaso Bianchi wanted for fraud in New York City. Wait, is that the Italian guy?"

I looked up to see Brice nodding at me.

"Is he one of the investors? And what is this?" I held up the other piece of paper that looked like a deed of sorts. "Is this for the Auld Mill property? This says it is protected land. There's a natural habitat of otters?"

"Aye," Brice said, softly, as though he wasn't used to speaking.

"Oh my God." Realization hit. "Munroe has no idea what he's walking into, does he? That's why you flipped out."

"Aye," Brice said, again, his eyes filling with tears once more.

"Shit. I have to go. I have to stop this." I grabbed my purse and shoved the papers inside, racing for the doors. "We need to talk about how you express your emotions, Brice. Don't do anything else until I get back, I have to fix this."

Slamming the doors behind me, I skidded to a halt by the bicycle. I knew that Munroe was meeting with the investors in a private back room at the Tipsy Thistle. By the time I rounded up Sophie, explained what I needed, and got her to drive me, I could already be there.

If I rode the bike.

Fear for Munroe's future far outweighed any trepidation I had about accepting this gift from him, and without another thought, I swung my leg over the bar and plopped my butt on the seat. It had been ages since I'd ridden a bike, as we'd only had two to pass among the siblings, but it was true what they said about old habits coming back easily.

After the first few tremulous pedals, my confidence grew, and I took off toward town, like a Kitchen Witch without her broom. The crows joined me, cawing above my head as they circled, my own personal cheering squad, and I raced for the pub.

I only hoped I wouldn't be too late.

CHAPTER TWENTY

Munroe

"Gentlemen, I have to admit, I have some reservations." I'd been surprised to see Tommaso as one of the investors when I'd arrived at the meeting today, and wondered why he hadn't mentioned it to me the night before. I suppose that made sense why he was in the area, as it had seemed odd that he was in town just for the soft opening of Lia's restaurant. Not that she wasn't fabulous, of course, but the castle had done no publicity on the restaurant yet.

"That's understandable," Tommaso said, spreading his hands wide. "It's not easy to start playing with the big boys."

The way he said it rankled me, and I assumed it was designed to do so. Even though he wore a kindly smile, I sensed that he was goading me, as though he wanted to see if I was capable of rising to the challenge. With him sat two other investors, both with proposals about how we could take Common Gin to the next level. My real estate agent had handed off the paperwork for me to submit an offer on the Auld Mill property once the meeting was finished. I'd hesitated there, as well, even though the property was lovely. Something was niggling at me, which usually meant I needed to take more time before I made a decision. As much as I wanted to start the process of opening a distillery in Loren Brae, I still needed to be smart. If that meant taking more time until I found the perfect property, then so be it.

"How did you come to hear of my plans to build here again?" The investors claimed that they had caught wind of my interest in another distillery for Common Gin, which had subsequently piqued their interest in taking my brand to international markets as well. They claimed it showed my willingness to expand into other markets, since I continued to build more properties under the Common Gin brand.

"Your agent," Craig, one investor, mentioned. He seemed the nicest of the three, but I wasn't necessarily fooled. There was something that shifted beneath his eyes that I didn't quite like.

"Your mother," Tommaso said, and I turned, raising an eyebrow at him.

"Mum mentioned it?" It appeared I'd have to speak with my mother about sharing business secrets. I'd mentioned the new distillery in passing to her when I'd first come to Loren Brae, and it surprised me that she'd viewed it as notable enough to share with an investor like Tommaso.

"She did. Your parents were at the club, and we had a chat."

"What do you think?" Craig asked, pushing the paperwork toward me. I leaned back in my chair and steepled my fingers in front of me as I thought about how I wanted to proceed. Much like in my dating life, I could move at a glacial speed when it came to business as well. I would rather take my time to make sure a deal felt right, than to impulsively jump into something. These investors were offering a significant opportunity, the likes of which would take Common Gin through the stratosphere, and there was a lot of money on the table. Not only would I be giving up shares of my own company, but I'd also have to buy in to a new conglomerate they wanted to form to introduce a few choice Scottish brands to international markets. The packaging was slick, the opportunity was apparent, and the little boy inside of me who wanted to show up his parents screamed at me to take the deal.

"Munroe, wait!"

I jumped to my feet as Lia crashed through the door, her hair wild around her face, her breath coming in pants.

"Lia, what's wrong?" My stomach dropped. Had the broonie hurt her after I left? I was an idiot for walking away. I'd known it at the time, and I shouldn't have gone to this meeting. She was what really mattered, and she could have been hurt further. I moved around the table and took her hands in mine. "Are you okay?"

"I'm fine, I'm *fine*," Lia promised me, gulping for air. She leaned to the side to see the three men in suits gaping at her, and then looked up at me with panicked eyes. "I need to talk to you."

"Um, now isn't really the best time. Can it wait?" I asked, relief filling me that she was safe.

"It really can't," Lia said. Dropping her hands, she dug in her handbag and pulled out a handful of papers. "You need to see these."

"What is going on? Is that the chef?" Tommaso asked.

"Just a moment, please." Taking Lia's arm, I pulled her from the room and back into the front area of the pub where Graham wiped bottles behind the bar.

"Just read them. Munroe, I'm so sorry," Lia said, and I held up my finger to silence her so I could focus on the words in front of me. To her credit, she quieted.

"What's going on?" Graham asked, coming to stand in front of me, and I held up my finger to him as well.

"You know, I have an excellent pickup line that involves one finger," Graham said.

"Wheesht," Lia and I said together, and Graham, to *his* credit, shut his mouth.

"Fraud," I read out loud, and flipped to the other paper. "The Auld Mill is protected land?"

"Aye, there's a whole family of otters up there. It's been protected for ages. Wait, were they trying to sell you that property? I don't think you can build on it at all." Graham leaned forward and took the papers from my shaky hands. "I didn't know you were looking up that way."

"I didn't say anything as I didn't want too many people weighing in on my decision," I said. I could kick myself for not running it past at least a few of my friends. Lesson learned. Turning to Lia, I took her by the shoulders. "Lia. Where did you get these papers?"

"Brice," Lia whispered, her voice apologetic.

"Bloody hell. We need to work on how he deals with problems," I grumbled. Reaching up, I pinched my nose as I thought about what to do. It was easy enough to not offer on the Auld Mill property, though I'd need to report the agent for misrepresentation of the land. But the bit with Tommaso was trickier. If I called him out for his criminal charges in front of the others, I had no idea what stream of events that could trigger. For all I knew, he could be with the Italian mob. I would need to handle this delicately.

Thankfully, I'd trusted my instincts and hadn't signed anything away yet.

"I'm sorry, Munroe," Lia whispered, clenching my arm. "I know how important this is to you. And, I wouldn't have come here if I thought Brice was making this up. Please, trust me. I don't want you to get screwed."

Bending, I brushed a kiss across her forehead, and then tilted her chin up so her pretty brown eyes met mine.

"I'll take care of it. Thank you for bringing this to me." With a glance at Graham, I pointed at the papers. "You're certain about Auld Mill being protected?"

"Aye. I went to the ceremony celebrating it and everything."

"Fair enough. Thank you both for that. I'll speak to you later." With that, I smoothed my lapels and took a deep breath, before returning to the meeting. Closing the door neatly behind me, I smiled apologetically at the room. "I'm so very sorry about that. Lia, my girlfriend, had an issue at her new restaurant she's opening. Tommaso knows the place."

"Delicious food," Tommaso said, kissing his fingers. "Brilliant restaurant. I hope everything is well?"

"Well enough. Just nerves with a new business." Smiling, I sat down at the table and picked up the paperwork as I scanned the documents. Clause after clause, tying me and Common Gin up with their companies for years to come. I didn't need to address the real estate aspect of this, as that would be handled with the agent, so really it was just whether I wanted to bring up Tommaso's criminal allegations or not. Under the ruse of reading the contract again, I came to my conclusion. One thing I'd learned about really rich people? They hated losing face. I wasn't going to call Tommaso out, but I also wasn't going to take this deal.

"Thank you, gentlemen, for coming here today and for offering me such a generous proposition. Respectfully, I will decline the offer."

"What?" Tommaso blinked at me in surprise.

"Oh, come on," Craig exploded. "This was all a waste of time? Coming to this empty little town to try and woo you into a deal? Or is this just you playing hardball? If you want to negotiate terms, we can negotiate terms. But don't just flat-out reject the proposal. We're offering you the world."

"I understand." I smiled at the table as I stood. "And I thank you for your offer. But here's the thing—I already have the world. Right here, in this empty little town. Common Gin was built on the idea that we were a friendly, *accessible* gin—made for the common man. A drink to be shared among friends, of all walks of life. And that's right where I'll keep it. I'm happy with my life, and I'm happy with where my business is at. Thank you, again, for your offer, but Common Gin is not available for investment opportunities."

"Boy." Tommaso stood and grabbed my arm as I turned

to leave. "Do you have any idea what you're walking away from? Your parents will be furious. If you'd taken this deal, they would have finally had a chance to brag about you."

"Och, I certainly wouldn't want that now, would I?" I grinned at him and pulled his hand from my shoulder. "Why break with tradition?"

"Is this about the girl? There's always another girl..." Tommaso trailed off as I whirled on him, my hands clenched in fists.

"Lia isn't just some girl, and she's worthy of your respect. You'll not speak her name again."

Tommaso backed up a step, which was smart seeing as I was easily a head taller than him, and with one brisk nod to the others in the room, I left.

"Where's Lia?" I demanded of Graham when I returned to the bar to find her gone.

"She left. All good in there?" Graham nodded to the closed doors behind me.

"Not likely. I'll pick up the tab though. Whatever you do, don't let them pay, and let them know *I* paid for it." I patted the top of the bar twice before hightailing it for the door. I wasn't interested in sticking around to hear Tommaso try and talk me out of it, lest I slip up and bring up what I knew of the criminal allegations against him. Frankly, that wasn't my problem to solve. Or, as my grandmother used to put it, "sweep your own stairs." Tommaso's problems were his own, and so long as I wasn't getting involved with his business, I no longer cared. What I did care about was finding Lia and thanking her for coming to help me. I knew it had taken her a lot, particularly after we'd left each other in a difficult moment, and her showing up for me had solidified what I'd already known.

Lia was the one for me.

Now, even if I had to bully her into it, I was going to make her realize that we could have a happy life together if she'd just give us a chance. If that meant that I could never buy her another gift, well, so be it.

Yeah, that wasn't happening. But I'd give it a go if that was what she really wanted.

Pulling to a stop at the castle, I was relieved to see the kitchen doors open. She'd once told me that where some people went to the gym or the bar when they were upset, she always went to her kitchen. Crows cawed above me, seeming to follow me to the kitchen, and cawed so loudly that I couldn't help but glance up at them. When I did, something dropped at my feet, and I crouched to see what it was.

Lia's grasshopper.

Fear gripped me, and I pocketed it, hitting the kitchen doors at a dead run and skidding to a stop when Lia jumped up, a startled look on her face.

"Munroe, is everything—"

"Lia." I rounded the table and gripped her shoulders, my breath catching as I looked down at this luminous woman. "Are you okay? You're not hurt?"

"No, I'm fine. You saw that Brice didn't hurt me," Lia said, and I shook my head, taking a moment to shake thoughts of her being hurt from my head. Did that mean she'd thrown the necklace away? Was she that angry at me for giving her the bike? Uncertainty threaded through me, and I stepped back, dropping my hands.

"Is he here?" I asked, turning to look around.

"Brice? I suspect so."

"I'd like to have a talk with him. Can you get him to come out?" I asked.

"I honestly don't know. He rarely shows himself," Lia said, turning from where her spells book was open in front of her. "Brice? Munroe is here. He'd like to speak to you. But only if you want to. You can ignore him if you want to, that's just fine with me. He was pretty scary earlier. So, it's your call."

"Gee, thanks," I muttered.

"Aye?"

Brice poked his head out from the darkened hallway, and I took a moment to look at the little guy. With a wrinkled face, wizened eyes, and threadbare hair, he was not at all pleasing to the eyes. And yet, he'd tried to protect Lia, and myself, on several occasions, even if his methods were less than desirable. I walked forward and crouched in front of him and sighed when he shrunk back. Holding out a finger, I waited, until Brice finally reached out. His entire palm circled my index finger.

"Thank you," I said, meeting his eyes. "I'm deeply sorry for my reaction before. You scared me because I thought you'd hurt Lia. I think you and I are much the same. We'll do anything to protect her. I'm sorry. Can you forgive me?"

Tears welled in his little eyes, and he nodded once.

"And thank you for your help today. It means a lot to me. Moving forward, let's work on a better system for how you communicate if there's trouble, okay?"

"I can stay?" The words were barely a whisper, and I turned to Lia, not sure if she'd caught what he'd said.

"Can he stay?"

"Of course he can stay," Lia said, dashing her palms against her eyes. "What kind of Kitchen Witch would I be without my broonie?"

When I turned back, Brice had disappeared, but his happy chattering confirmed he was pleased with the decision. Standing, I returned to Lia's side and leaned against the table. We still had things to discuss.

"Thank you, for coming today. I know it was scary to walk in there, to interrupt a meeting like that, but I am really grateful that you did. While I was already on the fence about the deal, you truly saved me."

"Oh, thank God," Lia said, pressing a hand to her chest. "I was so nervous. But I couldn't let them screw you."

"Of course not, because you love me." I grinned as a stubborn look came over Lia's face.

"I didn't say that. It was just wrong, okay? What they were doing was wrong." Lia sniffed and lifted her chin. My smile widened as I took in the defiant tilt to Lia's chin. Okay, she wasn't quite ready to break, was she?

"You know...I've always dreamed of having a family."

"What?" Lia's eyes widened in surprise.

"Yes, a family. Big or small, it doesn't matter. But I always dreamed of that. Even more so, I've dreamed of having a partner who loved me for me. Who saw me, exactly as I was, and said—*I love him*. Just like that. A partner who doesn't want my money or prestige but is happy to be with me and play board games and talk about aliens."

"Aliens?" Lia said, faintly.

"You've met my parents. You see how screwed up they are. They're cold, unforgiving. My whole life...I've desperately wanted something different. I thought it was their approval I needed or wanted, when now I realize it's just my own approval that I sought all along. I'm not a bad person, Lia. And all I want is a family. I think, well, I think I can find it here, in Loren Brae. With you."

Lia's eyes filled, but still, I didn't dare touch her.

"I don't need, or want, to go global with my brand. I already make more than enough money, and I love what I'm doing. I like being hands-on, and I love the company that I've built, from the ground up. Some things don't need to become bigger to be better. Common Gin is fine the way it is. You showed me today what family does for each other. I want a life, with you, if you're willing to take a chance on a future with me."

"Oh, Munroe," Lia said, shaking her head, and my heart fell.

"Is that a no?" I asked, my stomach twisting. Maybe I'd read her wrong all along. Maybe I was just a distraction for her until she moved on to the next.

"You want to dream together, don't you?" Lia whispered, tapping a finger on the book in front of her. I followed her finger to see a recipe for dreams.

"Is that..."

"Yes," Lia said, gulping a breath. "You see, I've never really allowed myself to dream. Not really. I've always told myself it was a luxury for other people. But I'm silly, you see? I'd been dreaming all along. I'd been dreaming that Suzette's would be mine one day, and that dream got stolen from me. It was easier for me to tell myself that dreams weren't for people like me. But I don't want to live a life like that. There's so much...good here. So much promise. The restaurant. The town. The people. You."

"You were making this recipe, weren't you?" I asked quietly, hope blooming.

"I was. I don't care if it's for me. I haven't read any rules that say I can't use magick for myself. And it isn't like I'm using magick to win the lottery or something. I'm doing this because I know my power and because I choose to use my magick on myself." Lia lifted that stubborn chin again, and never did I love a woman more.

"By all means, lass, then have at it."

And so she did, mixing and stirring, and brewing until she poured a golden liquid into a cup and took a deep breath, and then another.

"By the power of fire let it shine bright,
What dreams may come this very night,
Forever on, my heart shall be,
Filled with hope, so mote it be."

THERE WAS a small flash of light in the cup, the same as the night before, and then Lia held it to her lips. Pausing, she smiled at me.

"I want to dream with you, Munroe."

It took everything in my power to let her finish the cup, to not reach for her and hold her close for all time, but I'd learned something that day about powerful women.

They needed to come around to things in their own time.

When she'd finished, Lia carefully put down the cup, a

luminous glow on her face. I dug in my pocket and held out my hand.

"Will you be wanting this back then?"

"Oh, Munroe." Lia's hand came to her neck, shock crossing her face. "It must have fallen when I jumped on the bike. I was in such a hurry. Oh, the chain's broken. I'm sorry, I'll have it fixed–"

"I just needed to hear you didn't throw it away," I said, putting a finger to her lips to stop the flow of words.

"I can't wait to dream with you, my glorious Kitchen Witch." I replaced my finger with my lips, and leaned into the moment, everything quieting around me and my world once more becoming right. When the kiss heightened, I broke it before I took Lia on the prep table with the kitchen doors wide open. Given how often people stopped in to say hello, I wasn't sure Archie's poor heart could handle bearing witness to such an event.

"Munroe, look!" Lia said, and I glanced down to see her gaping at her kitchen knife where a third gold band shimmered in the handle. "I did it. I passed the challenges! I'm officially a part of the Order of Caledonia."

"And together, we'll save Loren Brae." I smiled and pulled Lia back into my arms, unwilling to let her be away from me in this moment. "You know, seeing your grasshopper reminded me of an idea that I've had. I think I know just the perfect place for the distillery."

"You do?" Lia looked up at me. "You still want to open a distillery in Loren Brae?"

"Of course I do. I did before I met you, and now you've given me even more reason to plant my roots here. Come on, let's go find Lachlan. I have an idea to run past him."

"Oh, right now?" Lia pushed out her lower lip, and I threw my head back and laughed, delight filling me that my little Kitchen Witch was grumpy about not getting my love. Scooping her up so that she squealed, I buried my face in her neck.

"We'll stop by your room first. Then, my love, we'll find the others and talk about our dreams together."

"I guess I do love you," Lia said, her voice muffled at my throat.

"What was that, I couldn't quite hear you?"

"You heard me," Lia grumbled, and I laughed, carrying her out of the kitchen, the same crows cawing as they followed us around the side of the castle.

"It's okay, grasshopper, you'll get used to saying it."

"I'm not your grasshopper." Lia's voice was indignant.

"I was just testing out a nickname. You don't like?"

"Moo!"

I almost dropped Lia as Clyde burst out of the wall. It was the first time I'd seen him since I'd been back, and he tossed his head proudly in the air. He danced forward and backward, positively delighted with our shock, and I slumped against the wall, trying to catch my breath.

"Damn it, Clyde! You made me wet my pants," Lia shrieked.

"Shower it is, then," I said, and Lia swore under her breath.

I laughed the entire way there.

EPILOGUE

Lia

"Come for a walk with me," Munroe said, tugging my hand and pulling me from where I was triple-checking my supplies order for the grand opening of Grasshopper, a garden-to-table restaurant focused largely on vegetarian meals. The nickname Grasshopper had stuck around, even though I steadfastly refused to answer to it, and it had been Sophie's idea to use it for the restaurant instead. I hadn't been certain it would be a good fit, what with MacAlpine Castle being as fancy and historical as it was, but Hilda and Archie had embraced the idea. I had to admit, I quite liked the name. It was a full circle moment, reminding me of where I'd come from, and the incident that had neatly changed the direction of my life.

"But..."

"You've gone over the order a million times. It's going

to be perfect, I promise," Munroe said, grabbing my hands and dragging me out of the kitchen and into the sunshine. It was a perfect late summer afternoon, and I had to admit that I probably needed the break. It was a shame to waste fine weather in Scotland, I'd quickly learned, and I took a few deep breaths of the fresh air as Munroe drew me more deeply into the gardens that ringed the castle.

"I just love these gardens. They're so fancy and far more elaborate than anything I've ever seen back home. I'm looking forward to growing my fresh herbs, though I confess, I'm going to have to lean on Shona a lot for that one. She said she doesn't mind if I bug her about it," I said, pausing to admire a peachy pink rose bush.

"I'm sure she won't. She's very lovely and seems pretty knowledgeable about her produce. I imagine she'd be quite helpful with your spells work as well."

"She has no idea how many ingredients she's going to have to source for me," I admitted. Every free moment I had, I was playing around with recipes in the book. It seemed a Kitchen Witch was sort of a hodgepodge kind of witch. Some recipes were for spells to help with healing, but others were much more ephemeral than that. Much like the one I'd done for dreams.

The Kelpies had quieted in the weeks after I'd finished my challenges, allowing Sophie more sleep, and me the chance to work on my magick without any pressure. Every day I felt I grew stronger, though I knew that Hilda and Archie were already making noises about locating the next of the Order. I had an idea who that might be but was nervous to suggest it as it seemed almost outlandish.

"It's been a joy to watch you work," Munroe said,

smiling down at me. For a moment, the sun highlighted his tawny hair, and I caught my breath, still kicking myself that this incredible man was mine. If you were wondering, my ladyparts were equally as delighted with my choice.

"It's been a joy to work. I've always loved cooking, creating, and all of that...but discovering my magick? That's been an entirely whole new layer. I feel like this rose," I said, running a finger across a velvet petal.

"You've bloomed quite beautifully," Munroe agreed, tugging me along the path. We wandered in silence for a while, appreciating the breezy afternoon, until we clambered up a small incline and Munroe nudged me toward a building that I hadn't seen before.

"What is this place? Is it a stable? I thought the stable was closer to the castle," I mused. "It's cool, isn't it? I just love all the stonework here. It's a constant reminder of history, isn't it?"

"It is." Munroe picked up something from a ledge by the door and I noticed a small ribbon tied across the rusted iron door handles.

"What's this?" I tilted my head at him in question as he handed me some scissors.

"This is a pair of scissors. They are a tool used to cut things, from gardening to in the kitchen–"

"Wheesht," I hissed at him, using my favorite new Scottish word. That and "tetchy." I loved pointing out when people were tetchy, which, let me tell you, rarely went over well. But it was such a fun word to say, the way it kind of caught on the tongue, and reflected the crabbiness of the mood it described. "Why are you handing me scissors?"

"To cut the ribbon," Munroe pointed out, a bland smile on his face.

"They can also be used as a murder weapon. Or to maim people. I do enjoy a good maiming, have I mentioned that?" I hefted the scissors, and Munroe's face paled.

"A time or two, yes. You've a bloodthirsty streak in you, don't you?"

"It's hard to say if it comes from the Italian or Scottish side." I narrowed my eyes at him.

"Go on, cut the ribbon, and I'll tell you."

"Fine." I cut the ribbon neatly in two and then pocketed the strips, just in case what he was going to tell me was meaningful. I liked to save little mementos like that.

"Welcome to Common Gin's newest distillery."

"*No*!" My mouth dropped open, and then I launched myself at him. Munroe dodged, quickly grabbing the scissors from my hand, and putting them aside, before pulling me into his arms. I planted a smacking kiss on his lips, my heart bursting with excitement for him. "Munroe! What a perfect idea. This is just fabulous. Of course, what an excellent location. It's so close to the castle and will just be an added layer of what we can offer tourists. Oh, I'm so excited. Plus we can work closely with each other."

"I wonder if I can do a grasshopper gin," Munroe mused, tapping a finger on his lips.

"Mmm, maybe we'll just stick to making the grasshopper mixed drink," I amended, suddenly fearful for all the grasshoppers in the area. While I appreciated the full circle nature of the grasshoppers and all, I didn't need to ingest them in any manner, liquid or solid.

"Probably for the best." Munroe laughed. He slid the door open and flipped on the light, and I eagerly stepped forward.

"Surprise!"

I dropped to the floor and gasped at where my entire family stood in the middle of the building, wide grins on their faces. *Listen, I don't want to bring up the wetting the pants thing again, but let's just say it was close, okay?* Then I was jumping up and flying across the room, my mom and dad catching me in a three-person hug.

"I can't believe you're here! How did you get here?" I shrieked, bouncing up and down in excitement. I turned, hooking an arm around Gio's head, and kissing Carlo on the cheek. Everyone spoke at once, and I didn't catch what anyone said, I was so overwhelmed with excitement at seeing them all. I hadn't realized just how much I'd missed my family, and now tears sprang to my eyes. Turning, I saw Munroe hanging shyly back.

"Was this you?" I asked, suspicion lacing my voice.

"First class, Lia! Can you believe it? Never have I been treated so fancy." Enzo shook his head. "That's a good guy you got there."

"You did this for me?" I walked over to Munroe, tears dripping down my cheeks. "You flew them all here?"

"Of course." Munroe shrugged. "I know how important your family is to you, and they're so proud of what you've done—"

"You impossibly perfect man." I threw my arms around him, and to my surprise, my family circled us in one massive hug. Munroe's body tensed under my arms, and I knew his innate shyness was kicking in. "Just lean into it, Munroe. They'll smother you with their love."

"He needs mothering," Mom whispered in my ear. "I can tell."

"Have at it, Ma. He won't know what to do with himself," I said, and Munroe drew back to look down at me with suspicion in his eyes.

"What won't I know to do?" Munroe asked.

"Nothing. Oh, I can't wait to show you everything." We broke the hug up, everyone talking over each other, and walked back outside. "Where are you guys staying?"

"Hilda's put us all up in the castle. Can you imagine?" Carlo shook his head. "A real freaking castle."

"I know. I felt the same way. Can you believe I live here?"

"I'm so proud of you, Pumpkin." My dad put his arm around my shoulder and took a deep breath, rubbing a hand at his chest. "This air. It's so fresh and clean. I can't believe I'm back in Scotland. I've missed it here. A beautiful place it is."

"Did you bring your kilt?" I angled my head up at him, wondering if he'd dress up for opening night.

"Did he? We all did." Luca punched me in the shoulder. "Your man got us all kilts too."

"You did?" I laughed up at Munroe, imagining him trying to wrestle with measurements for all of my brothers. I'm surprised he hadn't given up and just left them all in Boston. "That must have been fun."

"He's exceedingly patient," Mom put in. "You've picked a good one, Lia."

"Don't I know it," I said, smiling up at Munroe. "Come on, let me show you the restaurant. How do you feel about broonies?"

I'd made the decision to be honest with my family about my magick. I didn't like to lie to them, and I had nothing to hide, as far as I was concerned. My brothers could be difficult at times, but they knew how to keep a secret, and they'd never do anything to put me in a position of danger.

"Shut up. Do we get to meet the little guy? This is so cool." Luca bounded across the lawn like he was twelve years old.

Munroe wrapped an arm around my shoulders and pulled me into him as my family peppered us with questions, loud and rambunctious, as they spilled across the gardens.

"Just wait until they meet Clyde."

Munroe laughed and pressed a kiss to my head, and my heart sighed. My mother had been right all along.

Love was always the perfect ingredient.

Don't miss the opening of Lia's new restaurant!
Download the free bonus scene:
A Magickal Restaurant Opening
https://offer.triciaomalley.com/love

Who will the next member of the Order of Caledonia be? Read on for a sneak peek into the next book in the Enchanted Highlands series:

Wild Scottish Rose

WILD SCOTTISH ROSE

Sneak Peak – Wild Scottish Rose

Shona

"I *said* I wanted Calla lilies."

I tensed as the bride's voice cut through the din of chatter where my team, as well as the venue staff, were setting up the reception area for the wedding that evening. Turning, I pasted a polite smile on my face as the bride, Kennedy Williams of Dallas, Texas, bore down on me. Her pretty face was screwed up in anger and her eyes were alight with battle.

Life was going to be difficult for Kennedy if she got this angry over flowers.

"I'm certain that you didn't. But I'll just double-check the order form if you'd like confirmation?" I pulled up my phone and flipped through the orders which I had neatly organized in a file, even though I was well aware that *Miss* Kennedy Williams had ordered white roses for her centerpieces. The arrangements were simple and beautiful, as instructed on the order form, and I'd chosen roses at varying stages of bloom to add depth to the centerpieces. Even though white roses were the most common order I received from brides, I still enjoyed working with the flower. It was one of my favorites, after all. Even more exciting? An opportunity to decorate at Òran Mór, a fabulous reception venue in Glasgow housed in a renovated church. It was my first time traveling this far for a wedding, and I was hoping to enjoy a bit of the city after we finished setting up.

Life in Loren Brae was lovely, and while I enjoyed the pace, it was still nice to get to the city on occasion for some excitement. And *shopping*. My heart did a little dance thinking about how I'd carefully saved up to buy some extravagant lingerie. It was a secret passion of mine, because much of my life was spent mucking in the dirt, and it was useless to buy pretty clothes that would just get ruined. Now, my earlier excitement at working with the incredible team at Òran Mór, and the prospect of a shopping trip, dimmed. Already I could see my chance to shop being pulled away from me as I mentally readied myself to change all the arrangements right before the reception. It would be a mad dash, and I'd have to call in some favors from local florists, but it could be done if needed.

"White roses?" Kennedy sneered as I pulled up her order. "How positively boring. I definitely ordered the lilies."

"No," I began, turning my phone to show her the screen.

"Lilies? Aren't lilies for funerals?" A voice interrupted us, and a shiver danced across the back of my neck.

"What?" A look of confusion crossed Kennedy's face and she whirled on the man who approached us.

I suppose approach was a casual word for how this man strode confidently through the hall, outfitted in a perfectly fit tuxedo, with a tartan bow and matching pocket square. He moved like a panther, his eyes darting across the room, and seeming to take in every detail at once. When they landed on me, his assessment stopped, and a smile landed on his lips. Close-cropped dark hair, lively blue eyes, and broad shoulders completed the package and I found myself desperately wishing I'd dressed up.

Which was silly, really, considering that dressing up didn't make sense with the amount of manual labor it took to decorate an entire reception hall with flowers. It wasn't just putting vases of flowers on the tables–there were garlands to be hung, vines to be entwined, and lighting to be added. Frankly, I wasn't even sure I owned anything that this type of man would find appealing. Either way, jeans, a t-shirt, and trainers were the smart choice for my line of work. And that was me. Sensible to my core.

What was it about this man that instantly made me *not* want to be sensible?

"Lilies are traditionally used for funerals. You wouldn't want people to think that your marriage is a death, would you?" The man turned to Kennedy, who looked up at him with annoyance on her face.

"Damn it, Owen. Why do you always come in and screw things up when I'm just trying to get things handled?" Kennedy demanded.

"Kennedy, if I may? It does say here on your form that you ordered the roses. See?" I brandished my phone, hoping to head off an argument between these two, but neither bothered to glance my way.

"See? The pretty flower lady says you ordered roses. Frankly, I'm surprised at that choice as well," Owen said. He crossed his arms over his chest and gave Kennedy a wry smile.

"What's wrong with roses?" Kennedy demanded, immediately jumping ship from the lily train to roses. Relief passed through me. If she was going to defend roses, then maybe I'd be off the hook and could get back to decorating. Easing back a step, hoping to leave them to their argument, I caught the eye of my assistant who hovered nearby with a vase in hand and a questioning looking on her face. I gave her a subtle nod, and she continued to set up while I waited to hear the outcome of this discussion.

"Nothing, of course, as these vases are perfection in their own right." Owen slid me a grin and I'm pretty sure my insides melted. His American accent held a hint of the south and somewhere else, but I wasn't well-versed enough in accents to place it. I found myself wanting to inch closer, to be drawn into his hemisphere, just to listen to him talk.

Never had I met a man with so much charisma before.

Apparently, I wasn't the only one who felt this way, as I caught more than one of the event staff giving him appreciative looks.

"It's just that..." Owen continued, tapping a finger against his lips. "We're in Scotland, right? I'm surprised you didn't go with something more traditional to the venue."

My stomach dropped. If I had to run out and find thistles, I would, even if it meant cutting them from the side of the road.

"You're right," Kennedy gasped and gripped his arm. "What was I thinking? What should I add in?"

"Haggis, naturally."

My heart skipped a beat, and I pressed my lips together to hold back a burst of laughter. Surely the bride had to know that haggis was a dish, not a flower. My eyes widened as Kennedy whirled on me.

"*You*. I need you to get wild haggis for the centerpieces." Kennedy snapped her fingers at me, her eyes bright with determination, and I blinked at her as I tried to come up with an excuse that wouldn't embarrass the bride. She didn't seem like the type to be able to laugh at a joke at her own expense.

"Well..." I began and Owen cut me off.

"In fact, you'll probably want haggis added to the bridal bouquet as well. Oh, and the boutonnieres for the men. Maybe the bartenders could make a haggis drink?"

"Of course! Like my lavender-infused martinis that I love." Kennedy turned and stormed across the room to the bar, and I was grateful for the momentary reprieve, though now I had to come up with a way to tell her that I wasn't about to put meat flowers in her bouquet.

"I'm probably going to hell. But I do so love winding her up. I'm Owen, by the way." Owen held out his hand I took it automatically, though my stomach twisted in knots about how to deal with this latest catastrophe.

"Shona," I said, faintly, my eyes on where Kennedy berated one of the bartenders about a haggis martini.

"My apologies, Shona, that you have to deal with Kennedy. She's not always this difficult..." Owen trailed off as he squinted his eyes. "Actually, nevermind, she is. In fact, I'm now warming to the idea of haggis in her flowers."

"But...I can't...possibly..." I held my hands up, at a loss for words.

"I think you can do anything you put your mind to." Owen pursed his lips and studied me, clearly used to people falling in line with his plans. I wanted to, I *really* wanted to, because there was something about the wicked glint in his eyes that made me want to be naughty even just for a bit.

I was *so* done with weddings.

It wasn't that all of them were awful, or anything like that, I was just over doing flowers for weddings. The stress never lived up to the enjoyment for me. I'd much rather be back home, nurturing my plants, and selling my wares at farmers markets. It was my comfort zone and this...well, *this* was not what I needed right now.

"Shona!" Kennedy shouted from across the room, stomping her foot, and Owen intervened.

"I'll handle her. Just get your decorations out as you see fit. She'll be happy enough once she's married." It came out as an order, and I found my attraction to this man instantly diminishing. Men like him? Yeah, they were used to dealing with women like Kennedy. He could very well handle it while I stuck to what I knew best–plants.

"Yes, sir. Whatever you say sir." I infused enough syrupy sweetness in my voice, so Owen knew that I was annoyed with him and walked away.

"Sassy. I like it." Owen winked at me. Damn it, but I found the wink sexy, and I hated myself for doing so. It was so cliché. The wink. The charm. The casual ease in a tuxedo. Owen was not my type of people. Why I even found myself attracted to him was beyond me.

"Your opinion matters little to me," I surprised myself by saying, and the grin widened on Owen's face before he sauntered away. What was wrong with me? I'd just insulted a client's guest. That would *not* bode well for my business. Even if I'd promised myself that I was done with weddings, I still didn't want to get any bad online reviews.

"Why is the bride screaming about haggis?" my assistant whispered in my ear. I kept my eyes trained on Owen as he pulled Kennedy away from the bar.

"Who is that?" I asked, turning to unwrap the padding from around a vase.

"The one who knows exactly what he's about?" My assistant fanned her face, and I rolled my eyes. "That's the brother."

Of course it was. Nothing like directly insulting a family member. I'd have to apologize later. But for now, I needed to make a plan.

"Do we still have the extra bucket of white heather in the van?" The bride hadn't asked for it, but I typically brought some along in case any spots needed filling.

"We do. Are we adding it?"

"We are. If anyone asks...it's wild haggis."

AFTERWORD

I was lucky enough to write this book between recent trips to Scotland, and I can't tell you how much I enjoyed taking inspiration from my travels and putting it into this story. I can't decide who I enjoyed writing more–Lia or Munroe–but they both hold a very special place in my heart. I love how Lia is so determined to build something for herself, even to her own detriment of pushing others away, while Munroe wants nothing more than to be in her light. While I certainly love writing some brooding heroes, I have to say the cuddly energy of Munroe just lit me up. It was fun to write about a man who instantly knew what he wanted and never wavered from showing Lia just how much he cared for her. We all need people to stand for us like that, don't we?

I also want to thank everyone for the amazing response to the first book in this series, Wild Scottish Knight. I can't tell you how much joy I've had in writing these books and knowing that you all love them just as much really warms my heart. Lucky for me, Scotland is becoming my second home as we just purchased a small flat in Edinburgh. We'll be splitting our time between Scotland and the Caribbean, and I can't wait to see what inspiration comes from our travels.

Sparkle on, my friends! XX – Tricia

ALSO BY TRICIA O'MALLEY

THE ISLE OF DESTINY SERIES

Stone Song

Sword Song

Spear Song

Sphere Song

A completed series in Kindle Unlimited.

Available in audio, e-book & paperback!

"Love this series. I will read this multiple times. Keeps you on the edge of your seat. It has action, excitement and romance all in one series."

- Amazon Review

THE ENCHANTED HIGHLANDS

Wild Scottish Knight

Wild Scottish Love

Wild Scottish Rose

"I love everything Tricia O'Malley has ever written and "Wild Scottish Knight" is no exception. The new setting for this magical journey is Scotland, the home of her new husband and soulmate. Tricia's love for her husbands country shows in every word she writes. I have always wanted to visit Scotland but have never had the time and money. Having read "Wild Scottish Knight" I feel I have begun to to experience Scotland in a way few see it. I am ready to go see Loren Brae, the castle and all its magical creatures, for myself. Tricia O'Malley makes the fantasy world of Loren Brae seem real enough to touch!"

-Amazon Review

Available in audio, e-book, hardback, paperback and is included in your Kindle Unlimited subscription.

THE SIREN ISLAND SERIES

Good Girl

Up to No Good

A Good Chance

Good Moon Rising

Too Good to Be True

A Good Soul

In Good Time

THE ALTHEA ROSE SERIES

One Tequila

Tequila for Two

Tequila Will Kill Ya (Novella)

Three Tequilas

Tequila Shots & Valentine Knots (Novella)

Tequila Four

A Fifth of Tequila

A Sixer of Tequila

Seven Deadly Tequilas

Eight Ways to Tequila

Tequila for Christmas (Novella)

"Not my usual genre but couldn't resist the Florida Keys setting. I was hooked from the first page. A fun read with just the right amount of crazy! Will definitely follow this series."- Amazon Review

A completed series in Kindle Unlimited.

Available in audio, e-book & paperback!

THE MYSTIC COVE SERIES

Wild Irish Heart

Wild Irish Eyes

Wild Irish Soul

Wild Irish Rebel

Wild Irish Roots: Margaret & Sean

Wild Irish Witch

Wild Irish Grace

Wild Irish Dreamer

Wild Irish Christmas (Novella)

Wild Irish Sage

Wild Irish Renegade

Wild Irish Moon

"I have read thousands of books and a fair percentage have been romances. Until I read Wild Irish Heart, I never had a book actually make me believe in love."- Amazon Review

A completed series in Kindle Unlimited.

Available in audio, e-book & paperback!

STAND ALONE NOVELS

Ms. Bitch

"Ms. Bitch is sunshine in a book! An uplifting story of fighting your way through heartbreak and making your own version of happily-ever-after."

~Ann Charles, USA Today Bestselling Author

Starting Over Scottish

Grumpy. Meet Sunshine.

She's American. He's Scottish. She's looking for a fresh start. He's returning to rediscover his roots.

One Way Ticket

A funny and captivating beach read where booking a one-way ticket to paradise means starting over, letting go, and taking a chance on love...one more time

10 out of 10 - The BookLife Prize

ACKNOWLEDGMENTS

Thank you, as always, to my incredible readers for continuing on this lovely journey with me. I know I say it all the time, but I really do have the best readers. While I love nothing more than to put stories about love and light into the world, I can't help but feel so lucky to have that love mirrored back to me from all of you. Thank you, from the bottom of my heart, for your support. Even when I can't respond to every email or social media comment, please know that I feel your support.

Thank you to Marion, my fabulous editor, who constantly makes me laugh with her pointed feedback and entertaining comments.

Thank you to the Scotsman's family for their help with this story, from answering random questions about all things Scottish to proofing and editing the final product. You all do such a fabulous job in helping to make my books shine.

Finally, thank you to my handsome Scotsman, a man I'm lucky enough to call my partner, my best friend, and my soul mate. Love you forever.

CONTACT ME

I hope my books have added a little magick into your life. If you have a moment to add some to my day, you can help by telling your friends and leaving a review. Word-of-mouth is the most powerful way to share my stories. Thank you.

Love books? What about fun giveaways? Nope? Okay, can I entice you with underwater photos and cute dogs? Let's stay friends! Sign up for my newsletter and contact me at my website.

www.triciaomalley.com

Or find me on Facebook and Instagram.
@triciaomalleyauthor

Made in United States
North Haven, CT
18 August 2023

40465008R00193